THE LEGEND OF THE KESTREL

BY

PETER WACHT

Kestrel
Media Group, LLC

BOOK 1 OF THE SYLVAN CHRONICLES

Copyright 2019 © by Peter Wacht

Cover design by eBooklaunch.com

Published in the United States by Kestrel Media Group LLC.

Kestrel
Media Group, LLC

ISBN: 978-1-950236-00-8

eBook ISBN: 978-1-950236-01-5

Library of Congress Control Number: 2019900052

ALSO BY PETER WACHT

THE SYLVAN CHRONICLES

The Legend of the Kestrel

The Call of the Sylvana (forthcoming)

The Raptor of the Highlands (forthcoming)

The Makings of a Warrior (forthcoming)

The Lord of the Highlands (forthcoming)

The Lost Kestrel Found (forthcoming)

The Claiming of the Highlands (forthcoming)

The Fight Against the Dark (forthcoming)

The Defender of the Light (forthcoming)

all books in print

For Kathy.

Thank you for your support, belief and patience.

PROLOGUE

Death circled in the air. Silently. Patiently.

After sniffing the wind for any sign of danger, the jackrabbit emerged from its burrow and cautiously shuffled out onto the plain. The majestic mountains of the Highlands rose around it, casting a long shadow over much of the steppe. The tips of the snow-clad peaks stretched for the sky, only to fall short by the smallest of margins. A gust of wind blew across the tundra, and the jackrabbit perked its long ears. All was quiet. The jackrabbit stepped farther away from the safety of its burrow, satisfied that it would not be disturbed during its early morning foraging.

Without warning a dark shadow sped across the plain, then disappeared into the higher reaches. The jackrabbit fled in terror, leaping back into its burrow, unaware of how fate had spared its life. On most mornings, the raptor hunted, and the jackrabbit would have been its first meal. But not today. Today the raptor felt an unfamiliar urgency. Its strong wings, spanning seven feet, propelled it a thousand feet above the ground. The white feathers speckled with grey on the bird's underside blended perfectly with the sky. When visible, the raptor was a dangerous predator. When hidden, it was deadly, shooting down through the thin air like an arrow, its sharp claws outstretched for the kill.

Today it searched for different prey, yet it did not know why. It knew only to obey the urge pulling it to the east, an urge so strong it drowned out its instinct to hunt.

The raptor caught a current of air that carried it between two snow-covered peaks. The sun radiated off the orange, black and brown feathers covering its back. As it dodged around the mountaintops, a monstrous shadow trailed along, darkening the ground as it passed. The jackrabbit would have been an easy meal, but the bird of prey ignored it and continued east on its solitary journey.

A beautiful sight, the Highlands, but also dangerous. The rugged land hid untold riches — gold and silver, precious jewels and more. But, as the old saying went: If the Highlanders don't get you, nature will. For centuries many in search of treasure stole into the Highlands, hoping a few days' work would lead to a lifetime of luxury. For most, these dreams of fortune shattered before their eyes, the hard steel of the Highlanders or the treacherous terrain bringing these adventurers back to a cold, stark and unforgiving reality.

The Highlands was the raptor's domain; now its only home. Once, not too many years before, raptors lived in every kingdom from the Western Ocean to the Sea of Mist. But no more. Nobles and wealthy merchants paid dearly for the feathers of the mighty bird. Rumors of their magical powers abounded. Some believed the feathers, when ground down and mixed with a few select ingredients, served as an aphrodisiac. Others insisted that drinking the strange brew gave wisdom. Still others thought it brought riches. Though no one had ever proven the truth of these myths, the old beliefs died hard. As the years passed, so did these majestic birds, until none remained except those in the Highlands, protected by the harsh weather, the rough landscape and the Highlanders themselves, for the raptors had a special place in their hearts.

The raptor continued east, and as the hours passed, the sun drifted across the sky until the bird flew in front of it rather than behind. It traveled the winds, dodging in and out of the peaks that rose up before it, pulled on by its instinct. Finally it broke through the rocky peaks into a lush valley of green that stretched between the mountains for more than a league. A dark smudge appeared in the very center. Skimming over the treetops, the raptor's strong wings drew it closer, until the smudge became a huge rock that rose hundreds of feet into the air and dominated the valley. From a distance, it resembled a small mountain cut off from its brothers and sisters by forest. But as the raptor approached, riding the warmer air currents with its outstretched wings and moving slowly upward, the markings of man became clear.

To the untrained eye, the monolith appeared to be no more than a huge rock thrusting out of the earth. In truth, it was the Crag, the stronghold of the Highlanders. The Crag had never fallen to an enemy. Many an army had learned that lesson the hard way, leaving behind crushed bodies and broken spirits. Carved from the mountain, it was a formidable sight. The Highlanders had built their fortress on top of a long-dead volcano, taking great slabs of black stone from the plateau to form its walls. During the night, the citadel receded into the darkness, undecipherable from the gloom.

Eight towers formed the Crag's perimeter, joined together by the outer curtain. The wall was a hundred feet high and forty feet thick. In the center of the outer ward stood the central stronghold. Built in the shape of a square, its inner curtain stood fifty feet higher than the outside wall, its corners again supported by towers. One tower, though, standing on the eastern side closest to the sea, rose higher than the rest. Known as the Roost, on a clear day it was said that from its great height the Highlanders could peer halfway across the continent and gaze upon the shores of the Heartland Lake.

The raptor circled the tower, watching closely as horsemen galloped down the road twisting away from the citadel. The Marchers lit the huge torches placed alongside the causeway to help the unwary traveling in the dark find their way. When the Crag was under attack, this was the first obstacle invaders faced. The snakelike road created dozens of places ready-made for ambushes and rockslides, a common occurrence in this mountainous terrain. Turning its gaze from the soldiers, the raptor tightened its circles around the Roost until it found what it wanted — the ledge of the highest window — and settled silently on the stone outcropping. Night rapidly approached, but the raptor's eyes sparkled in the failing light. The intensity of the urge that had driven it across the Highlands increased. Looking down from its perch, the Raptor gazed into one of the rooms of the keep, its eyes fixing on a small boy. It had finally found the reason for its long flight.

CHAPTER ONE

Escape

Thomas swept his eyes across the room. The pitch black failed to impede his vision, his green, strangely glowing eyes easily picking out the details of his apartment. Large bookcases built into the wall flanked the door straight across from his bed. Books he had borrowed from his grandfather's library were strewn about the floor. He'd have to do something about that tomorrow. His grandfather didn't like it when he made such a mess. To the left of his bed against the wall stood a tall wardrobe that held most of his clothes. He still couldn't understand why he had to use it. He didn't really have that many clothes anyway, and when the servants put them on the top shelves, he actually had to climb up the door of the wardrobe to reach them. Also to the left was a large window hidden by dark drapes. On the other side of the bed sat a small writing table for his studies and a few personal items. The previous day's clothes were in a pile on the floor by his wardrobe, where he had thrown them before going to bed.

Thomas judged it was some time in the early morning, with dawn still several hours away. He had lain in bed for most of the night, unable to sleep. A feeling of unease plagued him, but he couldn't determine its source.

Restless, Thomas walked to the window, making a small slit in the drapes so he could see the moon and stars. It was a clear, cool night. Autumn was just a few days off. Thomas' thoughts drifted as he tried to remember all the constellations Rasoul had taught him the day before. He could locate the Archer and the Scorpion, but he couldn't find the Waterbearer or the Bear or the Ram. He was about to try again when the door to his room slowly swung open, the dim light from the lamp in the hall illuminating the entryway. Thomas' sense of foreboding almost overwhelmed his senses. A mixture of fear and curiosity surged through him. Moving silently to the pile of clothes by the side of his bed, Thomas pulled free the dagger his grandfather had given him on his last name day. It was made for a man, so to Thomas it felt like a sword in his hand. The one conceit the dagger contained was the carving on both sides of the blade — a raptor, marking it as the property of the Kestrels. Otherwise, it was a simple, well-made steel dagger set in a hilt of carved bone so it wouldn't slip from a sweaty hand. He was thankful for that. His palms were already wet, and cold sweat ran down his back. As the feeling of wickedness crept closer, Thomas stepped quietly back toward the window and slipped behind the drapes, dagger held at the ready.

It seemed like an eternity to Thomas, yet it was only a few seconds before two large shadows silently glided into his room. They wore black clothes with no markings. Black masks covered their faces. As they moved away from the door, Thomas saw two quick flashes of light. Blades.

A bolt of fear shot through Thomas. He considered staying where he was, hidden by the drapes. But that wouldn't do any good. They'd find him eventually.

Terror began to take hold, freezing his muscles, as he tried to figure out what to do. Then a new emotion fought its way to the surface, one that surprised him. Anger. Two men wanted to kill him while he slept. His anger flared within him, burning white hot and incinerating his fear. They might succeed, but he refused to make it easy for them. Remembering some of the lessons that he had coaxed out of Coban, he molded his anger into cool resolve. The two assassins were taking their time because of the dark. Maybe he could survive, if he took advantage of their weakness.

The lead attacker slunk toward the bed, one step at a time, careful not to make a sound. The second remained by the door, closing it. *A guard*, thought Thomas. *To ensure that if the first failed, he still wouldn't make it out of the room alive.* He could use that to his advantage as well. But he'd have to be quick. Very quick. Either man could kill him easily if he lost the element of surprise.

The assassin was almost to the bed. Thomas saw the man stretch out one hand, searching for the edge of the mattress. To the assassin, the piece of furniture was a dim shadow at best. The first attacker thought his prey was asleep in his bed. Once the assassin realized his target was not where he was supposed to be, Thomas knew he wouldn't stand much of a chance. He had to move fast. He squeezed the hilt of his dagger tightly in his hand, making sure he had a good grip. Remarkably, he was no longer sweating. The fear that had paralyzed him before was gone. There was only anger, a scorching anger that energized him.

The assassin was almost where Thomas should have been lying. Now. Now was the time to move. Thomas rushed out from behind the drapes on silent feet, running directly toward the second assassin standing in front of the door. Thomas stabbed with his dagger, taking the man in the side just above the hip. Remembering Coban's lesson, he gave the blade a sharp twist before tearing it out and grabbing the door handle with his free hand. As the blade bit deeply into the assassin's flesh, the man screamed in pain and surprise, never seeing the small blur surging toward him. He toppled to the floor in agony, clutching futilely at the wound, desperate to stop the blood pumping out of him.

Startled by the scream, the lead assassin jumped around, realizing his mistake. Seeing a small figure pulling the door open, he lunged for Thomas, grasping for his shirt. Thomas frantically unlatched the door and pulled it open. He could sense the assassin reaching for him, his hand only inches away. If the killer took hold, Thomas knew he would die. Before he could grab his escaping target, the assassin's foot slipped on a pile of books sitting in the middle of the floor, and he tumbled to the carpet. The man regained his feet in an instant and launched himself at the door, cursing under his breath. With a burst of speed Thomas ran out the door, pulling it closed.

The hallway lanterns had been turned off, leaving much of the corridor in darkness. Thomas turned quickly, running down the hallway toward his grandfather's rooms. He looked back, thankful the door to his room was still closed, but knowing it wouldn't remain so. The next thing he knew he was sitting on the floor, dazed. He felt as if he had run right into a stone wall.

The dagger still in his hand, Thomas looked up at his obstacle, shaking his head to regain his senses. To make it this far and fail wasn't fair. It just wasn't right! He brought his dagger up to strike, then sighed with relief. His grandfather stood before him, holding a large, bloody sword in one hand. With the other, he scooped Thomas up easily, holding him like a sack of flour under his left arm.

Just as Talyn had gotten Thomas settled against his hip, the door to his grandson's room slammed against the wall. The second assassin rushed out after his small prey. Talyn barely had to lift his arm as the assassin ran right onto his blade. Thomas glimpsed the look of surprise in his attacker's eyes. A boy had beaten him. Just a boy, he seemed to be saying. The man became a dead weight, so Talyn let him slide off the blade. Looking at the gaping wound in the man's chest, Thomas felt the bile rising in his throat and thought he was going to be sick. He had never seen anything like it before. To escape the growing feeling of nausea, Thomas remembered something that Coban had once explained to him: "When you don't know your enemy, caution leads to victory and recklessness to death." He promised himself that he would pay more attention to Coban's lessons in the future.

Sticking his head into the room, his grandfather noticed the other assassin lying dead inside the doorway. "You did well, Thomas," said Talyn. "Most Marchers don't get their first kill at such a young age." Thomas heard the pride in his grandfather's voice, and the sadness.

Talyn moved quickly toward the bed, picking up the clothes Thomas had worn the day before as well as his boots. He handed them to his grandson.

When the two attackers first entered his room, Thomas didn't have time to think about his actions or their consequences. He simply acted as he had been taught. As he replayed the events that took place only a few minutes before, his nausea worsened. He remembered the dagger entering the assassin's body, the sound of tearing flesh, the initial resistance and then how the blade slid in easily. That was quickly replaced by the look in the other assassin's eyes as his life slipped away; the look of surprise and fear, and perhaps even loss. As the events repeated themselves over and over in his mind, a thought kept running through his head: *He had killed a man. He had taken someone's life.*

Thomas was jolted from his thoughts as Talyn guided him down the hallway toward his own apartments. Talyn looked down at his grandson and saw the green cast of his face. He knew the cause. He had gone through much the same thing after his first kill. But then he had been fighting on the border; not in his own bedroom.

"Let it go, Thomas. You had no choice in the matter. If you hadn't killed him, he would have killed you."

"But—"

"No buts, Thomas. Killing a man is not an easy thing, but sometimes you have no choice. You're alive. That's all that matters now. You did the right thing. Feeling sorry for killing a man is the normal reaction. When you don't feel sorry, that's when you have to worry."

Talyn came to another intersection and stopped, motioning for Thomas to remain silent. Talyn's words made him feel a little better, but he couldn't get the images of the two dead men out of his mind. His grandfather was right, though. If he hadn't killed the assassin, he would be dead now. And the assassins would have been pleased with their success. That last realization hardened Thomas' determination.

The sounds of battle reached their ears, the clash of steel on steel and the cries of the wounded and dying echoing down the corridor. At the far end shadows danced along the wall. Though Talyn couldn't see the combatants, the shadows they created were undeniable. The attackers towered over his Marchers. From the picture before him, his men were fighting bravely but faring poorly against them. Rage swept across his face.

"Ogren," he breathed acidly, biting out the word.

Ogren? How could Ogren have entered the Crag? Thomas didn't have time to think on this new dilemma. Talyn ran through the hallway intersection and headed in a different direction, away from his private chambers. Instead he made for the small office behind the Hall of the Highland Lord.

"We've got to get you out of here, and we can't use the tunnel in my room," said Talyn as he trotted down the hallway. "At first I thought we could fight back, hold the reivers off, but now I can't take that chance. Not with Ogren in the Crag."

"You are the last of us, Thomas," continued Talyn. "You survived the assassins. Your father wasn't as lucky. We only have a few minutes before it's too late."

Finally reaching his study, Talyn slid to a halt. He knocked on the door three times. The door swung open, and they stepped through quickly before it closed on their heels.

His father wasn't as lucky as him? It took Thomas a few moments to realize what his grandfather had just told him. *You survived the assassins. Your father didn't.* Thomas thought he should feel something, finding out that his father was dead. Anything. Sorrow. Remorse. But he didn't. The news simply washed over him like a wave and was gone. He had spoken to his father no more than a dozen times in his entire life. *But he was still his father, and he should at least feel something. Shouldn't he? His father was dead, and he didn't feel a thing.*

As the door closed, Thomas heard the click of a lock turning into place. Abruptly, his grandfather stopped.

"Put those on, Thomas," he said, motioning to the bundle of clothes Thomas carried in his arms. "And quickly, now. We don't have much time."

Recognizing the urgency in his grandfather's voice, he pulled on his breeks. As he reached down for his boots, he looked around the dim room. A single lantern turned to its lowest setting glowed a soft yellow in the corner farthest from the door. Coban was there, a small gash on his forehead, his white shirt stained red in many places. Standing with him were a half dozen Marchers, also covered in blood, much of it their own he suspected. Pulling his shirt over his head, he listened to the conversation closely.

"Assassins," said Talyn, spitting the word out. "Thomas earned his first kill. And Ogren as well."

Coban just nodded, a grim look on his face, though his eyes gleamed at the mention of Thomas' success. He casually wiped away a trickle of blood that had run down his forehead onto his sleeve.

"There is only one way Ogren could have gotten into the Crag," said a Marcher.

"A traitor," answered Coban. The Marchers nodded. One of their own had let the Ogren into the Crag. It was unthinkable. Horrifying. And all too real.

"Whoever did this—"

"One of the postern gates was opened before an alarm could be given. The gate guards were the first to die," explained Coban, his eyes burning with rage. "When I find this traitor, death will be something he will look forward to." Talyn nodded, noting the grim expression on his friend's face.

Coban sighed, mostly out of frustration. As Swordmaster of the Highlands, the Marchers were his responsibility. He blamed himself for what had happened, though a part of him knew that it wasn't his fault. There was little he could have done to prevent it. Still, the idea of a traitor among his own Marchers made his stomach turn sour. If he lived through this, he promised himself that he would find whoever was responsible, and he'd take a long time killing him.

Talyn was having a harder time than Coban controlling his anger. Only a few weeks earlier he had sent more than half of the Marchers stationed at the Crag to the border with his son to eliminate the reivers harassing the outlying settlements. He had been blind, and it had cost him his son and his kingdom. He promised himself that it would not take his grandson as well.

Thomas was dressed and ready, now adjusting the sheath for his dagger though he still held it in his hand. After what had happened to him, Talyn wasn't surprised in the least. Talyn expected to see fear in his grandson's eyes, or maybe sadness over the death of his father, but both were missing. The only thing he could decipher was purpose. Nodding with pride, he still could not believe that the fate of the Highlands had fallen on such small shoulders.

Talyn walked to the wall behind his desk, where the single lantern struggled against the darkness. He had not done this in a long time, so it took him a few seconds to find the correct stone. Moving his left hand slowly along the carved blocks, he found the slight irregularity he was looking for. Pushing gently, a section of the wall just big enough for a man to walk through swung inward on silent hinges.

Thomas stepped forward, trying to get a better look at the hidden passageway. It was so dark, even he had a hard time making out the features of the corridor. Finally he did, though just barely. The passageway was not very large. Any man over six feet tall would have to stoop. The stone was roughly cut, and not at all like the finely carved slabs that made up the Crag.

The clash of steel invaded the room. The fighting had reached the far end of the corridor. It would soon enter the Hall of the Highland Lord.

"Quickly, my lord," said Coban. The Marchers with him grasped their swords nervously. "You must hurry."

Talyn nodded resignedly. He beckoned to Thomas, who walked hesitantly to him. Talyn knelt down and placed a hand comfortingly on his grandson's shoulder.

"Thomas, you have not been treated well here," began Talyn, obviously struggling with his words. He had never been very good at revealing his emotions, something Lora had always pointed out to him, yet now he did not have the time to learn. "It's too late to do anything about that, but I'm sorry. I apologize for your father and myself. I could have tried to do more."

Thomas looked closely at his grandfather, seeing the sadness in his eyes. He didn't think it was right for him to blame himself for the failures of others.

"What's done is done, grandfather," said Thomas. The maturity of Thomas' reply caught Talyn off-guard. "You told me stories and helped me with my lessons. I never thanked you for everything you did for me. I'm sorry."

Talyn stared at his little soldier in amazement. He had not shed a tear since the death of his wife those many years ago, but now he was having a hard time holding them back. His mind wandered, focusing on Lora, the woman who had stolen his heart and given him a son. She had died from a fever just a few years after Benlorin was born. She could never stay angry at him, no matter how hard she tried. *Would she be angry with him now for what he was about to do?* The sounds of battle drifted closer, making the Marchers even more anxious.

"Coban, please take the men out into the Hall. That's where we will make our stand."

"But, my lord!" protested Coban. "Please, use the tunnel. We can hold them long enough for you and Thomas to escape …"

Talyn cut him off sharply. "No, Coban. I will not abandon my home or my people. I will fight for the

15

Highlands, and when I fall, the fight will continue," he said, nodding toward Thomas.

Coban tried to think of some other argument, any argument, to get Talyn away from the Crag. He knew it was hopeless, though, short of knocking him out and carrying him through the passageway. All he could do was resign himself to what was about to happen and hope for the best. Dying didn't bother him. It was something he expected as Swordmaster. Talyn was another matter. He was the Highland Lord, and the Highlands couldn't afford to lose him. He looked from grandfather to grandson, noting the striking similarities. Thomas would never grow as tall as Talyn. Neverthe-less, what mattered most was there: the intelligence, the determination, the courage.

Coban walked slowly toward the door leading to the Hall of the Highland Lord, his men following quietly after him. As he pulled the door open, dozens of emotions played across his face at once. He turned back to his lord and his friend. Coban stiffened his back, then brought the blade of his sword to his forehead, bowing his head slightly to Talyn, and then Thomas, before slipping through the doorway. Each of the Marchers copied the example of their Swordmaster, saluting their lord, and the one who would have been their future lord. It was a sign of respect. Pride swelled in Talyn's chest. Not for himself, but for Thomas. The Marchers had acknowledged him for who he was, and Thomas for who he would be. Maybe some day, with luck, Thomas would reclaim what they had given him.

"Thomas, today you are a man," began Talyn, saying the words that he had been practicing in his mind for the last few minutes. Words he had never imagined he would have to utter. Words that could condemn a small boy if the wrong people found him. Talyn quickly clamped down on his emotions. Thomas stood straight as an arrow before him, backbone made of steel, a look of determination on his face.

"Thomas, today you are a man," he repeated. At the same time he pushed Thomas' shirtsleeve on his right arm up to the elbow. He pointed to the birthmark on Thomas' forearm, to the place where his skin was darker, almost sunburned in appearance. It was a relatively small mark, the raptor's claw, but it signified much. Thomas had always wondered about it. The raptor's claw always stood out. It marked him. He knew that. He just didn't understand yet how deeply.

"Remember that," said Talyn, pointing to the birthmark. "This marks you as a Kestrel, as the Lord of the Highlands. If certain people see this, they will kill you. Others will flock to your banner because of it. The trick is knowing beforehand what each person will do. Keep it hidden until it is time."

"Yes, grandfather," answered Thomas in a solemn voice, struck by the gravity of the discussion. But he was confused. "How will I know it is time?"

"You will know, Thomas," said Talyn. He smiled. He should have expected the question. "As a man, as a Kestrel Highlander, I give you these charges." Thomas stared into his grandfather's eyes. He was caught by the intensity of his gaze. It felt like his grandfather was trying to burn his words right into Thomas' soul. Slowly, ever so slowly, something within him stirred, an energy he had never felt before. His blood began to warm and speed through his veins. Thomas tried to

17

stand even straighter, sticking out his chest. The energy within him continued to build, though he didn't know where it came from. He relished the warmth and the feeling of power it gave him.

"This is the sword of the Kestrels, the Sword of the Highlands." Thomas examined the claymore his grandfather held before him. He had seen it many times before. It was a large two-handed sword with a double-edged blade. "It has been in our family since the time of Olafon, when the first High King gave the blade to one of our ancestors in recognition of the many services the Kestrels had performed for him. I charge you to bring it to safety and to guard it with your life. When the time comes for you to become Lord of the Highlands, if it still may be so, you will have this sword in your hand."

Thomas reached out with both hands to take the blade that Talyn extended to him hilt first. He had a hard time holding the heavy sword in his small hands. He could barely keep the tip from striking the floor, so he clutched it to his chest in order to balance the weight.

Smiling at Thomas' valiant effort, Talyn reached into the front pocket of his shirt and pulled out a slim, silver chain. On its end hung a finely carved talisman. Thomas moved a step closer to get a better look at it and was surprised how it shined brightly even in this dim light. The talisman was shaped like a rounded triangle, with the center showing what appeared to be the horn of a unicorn, the thick bottom of the horn spiraling up to a razor sharp point.

"This necklace belonged to your mother. It now belongs to you. She told me once that her mother gave it to her. She said that with this necklace, if you were ever in danger, you could follow its heat to safety. I hope it works for you as I assume it did for your mother."

Thomas bent his head slightly, which allowed Talyn to place the chain around his neck. A warmth enveloped him immediately, flowing through his entire body and mixing with the energy still coursing through his blood. After only a few seconds, most of the warmth disappeared, leaving in its wake a strange feeling, one that he had never experienced before. It felt as if someone was watching him.

"My second charge is for you to remember," said Talyn. "You are Thomas Kestrel, Lord of the Highlands upon my death, and I charge you to remember that and to make sure that others remember it as well."

"I will," replied Thomas in a quiet, determined voice. Talyn gave a satisfied nod. His grandson had a great deal of inner strength. It would serve him well in the days ahead.

"Good. Now I charge you to escape," said Talyn as he motioned to the dark tunnel behind him. "Go through this passageway until you come to the forest, then keep going. Get as far from the Crag as fast as you can, and stay away from anyone not of the Highlands. I wish I could give you more than this, but there's no time."

The sounds of battle grew louder. A dull thud echoed through the room. Whoever had attacked the Crag was breaking down the doors to the Hall of the Highland Lord.

"Now you must go."

"But I want to stay with you. I want to defend the Crag."

"No, Thomas. I'm sorry, but you must go. The Crag won't hold much longer. You're our only hope. You must go."

Thomas looked at his grandfather for a second, his words hitting him in the gut. There were tears in his grandfather's eyes. He stepped forward to give his grandfather a hug, but the sword he was carrying prevented it. It didn't stop Talyn, however, as he swept up his grandson in a bear hug, the tears now flowing freely down his cheeks.

"Goodbye, grandfather," whispered Thomas. His words made Talyn squeeze him even harder.

Talyn set him down as the pounding on the doors became deafening. Thomas turned toward the pitch-black passageway. The realization that he was never going to see his grandfather again filled him with a sadness that had escaped him when he had learned that his father had died. But his grandfather had said that he was a man, and he was going to act like one no matter how much it hurt.

Peering into the darkness, he took a few small steps forward until he stood at the very edge of the passageway, his eyes adjusting almost immediately, picking out the faint edges of the uncut rock that formed the tunnel. He breathed deeply and walked through quickly, his stride carrying him deeper into the darkness, and farther away from the only place he had ever called home, from the only person who had ever really cared about him. That thought made him afraid. He turned around and saw his grandfather standing in the opening, watching him, a sad expression on his face. His grandfather had given him several important tasks, and he refused to let him down.

Thomas raised the sword above his head with two hands, a newfound strength aiding him, and yelled as loud as he could, "I am Thomas Kestrel, Lord of the Highlands! The Highlands will not be forgotten!"

A smile touched his grandfather's lips as he gazed upon his little warrior. Pride for his grandson filled his heart, and he regretted not being able to see the man that he would become.

"For the Highlands!" he replied, answering his grandson's salute.

Thomas smiled as well as he brought the sword down and again held it against his chest so he could cradle it in his arms. He walked down the passageway, stepping with a new confidence deeper into the darkness; a little boy with the seriousness of a man, carrying a sword much too big for him.

As his grandson disappeared into the darkness, Talyn stepped away from the opening and released the hidden latch, allowing the wall to close. Now it was his turn to make his grandson proud. The Crag was his, and he would make his stand in the Hall of the Highland Lord. Talyn knew that his death approached, but he was safe in the knowledge that the Highlands would not die with him.

CHAPTER TWO

Awakening

A tall man walked silently through the forest as if he was a part of it. The heart trees did their best to trip him, their gnarled roots twisting across the forest floor. Climbing hundreds of feet into the air, the heart trees' trunks blocked a person's view for a hundred feet to either side. Thousands of years old, it was said that if you lay your ear against the trunk, you could hear the beating of the earth within it. There weren't many heart trees left, and the same story said that once they were gone, the earth would die as well.

The tall man didn't seem to notice the roots, stepping nimbly around them or over them as he focused his attention on a small plant he cupped in his hands, careful not to disturb it. He had been waiting for this particular plant to grow for a long time. It bloomed once every twenty years, and then for only a few days, which testified to its scarcity. Known as shadowsbreath, it blossomed in just a handful of places. Though a tiny plant, it held many peculiar qualities. The primary one being that if you took a single taste of it, you would die a painful death, the poison slowly rotting you from the inside out. Yet it held other characteristics as well that would assist him in his experiments. Dodging around the large trees that reared up to block his way or ducking under huge roots that sometimes rose as high as his head, he increased his pace. It was getting dark and he was anxious to be home. Autumn was almost upon the land and the nights were getting chilly.

He wore brown breeks and a dark blue shirt that covered a slim body. Though he did not look it, he had a deceptive strength. The cloak he wore helped to ward off the chill and swirled around him as he strode quickly toward his destination, its green and brown colors blending perfectly with the landscape. His piercing green eyes held an intensity that would have frightened most men and were accentuated by the sharp features of his face. The short black beard flecked with grey gave him an almost dastardly appearance. If anyone had the courage to tell him so, he would have smiled and thanked them for the compliment.

He soon entered a part of the forest where the trees did not grow so thickly, and he strode straight for a heart tree larger than the rest. It looked like any other, but he had no trouble picking out the door that stood almost in the tree's very center. He hated that door. When he had built it, he had made a mistake in its dimensions, and he didn't like making mistakes. Every time he went through the door he had to duck his head because the entry failed to accommodate his height. He could have replaced it, but chose not to. If nothing else, it reminded him of his fallibility. Next to it was a small window, now closed. If you looked up into its branches, a small chimney was visible halfway up the trunk. But again, you had to know what you were looking for in order to pick it out.

As he approached the door, he moved to the window first and looked inside. The smile that curled his lips gave him an even more forbidding look. Inside the unique dwelling stood the most beautiful woman he had ever seen, the woman who had stolen his heart. No more than five feet tall, she carried herself like a giant. Even as she stirred the evening stew in a large black kettle, she resembled a queen. Her dark chestnut hair covered one side of her face as she bent down to taste her cooking. As she swept her hair out of the way with a quick swipe of her hand, she revealed deep blue eyes. Eyes that the tall man had often gotten lost in time and time again, much to his pleasure. Saying she was beautiful did not do her justice.

Judging that the stew was done, the woman reached for two bowls. Suddenly, she straightened as if in pain, a look of shock crossing her face. The two bowls dropped from her hands and shattered on the floor. The woman staggered back against a table, one hand going to her throat.

In an instant the tall man rushed through the door, forgetting the plant he dropped and knocking his head against the frame in his haste. Ignoring the pain, he grabbed hold of his wife so she wouldn't fall.

"Rya, what's the matter?" he asked, trying to keep the panic that he felt rising in his throat from his voice. "What is it?"

"It's all right. I was just surprised," she said, her hand still clutching at her neck.

Rynlin pulled out a chair from underneath the table with his foot and helped his wife to sit. He knelt down next to her, his hands still on her petite waist, unwilling to let go.

"Rynlin, don't worry. Like I said, I was just surprised." Rya saw the concern in her husband's face, but she couldn't explain what had happened. Her emotions swirled within her, as if she were trying to control a hurricane. She held a necklace in her hand, a slim, silver necklace, and it felt warm against her skin, a warmth tainted by fear. She had not felt that warmth in ten years, a warmth that brought back memories of a daughter taken from her. A beautiful, strong-willed daughter. Doing her best to rein in the emotions running wild within her, she smiled at her husband to ease his worry.

"It's the necklace, Ryn. Marya's necklace. I can feel it. I haven't felt it in a decade, but I can feel it now." His wife's words forced Rynlin to his feet. She was smiling, smiling like he had not seen for years. *Marya's necklace. It couldn't be. She had died ten years before. It had to be a mistake.*

The necklaces had been in the Keldragan family for millennia. They were said to be made from the same magic that had created the world, though Rynlin didn't believe it. He did believe in what they could do, though. The necklaces were attuned to the members of the Keldragan family. Each necklace served as a beacon. You could tell who it was and where, anywhere in the Kingdoms.

When Marya had been old enough to understand, Rya had given her a necklace that matched her own. When they both wore them, they could feel the emotions, to a degree, of the other. And now she could feel the warmth of the necklace again, but it wasn't Marya. In a way, it felt as if it was a part of her, but there was another feeling there, an unfamiliar sensation.

"That's impossible," began Rynlin, "Marya is—" He couldn't finish the sentence. It was too painful for him.

"I know," said Rya. She kept her voice level, but her excitement was growing. "It's not Marya, but it feels like her in a way. It feels like a child, and we won't know for sure until we find whoever is wearing our daughter's necklace."

"We can't just go running off—" Rynlin would have said more, but the steely gaze he received from his wife cut him off. Rya looked even smaller than she was when she stood next to Rynlin, but she was not someone to cross when she made up her mind. "All right, just let me throw a few things into our traveling bags and we'll go."

"Good," said Rya. Her dazzling smile sent shivers through Rynlin's heart, even though he knew he had been bullied ... again. "I knew you'd see it my way. I'm just glad you've finally learned when not to argue."

Yes, his wife could have a very commanding presence about her when she wanted. And she liked to gloat sometimes. Nevertheless, he bit back a response and began searching for their travel bags and the few things they would need as Rya bent to clean the mess she had made. She then scooped out the remainder of the stew for a quick dinner. Each was lost in their own thoughts as they performed their respective tasks, but a single one dominated for both: Who was wearing their daughter's necklace?

CHAPTER THREE

UNLOCKED

Thomas traveled beneath the Crag, making his way through the darkness by tracing the outline of the tunnel with his eyes. He had not yet come across an intersection of trails, which buoyed his confidence. At least he didn't have to worry about getting lost. He had enough to worry about as it was.

The events that had pulled him from his bed just hours before continually ran through his mind, his grandfather's words burdening his soul. The growl of his stomach jarred him from his thoughts. He was walking in a daze and failed to pick up the scent that beckoned to him. Fresh air. The slight breeze brushing against his face made him increase his pace down the passageway.

He stopped abruptly, confronted by a massive door. He had almost stumbled right into it. Bands of steel held together large oak timbers. Running his hands over the door, he determined it was still in good condition, though in several places the timbers were cracked. The door didn't appear to have been opened for centuries.

That discovery worried him. If no one had used the door in such a long time, there was no guarantee he would be able to get out. What if he couldn't open the door? Thomas locked away his fears. His grandfather used to say that if you spent all your time worrying, you'd never get anything done. *His grandfather was gone.* Coban had explained once that when it appeared that a Highland fortification would fall, the Highland war leader fought to the death. Surrender was never an option. Thomas had not understood the logic of it all, and Coban couldn't explain it any better. He had just said that that's the way it was done, that's how the lord maintained his honor. *His grandfather was gone.* The conflicting emotions boiled up within him all at once. The sorrow and pain of losing the only person he had ever cared about fought with his desire to make his grandfather proud. He wanted to cry, but forced down the urge. He refused to cry. His grandfather was gone and that was that. He would have to make it on his own. His grandfather had said that he was a man now.

Turning his attention back to the door, he neatly sealed away the turmoil, leaving only the task at hand before him. Thomas ran his fingers along the edges of the door until he found a set of locks. Setting down the sword carefully, he took hold of the top bolt and tried to turn it. The bolt refused to budge. Irritated, he let out an oath that would have made Coban proud. If the locks had rusted shut, he'd never open the door. Kicking the ground in frustration, he noticed the tiny flakes of dry dirt that danced up from the floor. The tunnel was free of moisture. Therefore the locks would probably be free of rust as well, so they should move. Maybe he simply had to try something different. Taking hold of the top bolt with both hands, he redoubled his efforts, placing his foot against the door for additional leverage. At first nothing happened. Then, slowly, the bolt grudgingly gave way. His grip slipped off as the knob turned completely with a resounding click. Sweating heavily from the effort, but with a grin on his face, he set to work on the remaining four bolts. Thankfully, they weren't all as difficult as the first, and he completed the task in just a few minutes.

Taking a moment to catch his breath, Thomas listened for any sign of pursuit. Nothing. Thomas took hold of the handle and was about to pull the door wide when one of his grandfather's charges passed through his mind: *Trust no one who is not a Highlander.* It would probably be a good idea to exercise caution in other things as well. Especially since he wasn't sure where he was in relation to the Crag. He considered his options. While growing up, he had spent most of his time in the forest surrounding the Crag. He felt more comfortable in the forest, away from the folk who tended to stare and whisper behind his back.

He learned that he could extend his senses and know exactly what was around him for miles. It was a skill he had discovered quite by mistake. Perhaps it came from his mother, who the castle residents also talked about, shocked by some of the strange things that always seemed to happen around her. Although he had no way to explain this unique gift, he was more than happy to make use of it. While testing this skill in a glade below the Crag, he had glimpsed a blue jay as it flew from its nest in search of food, leaving behind three small eggs. Thomas had followed the image in his mind through the forest right to the nest, even though it was almost a mile away. Then he did it again, finding a beaver that did not want to be disturbed while it finished its dam; and then again, coming upon a beehive that had been knocked down from a tree branch by a hungry bear. Why couldn't he do the same thing now?

He attempted to concentrate, but to no avail as his mind remained focused on the events of the past few hours. Breathing deeply, he tried again, this time closing off everything except the part of his mind where this hidden ability lay. Though difficult at first, his efforts paid off. He succeeded in extending his senses to the door. Unfortunately, it was like running headfirst into a brick wall. No matter how hard he pushed he couldn't get past the steel in the door. Even with the large oak timbers, the door was still more metal than wood. Suddenly it hit him. When he was in the forest, he had no trouble at all stretching out his senses. Why? Because everything he was dealing with was a part of nature. The door was manmade. He shifted his attention away from the door to the rock wall. At first it felt very much like trying to push his senses through the steel door. He concentrated even more, closing out everything around him except for one particular section of rock. Much to his surprise, Thomas discovered minute crevices running through the stone, so small they were invisible to the naked eye. He immediately pushed his senses through. Although some of the crevices came to an end somewhere within the rock, many did not, and he was able to extend his senses beyond the stone. To his relief, this part of the forest was free of danger, at least for a time. Whoever had attacked the Highland fortress had not yet extended their reach to the glades beneath the Crag.

Letting go of his talent, he took hold of the door handle with both hands and pulled as hard as he could. Sweat popped up on his forehead and the veins in his neck strained from the effort. The door wouldn't budge. Thomas let go of the handle and rubbed his sweaty palms on his shirt. He took hold of the door again, this time setting one foot against the wall and pulling with all his might. He stood there for a moment, completely immobile, every muscle in his body screaming in protest. It wasn't working. He'd be stuck underneath the Crag for the rest of his short life. Without warning, he flew backwards, landing hard on the stone floor. The door opened with a tremendous screech of steel running across steel that echoed back down the passageway. He picked himself up from the floor, a huge grin on his face. The early morning sun just coming up over the Highlands greeted him.

Wiping some of the dirt from his clothes, he hurried to the opening. The passageway ended in one of the many small glades ringing the Crag. A small stream ran just to the left of the entrance, calling to him. He had not eaten since the night before and his thirst was getting the better of him. Stepping out into the light, Thomas knelt at the water's edge, savoring the cool liquid. He was in the middle of a thicket, the trees and bushes standing close to one another. He took several more swallows from the stream before getting back to his feet.

The trees and cliff blocked his view, so he wasn't quite sure where he was in relation to the Crag. Jumping across the tiny stream, Thomas reached for a low branch and pulled himself into one of the trees. After a few minutes of climbing, he was well above the cliff. The first thing he noticed was the smoke, which darkened the sky for several miles to the north. He saw the knoll where the Crag had once stood, but the Crag itself, and its twelve towers, was unrecognizable. Biting back tears, he assessed his situation in the calculated fashion his grandfather had taught him.

The Crag had fallen. The smoke that rose up around the knoll, and the few fires that remained, told him all he needed to know. His grandfather had bought him time to escape, and that's what he had to do now. If he stayed in one place long enough, and those reivers discovered he had escaped the Crag, they would come after him. It was only a matter of time.

Climbing down from his perch as quickly as he could, he jumped back across the stream and stepped inside the tunnel. He laid his sword down on the other side of the opening and then examined the door. When it swung shut, it would look exactly as if it were part of the cliff face, yet even if he pulled it closed, there was no guarantee that it would stay that way. Trusting to luck, he grabbed hold of the door and pulled as hard as he could. As it closed, Thomas heard the locks click back into place. One problem solved.

Another lay before him. Thomas looked down at the large sword. If he held it in his arms as he did going through the tunnel, it would catch on the branches and bushes of the forest, slow him down, and leave a clear path for anyone to follow. He had to take it with him, though. His grandfather had stressed how critical the sword was to his family. More important, he had told Thomas to guard it with his life. He didn't want to let his grandfather down.

He smiled again as an idea popped into his head. Unbuckling his belt, he removed it from his breeks. First, he put the buckle under the hilt, then pulled the strap through. Next, he did the same thing about a foot from the end of the blade. *Definitely not the most elegant of scabbards, but it would do.* He placed the strap over his shoulder and walked a few steps with the sword on his back. He would still have to be careful as he traveled through the forest. The hilt rose about a foot above his head, and the tip of the blade was no more than six inches from the ground. But it was still better than carrying it out in front of him. At least now he'd have less of a chance of leaving a trail.

The final dilemma was which way to go. Obviously, north was out of the question. He took a few steps to the south. A sudden chill passed through his body. Reaching under his shirt, he pulled out the amulet his grandfather had given him. It had grown ice cold in just those few steps. When he was traveling through the tunnel it had felt warm, but he had simply thought it was because of his exertion. Maybe there was more to it than that. Maybe what his grandfather had said about the amulet was true. He turned to the west. The amulet felt like an icicle. When he faced to the east it grew warm against his skin.

"Well," he said to no one in particular, "east it is." Through a break in the trees, Thomas saw a raptor circling lazily in the sky, swooping in and out of the low-hanging clouds. Taking solace in the large predator, Thomas leapt across the stream for the third time. Sword on his back, he slipped between the trees and made his way deeper into the forest using the amulet as his guide.

CHAPTER FOUR

AWAKENED

It was only early morning, but it appeared to be dusk. Most men refused to enter the Charnel Mountains, and those who did rarely returned. Any who traveled within ten miles of the forbidding peaks could sense the evil lurking there, hidden away from the sight of man, but always there. Watching, waiting, until it was too late.

Some said the Charnel Mountains were an abomination, caused by a tremendous magical battle between the forces of good and evil. Those who followed the light had won, but they could not destroy the dark. So instead they imprisoned their enemies in the mountains, sealing them away for eternity, or so they thought. Dark grey stone formed the mountains, the very tips of the monstrous peaks a sooty black.

The tallest of the mountains could not be seen completely, as fully a third of its mass rose up into the clouds. Known as Blackstone, that single peak had an even older name. Shadow's Reach. On certain winter days, when the sun was just right, the shadow of Blackstone reached out across much of the Northern Steppes, turning day into night and, for those lone travelers caught in that desolate land, life into a nightmare.

But today was different. A single ray of sunshine had fought its way through the thick clouds, shining down on Blackstone, illuminating the abandoned city. The sunlight flickered, struggling against the murky shadow. The shadow fought hard, but the light refused to yield, increasing in intensity with each passing second. The ray of light shone down through a glass dome situated on top of the largest building in the city, a massive structure that resembled a castle, yet in the place of crenellations stood gargoyles and other hideous creatures in gruesome poses. As the darkness dissipated, the room revealed its secrets. Massive marble columns stationed around its perimeter appeared. Black and white tiles as wide as a tall man covered the floor. If there were any doors, they remained hidden in the darkness.

The beam of sunshine settled on the room's most unique characteristic, a stone disk with an intricate design set in the very center of the floor. Two figures emerged from the cuts in the block, done with such excellent workmanship that they appeared lifelike. The first resembled a young man with a blazing sword of light. Opposing him was a tall man with a cruel face wielding a sword that swallowed the light. They were locked blade to blade, their faces no more than a fingerbreadth apart. The boy wore a look of determination, the man a grin of arrogance and sure victory. As the sun touched the stone it grew warm. A rumble began in the room, drifting out to the very edges of Blackstone. It was not an earthquake, for that was something of an end. Instead, it was a beginning.

CHAPTER FIVE

HIDEAWAY

The muscles in Thomas' legs burned in protest, angered by having to climb up and down the small mountains common to this part of the Highlands. He spent most of the day traveling to the east. He should have been thankful. These mountains weren't as tall or as steep as those to the west or north. Going in either of those directions would have made his life much more difficult. At least he didn't have to worry about the trees. After a few hours the forest had thinned out, which made the going somewhat easier. While he traveled through the dense thickets closer to the Crag, even with the sword strapped to his back, he had to keep stopping to untangle it from a vine or branch.

Along the way he had picked some berries to satisfy his grumbling stomach and he drank from every stream he came across. At what he had judged to be midafternoon, he took a short break by one stream and removed the strap from his shoulder. Taking a closer look at the blade, he read for the first time the words etched into the steel. He had always focused his attention on the raptors on each side of the blade, as well as in the pommel. Peering closely, he read the words out loud: "Strength and courage lead to freedom." As he trekked through the Highlands, those words danced around in his mind. No matter how hard he tried to think about something else, he couldn't escape them: *Strength and courage lead to freedom.* He had thought about their significance, hoping that doing so would banish them from his mind. The literal meaning was, of course, the most obvious. But he had a feeling that there was a deeper meaning, one that evaded his grasp.

The hours passed quickly as Thomas journeyed to the east. Though he still had several small mountains to climb, with each step the smell of the sea became stronger. When he had begun his journey, he had moved quickly, his fear of capture pushing him on. But his exhaustion slowed his pace now. As a result, his fear had ebbed. He tried to remain alert, but it was a losing battle. The events of the past night and day were wearing him down.

From time to time, Thomas extended his senses into the forest to make sure he was alone. Looking back over his shoulder and seeing the sun edge closer to the mountains, he judged that now was a good time to check again. Coming to a stop on top of a small hill, he allowed the essence of the forest to flow within him. Each time he had extended his senses during the day it had grown easier, the task becoming more familiar. He had also been able to push out his senses farther each time, now reaching for several miles around. Not far to the east, a river ran through the Highlands. The Southern River, he decided. On its bank a badger patiently stared at the water, waiting for a fish to swim within reach of its paws. He focused his senses on the way he had come. A frown settled on his face. Not too far behind him something felt wrong. It was the same feeling that had bothered him in the early morning that preceded the attack. He concentrated on that feeling.

There were men behind him, many men, traveling in what looked like a dozen groups, all cloaked in darkness. His fear returned, as did his energy. He abruptly lost control of his skill, wanting only to run. Thomas forced himself to relax and extended his senses once again. He couldn't afford to run blind. He had to know what he faced. Approximately ten groups of about twenty men each coming toward him in some sort of pattern. The path of one group slightly overlapped the path of another. Then he realized what was going on. They knew he was somewhere to the east of the Crag, but they weren't sure exactly where. To ensure that he didn't sneak around them, they had formed a loose semicircle to push him toward the river. Once the pincer groups reached the banks of the Southern River, he'd be easy to catch out in the open. A feeling of helplessness swept through him, and he struggled to beat it down. His odds of escaping had just narrowed considerably.

Still, if those following him didn't know exactly where he was, that meant he still had a chance. Thomas set off at a fast trot down the other side of the hill, judging that speed was his best ally now. If he could keep his distance from his pursuers until dark, then he would have the advantage.

He continued at a steady pace for several hours to conserve his energy, hoping desperately to stay ahead of his pursuers. Night approached quickly, and with every minute gone, the more confident he became. As he reached the bottom of a steep hill, he stopped at a tree that had fallen to the ground. His lungs burned. He would have done just about anything for a flask of water. He looked back in the direction he had just come, then ducked behind the fallen tree. On top of the hill, he made out the shapes of several dozen men, recognizing the black armor and clothing from the Crag. *Reivers.* They were gaining on him, and it was still at least an hour before full dark. If he kept running they would catch him before the sun set. His only choice was to hide.

When the reivers started their descent and disappeared from view, Thomas jumped out from behind the fallen tree. He ran through the forest as fast as he could, desperately looking for a place to hide. The sword on his back now felt like a dead weight, catching on vines and branches in his haste. It was slowing him down, but he couldn't get rid of it. He would do what his grandfather had asked of him. As the minutes passed, the shouts of the reivers following behind him became louder. He judged that they had closed the distance to no more than a half mile, but in the Highlands, with the ravines, valleys and mountains, sounds could be deceptive. Someone who was only a few hundred feet away could sound as if they were miles in the distance. The reivers might even be closer than that. He had passed several trees that he considered climbing, but none appealed to him. If they saw him in the branches, he would be an easy kill.

Thomas came to an abrupt stop as he broke through the trees, his feet only inches from slipping over a steep embankment into the Southern River. The reivers' voices grew louder. He struggled down the slope. The snapping branches and the crunch of dead leaves so close behind him pushed Thomas on. Looking vainly to the other side of the river, thoughts of swimming across were swept away. He would never make it before the reivers saw him. The river was too wide.

As he frantically searched for a solution, the shouts of the reivers behind him made it harder and harder to think. He wanted to run, but there was nowhere to go. Then, he looked down at his feet. He had actually stepped into the river without realizing it. Thomas examined the riverbank. To his left reeds swayed in the slight breeze of the late afternoon. Thomas picked one that looked right. He sliced off both ends with his dagger and walked farther into the river, careful not to bend or break any reeds as he moved among them. Putting his dagger back in its sheath, he judged he was in water deep enough for him to not be seen from the riverbank. He heard curses now mixed with shouts. The reivers were almost upon him. He placed one tip of the reed in his mouth, then submerged himself in the water, shrugging off the cold that immediately seeped into him. Now, he was actually glad to have the sword on his back. Its weight made it easier for him to stay underwater. As he took his first breath from the reed, the reivers broke through the trees and stopped at the edge of the river.

CHAPTER SIX

MEMORIES

Rynlin and Rya continued their journey along the coast of the Highlands as the sun moved closer to the horizon. They had traveled most of the way in silence, each occupied by their own thoughts. Rya spent much of her time wondering who wore the necklace. She glanced occasionally at Rynlin, noting his dark scowl. She guessed that curiosity was not his primary feeling at the moment. She would have thought that after ten years, his anger would have diminished at least to some degree, but she wasn't too sure now. When Rynlin had learned that Marya had run off to marry Benlorin against his wishes, he had been in a black mood for almost a year and had refused to speak with her, a tactic their daughter used against them as well. Then, when they had felt Marya die, Rynlin had taken it especially hard, believing that he was the cause. Nonsense, she knew. Still, it was a long time before they were both able to resume their lives. His anger and pain from the past had probably prevented Rynlin from feeling what she had felt when just hours before someone had put on the necklace that had once belonged to their daughter.

As she gazed up at the mountains rising on their right, memories of her daughter flooded her mind. She remembered when Marya was only three years old, wearing a dirty dress and no shoes, a huge grin on her face because she had grown a pretty purple flower from a seed in a matter of seconds. Rya knew then that the special abilities that ran through both her and Rynlin's blood had already manifested themselves in Marya, but she had still been taken by surprise by her strength. Marya had always been a headstrong child, which she knew came solely from her father. That's probably why Marya enjoyed spending time with her father so much. They were very much alike.

"Whoever it is," said Rya, trying to draw Rynlin out of his cloud, "he's afraid. And he's in danger."

"How do you know it's a he?" asked Rynlin, his skepticism unmistakable.

"If you spent some time paying attention to what was going on rather than reliving what happened ten years ago," replied Rya sharply, "you'd know it was a boy."

Rynlin smiled at his wife. She always seemed more beautiful when she was angry. That's probably why he had fallen in love with her so easily — the fire within her. Rynlin wiped the smile from his face. He didn't think she'd appreciate his grin.

"I can feel him," continued Rya. "He feels more like Marya the closer we get to him, but there's something different about him."

They both quickened their pace, the look of concern spreading on Rya's face. She almost tripped when Rynlin grabbed her wrist. She was about to offer him a few choice words about manners, but Rynlin's expression brought her up short.

"Slow down, Rya. There are others about."

She was so absorbed in figuring out who might be wearing her daughter's necklace, she had stopped paying attention to her surroundings. She glanced at her husband with a hard look, daring him to say something. Instead, he scanned the beach in front of them and the trees to the side, looking for signs of movement. At least he had grown somewhat smarter during the years. If he made a single joke about her almost falling face first in the sand, she would make him regret it.

Pulling her gently behind him, they stepped into the forest and slipped between two large oak trees. Crawling to the edge of a small drop, they looked down into the foliage. More than a dozen men clad in black leather armor combed the woods, sticking their blades into bushes and peering up into the branches.

"It looks like we're not the only ones looking for someone," whispered Rynlin. Rya nodded. The worry in Rynlin's eyes mirrored her own.

They waited until the black-clad soldiers moved away, then stepped forward among the trees. They continued to follow the feeling that emanated from their necklaces, pulling them south, the silver growing warmer with their every step.

CHAPTER SEVEN

A COMPANION

At first, hiding beneath the water seemed almost like a game. The extra weight of the sword guaranteed that Thomas did not have to worry about breaking the surface, and the reed proved to be an effective tool for breathing. After only a few minutes, though, the chilly water began to turn his body to ice. Each hesitant touch of the current sent a shiver through his body. Soon, he desperately wanted to rise to the surface. But he couldn't. Not yet.

He had been submerged for only a few minutes, and it was still an hour before full dark; plenty of time for the reivers to do a thorough search of both sides of the river. He thought of other things to ward off the chill, remembering hot summers swimming in a hidden pool in one of the glades by the Crag. It didn't help much. Eventually, he simply resigned himself to the mind-numbing, bone-chilling cold of the water, doing his best to wait for the dark.

Thomas saw through the glimmer of the water as the sun gradually began to fade, until almost everything around him was in darkness. The reeds that were no more than a fingerbreadth away had disappeared, growing indistinct in the cloudy water as the day's shadows lengthened. Ever so slowly he stuck his head out of the water, the current pushing small waves up against his nose as they flowed toward the shore. Remaining motionless, he picked out several dark shadows on the riverbank no more than thirty feet away.

His breath caught in his throat. The reivers were still looking for him. Had his ruse failed? He hoped that with the darkness and the reeds surrounding him, he would remain unseen. To be safe, though, he unsheathed his knife, holding it in his hand just below the surface of the water.

"He couldn't have crossed it," said one of the black-armored men, spitting into the river to emphasize his point. "Not at his age. If he tried, he drowned." Several of the soldiers murmured their assent, others just nodded. They waited for another reiver to speak.

This was Thomas' first opportunity to get a good look at those who had attacked the Crag and killed his grandfather. The hate that filled his heart burned off some of the chill that had settled within his bones. His anger pushed him forward, the desire for revenge consuming him. These men had killed his grandfather.

The arrival of several more reivers on the shore snapped Thomas from his thoughts. He realized that he was now out of the water to his neck. He had taken a step forward, as if he was going to attack a dozen trained warriors by himself. Cursing himself for his stupidity, he quietly settled back into his watery hiding place.

He let the heat of his anger simmer. He felt like a cauldron; his insides were on fire, a roiling, boiling mass licked by a white-hot flame. He contented himself with studying his pursuers. Revenge would have to wait for another time. Most of the reivers carried short swords, though a few preferred battle-axes.

All of the reivers wore black armor, with their shoulders and upper body covered in steel plates or hardened leather and their thighs protected by chain mail. Flexibility and speed. The plate armor would stop most attacker's blows in battle, and the chain mail lessened the overall weight, allowing the men to move faster than expected for longer periods of time. Again, his grandfather's lessons had proven useful. Now he understood how they could follow after him so quickly. He wasn't strong enough yet to use his grandfather's sword properly, and even if he was lucky enough to succeed, he could swing with all his might and it would barely dent those plates. If he was quick with his dagger, though, one careful stab could slip right through the gaps. If you knew what you were doing, you didn't have to strike a man in the heart to kill him.

"Perhaps you're right, Oclan. Perhaps he did try to cross the river, and he drowned for his efforts." A single reiver stood by himself at the very edge of the river. He appeared to be the leader of this group. "Then again, maybe he didn't. Do you want to be the one to tell Lord Chertney that the boy drowned, only to find out later that he didn't?" The question was filled with menace. Oclan stepped back, though he wasn't one to be easily intimidated. A tall, massive man, his body dwarfed the armor he wore.

The reivers had the grizzled features of men used to battle, their arms and faces covered with the scars of war. They had long ago forgotten their fear, and that had helped them stay alive. But now, at the mention of Lord Chertney, they looked like raw recruits seeing a corpse for the first time. Their faces had gone a deathly pale, with some running their hands nervously over the hilts of their weapons. Others wiped their sleeves across their foreheads, catching the droplets of perspiration that had formed.

"No, Akala," said Oclan in a whisper, unable to meet his leader's harsh gaze.

"A very smart decision, Oclan. You're right, though. The boy probably didn't make it this far," said Akala, speaking with all the confidence he could muster. He was worried. They should have found the boy by now. When they had discovered the tunnel, the boy was no more than a half-day ahead. They should have already been back at the Crag with their prize. "The river is our new line. We'll backtrack until we reach the Crag. He's probably holed up somewhere along the way."

"Finding him won't be easy in the dark," said another soldier. "I've heard a few of the stories about this boy. He enjoys the dark more than the sunlight, his eyes glowing a dark green. They say he's a goblin when the full moon shines."

Akala stared at the reiver. The soldier averted his eyes, unable to withstand the malevolent gaze.

"Yes, I've heard those stories about the boy as well, Rolan. But we don't have much choice, do we? Personally, I'm more concerned about the stories involving Lord Chertney. Do you want to find out if those are true?"

Rolan shook his head emphatically. Several of the reivers imitated the soldier instinctively. Lord Chertney was one person they would avoid at all costs.

"Then we begin our search again," said Akala, walking swiftly toward the forest. His men branched out to either side. "Keep your eyes and ears open. We can't afford to let him get by us. Oclan, sound your horn. Let the other groups know our plan. If we do this right, we'll catch him between here and the Crag. Then we won't have to worry about Lord Chertney."

Akala shouted out several more orders, but Thomas could no longer hear them. The trees of the forest swallowed whatever remaining commands he had given. Thomas breathed a sigh of relief. He had escaped, for now.

He waited a full ten minutes before emerging from the water, just to make sure he was alone. Lips blue and teeth chattering uncontrollably, he desperately wished for a cloak. It was almost full dark, with just a touch of red in the western sky. He had to look at his hand in order to have it loosen its grip on the dagger he still held, as it wouldn't let go easily. The wind, which carried a chill from the north, had picked up. He couldn't stop shivering. The sword made it feel like he had strapped a huge icicle to his back. Tonight was a time for a fire. But he couldn't take the chance of it being seen. Better to be cold than dead. Then again, the only difference between the cold and a steel blade was that the cold took longer to kill you.

Thomas started to walk north through the shallow water running along the bank, just a few feet from the river's edge. He didn't want to leave tracks for anyone to follow in the soft mud and dirt of the shore. The necklace pulled him in that direction. In fact, the necklace was the only part of him that felt warm. He had never before seen the Southern River, and he now had a tremendous desire to never see it again. Having wished for water earlier in the day, Thomas had forgotten that you often got what you asked for, just not in the way you expected. The Southern River was the only river of significance in the Highlands, fully a mile wide. The Southern River. He wondered who had named it. It actually was located in the northern part of the Highlands and ran all the way through the Northern Steppes to the base of the Charnel Mountains where it disappeared. If anything, it should have been called the Northern River. Thomas focused on this new riddle, finding that with his mind occupied, he had an easier time ignoring the cold that had permeated every part of his body. He couldn't even feel the water he was walking through. His feet were too numb from the cold.

He remembered what Rasoul had taught him about the river. The one thing that stood out in his mind was that all the other rivers that ran through the kingdoms flowed from north to south. The Southern River flowed from south to north. Perhaps that was it, he reasoned. Whoever had named it had wanted to stress the difference, with the source of the river near the coast and its end somewhere in the Charnel Mountains, rather than the other way around. The way you would have expected it to be. Thomas reminded himself that nothing was ever the way you expected it to be.

A quick movement among the trees jarred Thomas from his thoughts. A reiver burst through the brush, coming to stand on the bank no more than fifty feet

49

from where Thomas had stopped. He held an evil-looking battle-axe in his hands. The reiver must have been separated from his search party and either hadn't heard the horn or simply ignored it. Whatever the reason, Thomas was trapped. All the reiver had to do was turn in his direction and all his efforts to escape would have been for naught. Yes, he had killed an assassin the night before. But that was when he had the advantage, and surprise as much as skill had been the reason for his success. He wasn't arrogant enough to think that he could defeat a reiver one on one and survive with just a dagger, especially with the icicle on his back slowing him down.

The reiver continued to look in the other direction, examining the trees and bushes running along the river for any sign of passage. Thomas only had seconds before the black-clad soldier turned in his direction. Then he would see his prey standing right before him, much like a deer cornered by a mountain cat. Even with the approaching nightfall, Thomas would be hard to miss. Feeling the current of the river tug gently at his legs, he wished with all his heart that he could be anything else just for that moment.

Staring at the water, without knowing what he was doing, he began to extend his senses, much as he did earlier in the day when he wanted to see what was going on in the forest. But this time, rather than pushing his senses outward, he pulled them inward, within himself. He focused all of his concentration on his immediate surroundings, pouring all of his energy, all of himself, into the river. He imagined the feeling of being submerged by the water, something he found very easy to do just then, since his body still felt like it was in the river's grasp. A picture formed in his mind of himself standing in the river with the water flowing all around him, as if it was covering him completely. Quickly the image changed, until the shape of his body became invisible in the black water, though he had not moved a step.

Not realizing he had closed his eyes, he opened them. The reiver was just turning toward him. Thomas held his breath as the image he had formed, of him actually becoming part of the river, remained in his mind. The reiver's eyes passed right over him. The reiver was staring directly at him, but he made no move to attack. Whatever he had done had worked. Thomas smiled. So far today his luck had held. He looked down at his feet. He could see himself clearly — his hands, his legs, his body — but the reiver saw only the river.

Though the reiver took a few steps toward him, his eyes were no longer on Thomas. The soldier was trying to look farther down the bank of the river. Thomas was so close, he could pick out the individual links forming the man's armor. He fingered his dagger nervously. Maybe his trick wasn't as effective as he thought. He relaxed somewhat. The reiver was still completely unaware that the one he was looking for was within arm's reach. Thomas concentrated on maintaining the image he held in his mind. Now was not the time to make a foolish mistake. It wasn't long before the reiver sighed in frustration, then turned and trotted back into the forest. Thomas waited several minutes, giving the reiver time to move deeper into the trees, before releasing the image from his mind. Whatever he had done had worked, but it certainly did take a lot of energy. He felt more exhausted than ever.

He needed time to think. What he had done was similar to extending his senses into the forest around him, but it was also different, requiring more strength and concentration. He had to figure out what he had done, how he had done it and if he could do it again. He was sure he could. And if so, maybe he could do some other things that he had never considered before.

Now was not the time to ponder his newfound abilities, however. He had only one immediate concern, and that was putting as much distance as possible between himself and the reivers. Night had finally covered the land, giving the trees of the forest dark and sinister shapes. Before yesterday, he might have felt some nervousness about being so far from the Crag, from what he thought of as home. But not anymore. Not after everything he had gone through. Now he welcomed the darkness.

Thomas began his journey along the river once again, careful to walk in the water to prevent any sign of his passage, allowing the warmth of the necklace to guide him. He had considered finding a place to sleep, but he didn't want to take the chance. If he did stop he would have to start a fire; otherwise he'd freeze to death since he was soaked to the bone. But he couldn't do that with his pursuers so close. At least if he kept walking he could improve his chances of escape and still work some warmth back into his body, however meager it might be. Judging by the current temperature, frost would greet him in the morning. The reivers certainly would enjoy that. Their prey had escaped, only to freeze to death during the night.

As the hours passed his fear and lack of sleep began to affect his mind. He felt like he was living in a dark cloud, and his eyes kept playing tricks on him. Several trees looked like men, setting his heart racing. And his thoughts were no better. More than once he thought he saw his grandfather's ghost standing in front of him. He didn't even remember when he had walked out of the river and into the forest. He only knew that he should follow the warmth of his necklace, now to the northeast. Thomas no longer thought of anything. He was too tired. He let his instincts take over, trusting his feet would find the best possible route on their own.

The ghost of his grandfather and the shadowy reivers finally left him, only to be replaced by something else. He envisioned his grandfather standing on the rock in the Hall of the Highland Lord, its walls and ceiling consumed by flames that licked higher and higher. His grandfather saw him there and beckoned to him, yelling that he should enter the Hall, now more flames than anything else. But Thomas didn't, and he saw the hurt in his grandfather's eyes, the betrayal. Soon, all that remained were yellow-orange flames. His grandfather was gone, consumed by the fire.

Thomas seemed to open his eyes for the first time all night. He stopped for a moment to get his bearings and clear the cobwebs from his head. The sky was just beginning to color a bright yellow-orange in the east. He now stood on the summit of one of the last Highland mountains on the coast. To his right, the dark blue glitter of the Sea of Mist dazzled him.

He had walked through the night, not exactly knowing where his feet were going, but still ending up where he wanted to be. His breath frosted in the cold air.

His clothes were still wet, but he had not caught a chill. Another thing to be thankful for. The rising sun just beginning to emerge from behind the mountaintops warmed him. He had escaped, at least for now. He chose to ignore the fact that he wasn't sure where he was going or what he would do when he got there, or even if he would know when he got there. He took a moment to appreciate his home. The home he was now responsible for. The Crag was simply a manmade structure. The magnificent mountains rising up to meet the sky and the lush forest that covered the land were really the center of the Highlands, its core, its heart. It was a beautiful country, one that he did not want to lose.

Thomas started to make his way down the slope, placing his feet carefully because of the rocky scrabble under his boots and the steep drop on either side. His stomach reminded him that he hadn't eaten anything since hiding in the Southern River, so he promised himself that once he got into the next valley, he would find some food and fresh water.

He reached the base of the mountain by midday and located a small stream and some berries he could munch on as he continued his journey to the northeast. It was a lot easier staying awake when the sun was up. The salty smell of the sea tickled his nose with every gust of wind. The Sea of Mist was no more than a mile away. He stopped a moment to get a closer look at a particular tree. A heart tree. That was strange indeed. There were probably only a few hundred in the Highlands, and his grandfather had said they were out of place. Someone long ago had tried to plant groves of them, but only a few had survived. Those that did were truly magnificent, rising several hundred feet into the air, their trunks sometimes a hundred feet around and their roots growing as tall as a man above ground and then plunging for thousands of feet below. Many believed that these trees were the heart of the forest. Without them, the forest would wither and die.

As Thomas walked slowly around the base of the tree, trying to see up through the branches to get an idea as to just how tall this tree was, he heard a rustle in the bushes behind him. His dagger instantly appeared in his hand. He stood there on his toes, waiting to see what had caused the noise. Hearing the rustle again, he became curious and stepped on silent feet to the bushes. Whatever had made the noise was on the other side. He tried to peer through the dense foliage, but to no avail. Stepping through the undergrowth, careful not to disturb the branches or leaves, the scene surprised him.

A large black wolf lay dead beneath a tree, eyes staring sightlessly up at the sky. Several arrows stuck out from the wolf's side. Reivers. The sight before him made him angry. Killing to eat was one thing; killing for sport was another. A squawk made him twist to his left, dagger held out before him. Thomas let out a slow breath and put his dagger back in its sheath. A vulture had followed the scent of death and now stood on the ground several feet away. In front of the vulture stood a wolf pup covered in thick black fur except for a streak of white that ran across its face. The vulture was surprised by the ferocity of the little wolf pup, standing there growling, teeth bared, ready to defend his dead mother. The vulture wasn't sure what to do — ignore the pup or kill it? Thomas made the decision for it.

He ran forward, yelling and flapping his arms. Startled, the vulture flew into the sky, its powerful wings taking it quickly through the trees. It gave one last squawk of anger before it went in search of easier prey. Looking down, Thomas saw that the pup had now turned its attention on him, stepping forward slowly, growling. Thomas moved away from the pup, not wanting to upset the little wolf. Satisfied by the retreat, the pup walked over to his mother's body and curled up by her paws. His eyes remained on Thomas, though, ready to attack if he came any closer. Thomas examined the wolf pup for several minutes, trying to figure out some way to show that he wasn't an enemy. He felt sorry for him. He had just lost his family as well.

A thought occurred to him. If he could thrust out his senses and actually see what was going on within the forest, why couldn't he use the same ability to communicate with animals? Trying something new had already worked once at the river, so what did he have to lose? Concentrating, he extended his senses, getting a feel for all the hidden activity of the forest. But rather than pushing out his senses he focused on the pup instead. The wolf was now on his feet, staring at him. It didn't know what to make of the brief mental contact. Thomas wasn't sure as well. He had done it. He had actually reached into the pup's mind and felt all the emotions surging through there. The anger, the pain of his mother's death, then the surprise of having Thomas there as well. He had not actually spoken to the wolf, but had instead used emotion to communicate. It had worked. He couldn't stop himself from smiling.

Getting a grip on his excitement, Thomas reached out again. Using his emotions, he expressed his sorrow at the pup's plight and his anger at those who had committed the murder. The pup continued to stare at the boy who had invaded his mind. Thomas then revealed his own sorrow and pain at the loss of his grandfather. Thomas thought that this time he felt something in his own mind, some emotion the wolf had sent back to him. Kneeling down, Thomas extended his hand, waiting to see what the wolf would do. The pup still stared at him, even shaking his head once as if to make sense of what was going on. Then, slowly, the wolf took a few steps toward him, sniffing the ground along the way. Finally, with the wolf no more than inches from his hand, Thomas communicated a feeling of friendship to the little ball of fur. The wolf stared up at him for a long moment before sniffing Thomas' extended hand. Then, ever so hesitantly, Thomas thought he felt a touch in his mind, that of friendship as well.

"I'm sorry about your mother, little one," said Thomas. "I've lost my family, too. Well, my grandfather anyway. But I guess one person counts as a family."

The pup nodded his head. Thomas felt in his mind an acceptance, as if there was little difference between them. Thomas smiled down at his new friend.

"Let's see if we can do something about your mother so she's isn't bothered again," said Thomas, rising to his feet. He knew that he couldn't afford to be in one place for too long a time, but he ignored the warning. Right now more than anything he needed a friend. Extending his senses, he found a small stream just off to the right. Before walking through the bushes, he motioned for the pup to stay where he was.

He was in luck. The streambed was dry since the fall rains had not yet arrived, and on its edge lay several large rocks. Thomas collected as many as he could, went back through the brush and then set them against the pup's mother. After the first trip, Thomas took off the sword hanging from his back so he could move more easily through the bushes. The wolf watched his work, until finally his mother was protected from scavengers. Thomas didn't have any way to dig into the ground to make a grave, so the rocks would have to do. Looking at the small pup, which stared intently at the rocks, Thomas perceived a touch of thanks in his mind.

"It looks like we are brothers of a sort," said Thomas, strapping his sword onto his back again. The wolf rose from the ground and stretched his legs. "It's time to go, I think."

Turning to the northeast, Thomas set off once again. But this time, a small wolf pup followed at his heels.

CHAPTER EIGHT

FAILURE

Akala and his reivers returned to the Crag in frustration. They had failed. If the boy had been found, a horn would have sounded. Akala had wished desperately for success, to hear that horn. As he played it all through his mind again he knew that he had done everything he could. He had divided his men into parties to cover a larger area more thoroughly, giving each a specific part of the forest to search. A small boy shouldn't have been able to escape, but he had. The thought of reporting his failure to Lord Chertney made his throat dry, fear gripping him for the first time in years. Akala had seen death hundreds of times as a soldier, thousands probably. It didn't frighten him as it did other people. But Chertney scared him. He took solace in the knowledge that Chertney terrified all of his men as well.

Akala walked through the still-smoldering buildings that once formed the boundary of the inner courtyard as he reached the place where the outer curtain of the Crag should have been. In many places, tall, graceful towers were now nothing more than piles of rubble. A group of women and children huddled off to the side, close to where the gate had once stood.

Most were covered in blood and bruises. Those who could work would probably be sent to the mines. The Highlands was a rich land, but you couldn't tell that from its harsh exterior. You had to dig for it. And he knew the men he fought for would begin that enterprise as soon as possible. He did not envy the fate of those who could not work. Ogren remained on the plateau.

On the far side of the plain reivers were forming into battle groups, this time to pursue any Marchers who had escaped. A small voice screamed a warning in the back of his head. He was the leader of the reivers. It fell to him to make the necessary preparations for this next task. But he had not been called back. He set his worry aside as best he could. He must deal with his failure first. Then he could find out who had usurped his authority and make an example of him.

Walking across the drawbridge, Akala strode toward the large black tent that sat in front of the entrance to the Hall of the Highland Lord. A single white pennant flew at its top with a black sword sewn along its length. Just looking at the pennant made him shiver. The mark of Lord Chertney could do that to the strongest of men. Drawing closer to the tent, he saw two Ogren standing on both sides of the flap that served as the entrance. Sweat began to drip down his face. He wiped his forehead with his sleeve. It was a cool afternoon, but to him it felt like he had stepped into a fire pit. Glancing back, he was glad to see that his men felt much the same way.

There was only one way to advance in the army of reivers that Chertney commanded, the Army of the Black Sword as it was called. You had to defeat your superior in a duel. That's how Akala had achieved his rank, and he knew that Oclan wanted it. Before entering the Highlands, he thought Oclan might actually challenge him. But Oclan had chosen not to. Nevertheless, he had become more difficult to deal with. Many times Akala had wanted to kill the bastard and be done with it. That was the easiest way to eliminate this latest threat to his power. The two large axes of the Ogren, their blades shining wickedly in the waning afternoon light, brought Akala to a halt and his thoughts to more immediate concerns. The Ogren regarded him with what looked like hunger. He guessed that this was how a chicken felt, right before the farmer cut off its head.

"Enter," said a deep voice from within the tent. Instantly, the Ogren removed their axes from his path, though they continued to look at him and his men as if they were pieces of meat. He actually felt sorry for those Highlanders by the wall. He wouldn't wish their fate on anyone. Stepping inside the tent, his men right behind him, they nearly walked right over him as he stopped just within the entrance so his eyes could adjust to the dim light.

"You've failed, Akala."

A dark figure stepped forward from the other side of the tent. If Akala had not seen the movement, Lord Chertney would still be invisible. Chertney was a tall man, almost wraithlike in appearance, with long black hair and a mustache that curled at the edges. His intense black eyes were hypnotic. Akala had served Chertney for years, and he had never seen him dressed in anything but midnight black. His breeks and shirt were covered by worn black armor, the dents and scratches from the battle two, almost three days before, still visible. The sword at his side made Akala uneasy. Though it was sheathed, he had seen it many times before. Made from the blackest steel, a single scratch would kill a man, much like certain poisons, though death by poison would be less painful than a touch from that blade. Chertney moved like a snake as he came to stand before Akala. A very poisonous snake, Akala reminded himself.

"No excuses, Akala?" asked Chertney, his voice menacing. "You've never failed me before."

"We tried, Lord Chertney," said Akala, having a hard time getting the words out. His throat was as parched as the desert. "We truly did. But the boy was too quick for us."

"You let a boy escape," said Chertney. An evil smile spread across his face as he walked toward the back of the tent, forcing Akala and his men to squint in order to pick him out from the black cloth. To Akala, it seemed as if he spoke to a floating head. "A very important boy, Akala. I cannot have a man bested by a boy leading my men."

Whipping around, Chertney extended his hand and mumbled a few words under his breath.

Akala had no time to react as something invisible seized his throat. It felt like a hand, but there was nothing there that he could see. The grip grew tighter and tighter. Akala struggled to breathe, clutching at his throat. His men looked on in horror as their leader's face slowly turned blue, yet no one stepped forward to help him. Akala's futile efforts grew weaker. Gasping for air, his eyes bulged, until finally he slumped to the carpet.

The reivers stared down at their former leader in horror. They had seen men die before, but never like this. Chertney's voice immediately pulled their eyes from the corpse.

"When I give an order, I expect it to be carried out. Do you understand the consequences if you fail?"

"Yes, my lord," they said, stumbling over one another in their fear. They'd do anything to avoid Akala's fate.

"Good," said Chertney, casually stepping over Akala's body. He smiled, seeing the beads of sweat running down their faces. He enjoyed making people afraid. "Oclan, you now lead the reivers. I want the lower Highlands cleared of Marchers. Is that understood?"

"Yes, Lord Chertney!" said Oclan, shouting out the words.

"Then take your men and get to work. Or do you wish to share the fate of your former commander?"

"No, my lord," said Oclan, already pushing his men out through the flap, wanting nothing so much in life than to be out of that tent. After the reivers had gone, Chertney looked down at Akala, studying the man's face in death.

"As I expected," he said absently. "It looks as if I will need some additional assistance with this small task. We can't have the heir to the Highland throne running around free, now can we? A troublesome boy, this one. When I get my hands on him, he will have wished he died as he was supposed to in the Crag."

His master had made it very clear that the boy was to die in the attack. There were to be no mistakes in that respect. At the time, he had thought nothing of it. His master didn't like his servants to think. He liked them to perform their tasks. But now he had to think. Why would his master want a boy dead more than Talyn Kestrel, the actual Lord of the Highlands? When asked what fate Kestrel was to have, his master had said that if he wasn't killed in the attack, Chertney could do what he wanted with him. But not the boy. The boy was to die immediately. He would have liked to ponder it more, to see if there was something he was missing that he could turn to his advantage, but he was interrupted.

"Have you completed your task, Lord Chertney?" asked John Killeran, the nasal quality of his voice becoming more evident as he followed his overlarge nose into the tent. "I would hate to report to the High King that you've failed. Have you gained control of the Highlands as ordered?"

Chertney turned slowly toward the entrance, once again cursing his luck at having to deal with this man. This man who played at lord. Killeran supposedly served the King of Dunmoor, the kingdom that bordered the Inland Sea and Fal Carrach. But he had no illusions that Killeran served only himself, which explained why he was now in league with the High King. Chertney had the sudden urge to kill the man, to wipe that condescending smile from his ratlike face with a single slice of his blade across the throat. The arrogance and condescension apparent in Killeran's every movement set his temper boiling. Instead, he took a long breath before answering.

"The Crag has fallen, and most of the Marchers garrisoned there are dead," replied Chertney in a calm voice, struggling to rein in his anger. His voice became colder as he thought of slicing that large nose off of Killeran's face. Perhaps another time. "Some of the Marchers escaped, and there were already several large squads of Marchers out scouring the countryside for us in the last few weeks. I've gotten reports that they're heading to the higher passes. Unfortunately, we don't have the resources to go after them all."

Killeran's face darkened as he listened to Chertney's report. "The High King will not be happy, Chertney."

"We will eliminate as many Marchers as we can. You will have to deal with whatever scraps remain," said Chertney, ignoring Killeran's glare.

The urge to kill the sniveling lord grew stronger. His master had ordered him to help the High King take the Crag. He had not told him to conquer the Highlands. Killeran had done little but complain and question Chertney's orders since he had started to secretly move groups of reivers and Ogren into the Highlands to prepare for the attack. And Lord Nose had been noticeably absent during the assault. Killeran wore the same armor as he had when the battle began, a gleaming silver breastplate and thigh guards with a long billowy white cloak running down his back. If not for his nose and his cold eyes, with his broad shoulders and curly brown hair, Lord Johin Killeran might have been considered a dashing figure. Yet, the vanity and arrogance stripped that away. Chertney was certain that Killeran had never removed his sword from its sheath

65

since the attack on the Crag began. Killeran had worked years to develop his reputation as a deadly swordsman. Chertney thought it was just that — a reputation.

"Do I need to explain it to you again?" asked Killeran in mocking disbelief. "The High King not only wanted the Crag destroyed, but he wanted the Marchers eliminated as well. This is the perfect opportunity to get rid of them. They may be considered the greatest warriors in the Kingdoms, but there aren't that many of them. By destroying the Marchers, we destroy any resistance. That means the High King can begin mining this horrid land in peace. If the Marchers remain, even just a small group, it will make my task that much harder. How is the High King supposed to advance his plans if he doesn't have the financial resources to support them?"

Chertney stood calmly through Killeran's lecture, but his insides churned angrily. He realized that he was massaging the hilt of his sword, so he took his hand away. He'd have to bear with this insolent worm just a little longer. If he was lucky, sometime in the future his master would allow him to kill Killeran. He'd do it now, but he knew the consequences of going against his master's wishes. He'd seen it many times before. You would think that after a time you would become desensitized to something like that. Chertney definitely enjoyed suffering, or rather, making other people suffer. But thinking about what his master did to those who did not obey his orders almost made him ill. He pushed those thoughts from his mind, reminding himself that for now his master was allied to the High King. However, alliances with his master did not last forever.

Soon things would change. Then Killeran would be fair game.

"Why are you smiling?" demanded Killeran, taking a step back from Chertney and almost tripping over something on the floor. He jumped back in surprise, not having seen the body of the dead reiver when he walked in. The man's eyes stared straight up in shock, his face blue, yet there was no discernible mark on him.

Killeran had heard rumors that Chertney was a warlock, a master of Dark Magic. The body and Chertney's smile, cold and harsh, confirmed it. Killeran quickly surmised that Chertney was more powerful than he. Instead of frightening him as it should, it infuriated him. He hated anyone who had more power than he did.

"And your other task?" asked Killeran. "Have you at least completed that?" The stony look on Chertney's face did not faze him, though he did take a few more steps backwards, so he would be closer to the tent flap.

Chertney thought of letting the Ogren take care of Killeran. Perhaps he could even make it look like an accident. There was not much you could do when Ogren were hungry, except stay out of the way. Chertney told himself to stop wishing. The sooner he finished this meeting, the sooner he would be rid of Killeran.

"The Lord of the Highlands is dead," replied Chertney, pointing to a table in the back of the room, "As is Benlorin Kestrel."

Killeran stepped toward the back of the tent, unable to make out the objects sitting on the table from where he was. He immediately leapt back, swallowing several times as gorge rose in his throat. Chertney had placed the heads of Talyn and Benlorin Kestrel on spikes stuck into the wood. Pools of congealed blood had formed beneath each one. But there was a third spike, and it was empty.

"And the grandson?" asked Killeran, unable to tear his eyes from the grisly sight.

"He's still missing."

"Missing," whispered Killeran. Things were not working out as he had planned. Having squads of Marchers roaming the Highlands was bad enough, but they could be dealt with. Yes, the High King wanted the riches of the Highlands, but he also wanted the Highlands for himself. Then he could turn his attention to the other kingdoms. But the Highlands was the first step. The most important step. If that boy remained free, the High King would have a hard time making a legitimate claim. "How could he be missing?"

"He escaped through a tunnel beneath the Hall of the Highland Lord," replied Chertney.

"He escaped," repeated Killeran, shaking his head in disbelief. How could a boy, no more than ten years old, escape? "Is there anything else that you have failed to do that you have not yet told me?"

Chertney again struggled to control his anger. This worm should be stepped on. He promised himself that Killeran would die, and he would feel a great deal more pain than the reiver lying at his feet.

"The boy will be found and killed," said Chertney simply. "You need not worry about that."

"Not worry. Not worry! And why should I not worry about that?" asked Killeran, letting out a nervous laugh. "You have failed to accomplish your simple tasks, but I'm not supposed to worry about the heir to the Highland throne running free?"

"He will be dead soon enough," said Chertney. This time it was his turn to smile. "I've got a surprise for him. He may have escaped my reivers, but his luck will soon run out."

"And just what exactly is this—" Killeran's words died in his mouth. Chertney motioned to the very back corner of the tent. A figure coalesced out of the darkness, a figure that made Killeran's entire body turn cold. He had heard of creatures like this before, but he had never seen one. He had never wanted to see one. Now he was certain the stories about Chertney were true, as well as the rumors as to just who his master was. It was dangerous enough to have a secret alliance with the High King. That paled in comparison to this. He would have to be much more careful in the future now that he knew where he truly stood in the scheme of things.

"No one can escape from a Nightstalker," said Chertney. The creature stepped into the dim light. A silent battle ensued as the torches struggled to light the space around the creature. It was well over eight feet tall, its body the color of black granite. Raven-black scales covered its body. The only way to see it was to look at its head. Unless it was caught in the sunlight, the Nightstalker was invisible, its body automatically adapting to the darkness around it. But you could never miss the eyes. The blood-red eyes that glowed in the dark.

Chertney was having a hard time seeing the powerfully built beast himself, except for the bright red eyes and the sharp white teeth that protruded from its jaws. Something large stuck up over the head of the creature, and then Killeran realized what it was. Wings. Large, black leathery wings that were now folded together. He looked down at the creature's hands and took an involuntary step backward. He was now almost completely outside the tent. Instead of hands, the creature had claws that could easily tear a man apart. The Nightstalker was created for one purpose, and one purpose only — to kill.

"As you can see," said Chertney, "the boy will not be alive much longer. Do you remember your history, Killeran? Do you know what a Nightstalker can do?" Chertney continued before Killeran could reply. "My master created these creatures to be his assassins. They're very good at what they do. They can cover great distances quickly. They fade in and out of darkness. Tremendous strength. Best of all, when a Nightstalker is given prey, it will hunt until its task is complete, no matter how long it takes. It never takes very long, though. So, as you can see, Lord Killeran, you have nothing to worry about regarding the boy. He will not be with us much longer."

CHAPTER NINE

NEW BEGINNING

It took Thomas several hours to build the grave, so it was not until midafternoon that he and his new friend started their journey. Night was almost upon them. Thomas walked under the trees, cradling the small pup in his arms. The wolf had followed him for a good distance, but eventually it had become too much of a struggle for him. Thomas felt the warmth of the pup against his chest. At least tonight, if there weren't any surprises, he might actually get some sleep. Even better, his clothes had dried during the day and his walking had driven the chill from his body. Nevertheless, the events of the last few days had taken their toll on Thomas. The exhaustion that was slowly gaining control of his body dampened his desire to continue. As the sun sank in the west, he knew that he would have to stop soon and catch a rabbit. He could survive on berries and nuts if he had to, but his little friend could not, and by the look of him the pup had not eaten in several days.

Finding it harder and harder to keep his eyes open, Thomas walked into a large glade with a small stream running through it, drawn by the sound of rushing water. He was halfway to the stream when he realized he was not alone. Thomas immediately backed away. The wolf pup, sensing his worry, came awake.

Two people stood before him. They had already started a small fire by the stream. The wonderful smells coming from the pot that hung over the flames made his stomach growl in protest. He heard the same noise coming from the pup. Thomas licked his lips as the breeze blew another whiff of the stew past him.

He studied the two people for several long moments, thankful that neither had yet approached him. They seemed content to study him. Thomas sensed that they had measured him from head to toe, inside and out, in seconds. A tall man stood behind the fire, having risen from where he was tasting the stew with a wooden spoon. He had dark hair and a short black beard salted with grey. His green eyes held an intensity that Thomas found frightening, as if he could see things about Thomas that Thomas didn't even know about himself. The dark man also wore a cloak that blended in perfectly with his surroundings. It seemed to Thomas as if he was only looking at a head. The man appeared dangerous. It was the woman, though, who knocked him off balance. Standing next to the man, she appeared short, though her presence made up for her lack of stature. Her long, chestnut hair flowed halfway down her back, the curls hanging over her eyes for her to habitually brush away. He was taken by her blue eyes. They held a natural warmth that Thomas had never seen before in anyone else.

She was a beautiful woman, but that's not what unsettled him. It was his memories. His grandfather had told him stories about his mother, about her chestnut-colored hair and blue eyes. He had never met her, so he had created an image of what he thought she looked like in his mind. The image now stood before him.

The man standing behind the fire stepped around it, moving next to the woman. Thomas let his new friend down and placed his hand on the hilt of his dagger. The pup bared its teeth and positioned himself several feet in front of Thomas, once again letting out a whisper of a growl. Thomas studied the man and woman carefully. The woman gave the man a quick look of exasperation, as if she didn't want him to come around the fire. But he ignored her. The man continued to examine Thomas. This man with the hard green eyes did a better job of making Thomas feel afraid than the reivers.

Thomas attempted to look at ease, but with the intense scrutiny he was under, he kept shifting his balance from one foot to the other. He told himself to remain calm, to be ready for anything. He looked quickly to see if there were others. If need be, he could scoop up the wolf pup and escape into the trees before the man or woman could catch him. But the two strangers simply continued to study him. He felt like they were taking in everything about him and cataloging it away for future use, from his clothes to the color of his hair to the way he stood. Finally, Thomas grew tired of it. He didn't like being on display, so he adopted the same pose as the other two. His face took on an inquiring look, and he shifted his feet so he stood akimbo, a challenging glare in his eyes. At the same time, he took another hard look at them. They didn't carry any weapons, at least none that were visible. That surprised him. Thomas didn't know if he should be worried about that or not.

Seeing Thomas adjust his stance, the man grinned. He appeared pleased by Thomas' change in posture. Thomas tried to guess just how old these two strangers were, but he found it to be an impossible task. They did not look old, but there was a part of him that could feel the wisdom and knowledge they both carried. A wisdom and knowledge not normal for people of their appearance. The wolf pup remained poised before Thomas, growling in warning, ready to defend his newfound friend.

Finally, the woman walked toward him. Thomas had his dagger in hand before she had moved more than a few feet, the growl from the little wolf increasing in volume. The woman stopped, surprised at the speed with which Thomas had moved to defend himself. She had initially seen him as a young boy. Now, she revised her assessment. And she didn't like it when she was wrong. She told herself that she'd have to be more careful with her judgments in the future, especially concerning the young man standing before her.

"It seems that we have found two little wolves," said the man, a touch of amusement in his voice.

"We will not hurt you, child," said the woman. "In fact, we were looking for you."

Thomas was not surprised. Most people stayed away from this part of the Highlands if they could. It was dangerous terrain, and it was close to both the Northern Steppes and the Isle of Mist, two places that most people avoided at any cost.

"Others are looking for me as well," said Thomas. "Why should I trust you? You're not Highlanders."

"You're right, boy," replied the man, returning to the pot hanging over the fire. He picked up the wooden spoon again and stirred the bubbling stew. "You shouldn't."

The woman gave the man a frosty glare, a look that could freeze water in the middle of summer. When the man saw the look, he instantly regretted his words. He could never understand how a woman could put so much into a single glare. The man stared at the stew, intent on his task.

Satisfied that she would no longer be interrupted, the woman turned back to Thomas, her glare now a welcoming smile.

"We won't hurt you, child. My name is Rya, and this is Rynlin," she said, motioning toward the man who continued to have an inordinate amount of interest in the fragrant stew.

The woman waited expectantly for the boy to give his name, but he did not. His expression became more suspicious, and the grip on his dagger remained tight. She looked to Rynlin for help, but he shrugged. She gave him an angry glare. Rynlin once again came to the conclusion that no matter what you did, you could never fully please a woman, even if you were doing exactly what she wanted.

When they had gotten to the clearing and made camp, knowing that the boy would be there within the hour, Rya had said very clearly that she would handle matters, and that Rynlin should do his best not to get in the way. Well, maybe he could prove helpful after all. He stole a quick glance at Thomas and caught him glancing at the stew. Rynlin motioned to the stew with his head.

"You look hungry, child," said Rya, picking up on her husband's hint. "Join us for a meal."

The boy continued to stare at her. Standing on the balls of his feet, he looked like a rabbit about to run. Rya corrected herself again. A rabbit with a bite and a very interesting friend. Seeing that the boy would not be swayed with words, she moved over to the fire and pulled a few things from her pack. As Rynlin stirred the stew, she took out a small cutting board. Rya used her belt knife to slice several thick pieces from a loaf of bread and a block of cheese. With a final taste from the wooden spoon, Rynlin nodded to himself and used a cloth to lift the pot from the fire and set it down on a rock. He then scooped the stew into three bowls. He took one to his wife, placed another bowl and a few slices of bread and cheese on a rock on the other side of the fire, then settled himself next to Rya on a large rock jutting out over the stream. The boy had still not moved. Rynlin shrugged his shoulders at his wife's unasked question and then began to enjoy his evening meal.

The wonderful smell of the stew set Thomas' stomach churning. He knew that the pup was hungry as well, but was not going to move forward unless Thomas did so. The stew smelled delicious, and he'd do anything for a piece of bread or cheese. He hadn't eaten a real meal in two days, and he was certain that the wolf pup had gone even longer than that. The man and woman — Rynlin and Rya — were comfortably seated on the other side of the fire. Thomas judged it safe enough to eat a few bites if he kept an eye on his two hosts. He walked to the rock and the wolf pup followed. When he looked down at the stew, his stomach growled in protest once again. Confirming that Rynlin and Rya remained seated, he lifted the wolf onto the rock. Then he picked out several pieces of meat from the stew for his friend. Thomas remained standing. He didn't want to be caught by surprise.

Hesitantly, he took a bite. It was probably the best bowl of stew he had ever tasted, and whether that was because it really was or he was too hungry to tell the difference didn't matter. His little friend was probably thinking much the same thing. The pup had already eaten the pieces of meat Thomas had selected for him. Thomas picked out some more before munching on the bread and cheese. He kept an eye on the two strangers, ready to make a run for it, but they seemed content to eat their meals and watch him. The three ate their suppers in silence, Thomas not wanting to speak and Rya and Rynlin not sure how to begin. In only a few minutes everyone had eaten their fill. Thomas used a piece of bread to get the last of the stew from his bowl, smiling as the wolf pup lay down on the rock and licked a few drops of stew from his muzzle.

"Who's your friend, boy?" asked Rynlin, taking a final spoonful from his bowl before setting it down on the rock.

Idly scratching behind the wolf pup's ears, Thomas thought for a moment. He hadn't decided on a name yet.

"Beluil," he replied. The pup looked at him then, and a feeling of approval ran through Thomas' mind.

"That's a good name," said Rynlin. "And you, boy? What's your name?"

Thomas eyed the tall man with suspicion, his hand instinctively going to the hilt of his dagger. Yet even after everything he had been through in the last two days and the warning from his grandfather, he felt he could trust these two. There was just something about them that made Thomas feel safe. Even though the man had a forbidding appearance, they didn't seem to be a threat. Thomas glanced quickly at the woman, who was holding her breath. Thomas returned his gaze to the man. He judged that if this stranger was ever going to do something, he would have done it by now. He also knew that even if he were standing thirty feet back from where he was now, the man would have caught him before he reached the safety of the trees. But the one called Rynlin hadn't bothered to try.

His grandfather had warned him about trusting anyone not of the Highlands, but these two did not look like reivers. And more important, the reivers gave off a feeling of evil. These two strangers did not. In fact, the forest seemed to accept them much as it did him. And the woman had a kind face. The more he looked at the woman, the more his mind drifted to memories of his mother. He knew that he was having a hard time concentrating now that his belly was full and that the need for sleep was catching up to him. He had to start trusting someone, at least to a certain extent. Besides, he had no idea where he was going or when he would get there.

The necklace! He hadn't thought about the necklace since he entered the clearing. It now felt very warm against his skin, even hot. Reaching into his shirt, he pulled it out just to make sure. As he held it in his hand, it became even warmer. He sensed that he had reached his destination, but he couldn't explain why.

"Thomas," he said, letting the necklace drop from his hand.

"Thomas," repeated Rya, savoring the name, almost as if she were tasting a bottle of wine for the first time. "That, too, is a good name."

"And your last name, Thomas?" asked Rynlin.

Thomas looked at Rynlin, this time focusing on his eyes. Those eyes seemed to hold the answers to many questions, questions Thomas didn't even know to ask.

"I think you already know that," said Thomas.

Rynlin smiled. He was indeed a very smart boy.

"You have two last names," said Rynlin, adopting a pedantic tone, "though you probably only use one. If you used your mother's last name, it would be Keldragan. But since you were raised in the Highlands, where most go by the names of their fathers, you more likely use the second. Kestrel. Your name is Thomas Kestrel."

Thomas smiled. He was not surprised that the tall man's guess would be right; that this forbidding man would know his name, though he had not heard anyone ever speak the name Keldragan, except for his grandfather. That indeed was his mother's name, though he had never used it. He didn't think most of the people in the Crag knew his mother's last name. He didn't have time to wonder how this man, who was obviously not a Highlander, could know such a thing. The woman immediately followed with a question of her own.

"That's a beautiful necklace, Thomas. Where did you come by it?"

Thomas fingered the amulet hanging at the end of the silver chain, having forgotten to tuck it back under his shirt. He had not expected the question. He examined the amulet carefully for a moment, taking in the workmanship, the skill required to carve the unicorn's horn so delicately into the soft metal. He had only worn it for two days, but it already felt like it was a part of him. That it was him, in a way.

"It was my mother's," he answered, still examining the amulet. He ran a finger along the twists of the unicorn's horn. "My grandfather gave it to me." Almost as an afterthought, he added, "Right before he died."

The finality of his words brought tears to Rya's eyes, and surprisingly Thomas saw a look of sadness cross Rynlin's face as well.

"Do you know what that necklace can do, Thomas?" asked Rya, gaining control of her emotions. He was looking at her intently now. For some reason Thomas felt a closeness to her that he had never felt with anyone else before, even his grandfather. She didn't give him a chance to answer.

"It's a very old necklace, Thomas. More than a thousand years old, in fact. It's actually a tool, rather than jewelry. It belongs to a very old family, one that is rarely mentioned now, if even remembered, though some of its members still walk the Kingdoms." Thomas was captured by her eyes and listened to her words intently. A part of him knew that this story connected to him in some way.

"Did your grandfather tell you what it could do, Thomas?"

"Yes," he said in a quiet voice, still not sure where this discussion was going. "When he gave it to me, we were under attack. The Crag, I mean." He looked over at Rynlin. At the mention of an attack, the tall man sat up straight. He resembled a lion ready to pounce. "He wanted me to escape, but he wouldn't go with me. So he gave me the necklace and said that I should follow it to safety. If I walked in a direction that was dangerous, it would grow cold. If I walked in a direction that led to safety, it would grow warm. That's how I ended up here."

Rya nodded, "Yes, that is one of the things it can do. It was originally created by this family for that specific reason. You see, Thomas, this family had a history that involved the Talent."

The word Talent opened a door in Thomas' mind. It felt like everything was clicking in place, but he still wasn't sure how. The history books had talked of the Talent, another word for the natural magic or power of the world. While thinking about that word — Talent — he thought that perhaps it was the correct term for what he could do. He didn't know why; it just seemed right. Many people said that there was no one left who could use the Talent, and that those who could were warlocks, the servants of the Shadow Lord. But his grandfather had said that those people were naive. If you didn't understand something, it was easier to go through life denying its existence. His grandfather had confirmed that the Talent was still alive in the world, and that using it didn't mean you were evil. It was how you used the Talent that determined if the user was good or evil.

"This family served a particular purpose in the world, and as a part of that purpose, the necklaces proved necessary. Rynlin and I are a part of that family," she said, pulling an identical necklace from beneath her shirt. Rynlin mimicked her action. Thomas saw how the light of the fire danced across the silver of Rynlin's necklace. All three looked exactly the same.

"When our daughter was a young girl, Rynlin and I gave her a necklace just like the ones we wear now. She was a beautiful girl, with sharp blue eyes and chestnut-colored hair. In fact, she smiled just as you do."

Thomas' mind churned at a furious pace. Everything was coming at him so fast, he did not have time to think. The description of Rya's daughter immediately brought to mind the image he had created of his mother. Unwittingly, he whispered, "Marya."

"Yes, Thomas," said Rya. A tear streaked slowly down her cheek, though she was smiling. "Our daughter's name was Marya, and your mother's name was Marya. Your father's name was Benlorin, but Marya was your mother. You're wearing Marya's necklace, Thomas. You're wearing our daughter's necklace."

Ever since he had walked into the clearing and met these two strangers, he had done his best to control his emotions. His grandfather had always said that you could judge a man by his face, and if you could hide what you intended to do from those around you, you had the advantage. Thomas had tried to do this, and he thought that he had succeeded for the most part. But Rya's words knocked away the wall he had put up around his emotions. The shock of the realization that ran across his mind registered clearly on his face.

"Yes, Thomas," said Rya. "I can see that you understand now. Our daughter, Marya, was your mother."

Before the last word had left her lips, Rya was up and across the fire in an instant, sweeping Thomas up in a fierce hug. Tears of joy ran down her face. Thomas could not escape her grasp, and he wasn't sure he wanted to. He kept hearing Rya whisper into his hair, "I have a grandson. I have a grandson." His fear, sorrow and exertion fell on him all at once. For the first time in two days, Thomas fell asleep.

Rynlin watched the look of joy spread across his wife's face as she pulled her grandson into her arms. He hadn't seen his wife smile like that in a long time, since Marya had died, in fact. Thomas' face, his eyes, the way he stood, all reminded him of his daughter. He wanted to move across the fire and join his wife, but he couldn't make himself move. He could only stare at Thomas and marvel at the resemblance. He didn't know what to say or do. He had never had a grandchild before, and the surprise of finding one immobilized him.

Rya adapted to surprises much better than he did. What galled him the most, though, was that he always knew what to say or do. So why couldn't he do anything but watch his wife cradle Thomas in her arms? A small smile crept onto Rynlin's face. He told himself that he was smiling for his wife, because she was so happy, but a voice in his head told him he was a liar. And if he denied it, he knew in his heart that the voice would win the ensuing argument. Just then, Rynlin saw a movement off to his left, up in the trees. A large raptor had settled onto one of the branches, its sharp claws digging into the bark. The raptor's keen eyes took in the scene before it, watching closely. Rynlin stared at the bird in amazement. He knew that this wasn't a coincidence. After a few long moments the bird nodded its approval. It then turned its attention to Rynlin. When they locked eyes, Rynlin noticed the warning. Silently, the raptor took flight, but its eyes remained with Rynlin. First a wolf and now a raptor. This was indeed a unique little boy.

After a few minutes, his mind turned to other things, the first being Thomas' report of the attack on the Crag. He had met Talyn Kestrel a few times before and respected him. He was a good man and a good ruler. If Thomas had been forced to escape, then Talyn was dead, because he knew that Talyn would have done everything in his power to protect him. When Marya had run off with Benlorin Kestrel against his wishes, he had thought of bringing her back, though he knew it would do no good. She would have simply run off again. But as a father, he still had to try. Talyn Kestrel had convinced him that his daughter would be all right that night he had snuck into the Crag to find his daughter and talk some sense into her.

Rynlin had found Talyn waiting for him just outside the door that led to the rooms Benlorin and Marya shared. Talyn had known that he would come. Rynlin laughed to himself as he remembered the scene. The hallway almost completely dark, except for a few lanterns where the corridors crossed. Those lanterns had intrigued him immediately, and he had spent more time talking with Talyn about them than about his daughter. In the end, he had left satisfied that his daughter would be taken care of and that he needn't worry. Talyn had promised to treat her like a daughter, and that was enough for Rynlin.

He mentally kicked himself for being too stubborn to visit her during the year that preceded her death. It was his own stubbornness that had kept him away, and the only person that matched him in stubbornness was Marya. For the thousandth time he told himself he should have gone and made peace with her. But he hadn't. And he had lost her. Looking across the fire, Rya had risen from her seat and placed Thomas close to the fire, bundling him in several blankets. She sat next to him and watched him sleep. Worrying about the past solved nothing. He had a second chance, and this time he wouldn't make the same mistake.

Getting up from his seat on the rock, he wiped a few crumbs of bread from his shirt. He then stretched his back to remove the kinks. He was no longer a young man, and sitting on a hard rock for a long time was not his idea of comfort.

"You're going to take a look?" asked Rya quietly, not wanting to disturb her grandson's slumber.

He nodded.

"Be careful," she said.

Rynlin smiled at that. She had said it so many times in the past, and he had always come back safely. Yet she still worried about him. Glancing a final time at his grandson, Rynlin walked silently into the brush surrounding the clearing.

CHAPTER TEN

CONFIRMATION

The smell of smoke and burnt wood made it hard to breathe as Rynlin crept noiselessly to the edge of a grove of trees on the plateau holding the Crag. An evening fog covered much of the land, serving as a shroud for what was once the stronghold of the Lord of the Highlands. The forbidding structure had become a wasteland. Thomas' report that the Crag had been attacked surprised Rynlin. The Crag had never fallen, and the tale-tellers liked to say that it never would. But the tale-tellers had been wrong. What bothered Rynlin even more, though, was that he couldn't figure out how it happened.

Because of the Crag's location, no matter how large the encroaching army, only a small portion of the attacking force could actually march up onto the plateau and attack the stronghold at one time. Even then, the walls were so thick that siege engines or catapults had little effect. The Crag even had its own water supply from a spring running directly into its main well. And knowing Talyn, he had at least a year's supply of food stored away.

Rynlin slowly moved east along the edge of the small forest, studying what had once been the greatest fortress in all the Kingdoms. He saw several large holes in the walls, something that only a few days before was inconceivable. Most were large enough for more than a dozen men to walk through standing abreast of one another. Through the holes, Rynlin picked out a few of the buildings of the inner ward. Those made of wood had burned to the ground. Rynlin turned north in his reconnaissance and finally found what he was looking for. The inner wall had also been blown apart, revealing what was left of the main fortress. A single wall remained standing; the rest was a pile of rubble.

Rynlin became more and more uneasy as he continued his investigation. There was only one weapon that could do that kind of damage to a wall. The Talent, or Dark Magic more likely. In his heart he knew it was Dark Magic. But even then, it would have required more than a dozen warlocks working together. That in itself would have worried him, since anyone using Dark Magic against the Crag did so for only one reason, a reason he didn't want to consider. That realization sent a shiver of fear through Rynlin. If his assessment proved accurate, the destruction of the Crag was the least of his worries.

What bothered him more at that moment was the fact that those who had destroyed the Crag were still on the plateau. Maybe not the warlocks, but the others who had attacked the Crag remained. Men were involved. He knew that from the reivers. But his instincts told him something else as well. Then he knew what was wrong. It was so obvious he had completely missed it. The lights. There were no lights. When it was dark, men preferred lights. Rynlin stole a quick glance at one of the holes in the outer curtain. Yes, he was right. Each hole was at least twelve to fifteen feet high. The warlocks had made such large holes for a reason. And doing so required a tremendous amount of strength. There were not many warlocks who could do such a thing on their own, and even working with a dozen or more it would be a tiring exercise. Men didn't need holes that big to walk through, and they required light during the night. Some other, more dangerous creatures, didn't.

Rynlin dove to the ground as the blade of an axe swept through the air where his head had been only a second before. Rolling back to his feet, he heard the massive blade land solidly in a tree. He cursed himself for a fool. He had been so busy trying to figure out how the Crag had fallen that he had not paid enough attention to his surroundings. Ogren! That's what had conquered the Crag. The reivers were only a small part of it. Once Ogren had gotten inside, the Marchers were doomed. That's what needed such large holes. That's what preferred the darkness to the light. And that's what he fought now.

The monster roared in anger as it struggled to pull its axe free. Twice the size of a man, its heavily muscled body covered in fur, Ogren were truly hideous creatures. They lacked intelligence, but their strength more than made up for that shortcoming. Their massive shoulders and upper body sometimes proved too heavy for their spines, forcing them to walk hunched over. Their chiseled, beast-like faces looked like they had been carved from rock. Long sharp tusks protruded from their lower lips to curl around their cheeks. Ogren were efficient soldiers. They enjoyed killing, and they ate what they killed. A single man did not willingly fight an Ogren, not if he wanted to live. But Rynlin didn't have a choice.

As the Ogren worked its axe free, seemingly oblivious to everything else, Rynlin gathered his will. Extending his hand, a stream of fire shot out, enveloping the Ogren in flames. The creature screamed in agony as its flesh burned. The creature fell to the ground, desperately beating at the fire covering its body. The pieces of armor it had worn had already melted, and bits of charred flesh began to peel away from its body.

Rynlin trotted deeper into the forest, moving away from the Crag as fast as he could. The beast's dying screams had brought life to the plateau. Torches had appeared on the inside of the Crag. Someone was coming to investigate. If any warlocks remained here, one look at the Ogren would tell them all they needed to know about the intruder. The thought of taking on the bastards who were responsible for destroying the Crag appealed to him, but being surrounded by Ogren and whatever else had been used to conquer the Crag was not his idea of fun. Besides, if one Ogren was about, then others would be as well. And they loved to hunt at night.

Several hours later an exhausted Rynlin walked back into the clearing where Thomas lay asleep. Rya still sat by the fire, watching over her grandson. Seeing the dirt covering his clothes and the rip in his breeks from his roll to the ground, Rya rushed to her husband's side. Satisfied by a quick examination that he was all right, she led her husband over to a rock by the fire before letting him speak.

"What the boy says is true, Rya. The Crag is destroyed."

"But how?" she asked, surprised at hearing the news. Conquered, perhaps, but she couldn't imagine the Crag actually being destroyed.

"Dark Magic and Ogren," was all Rynlin said, and the look of disapproval that Rya gave him told him that she understood. "It looks as if our newfound grandson is the Lord of the Highlands." He motioned to the sword that Thomas was curled up next to, his small hands actually holding onto the hilt of the large blade. "I don't think his life will be getting any easier."

"I know," said Rya, "but he doesn't have to worry about that for a while. Once we get home he'll be safe."

"For a time," replied Rynlin. "For a time."

CHAPTER ELEVEN

STRATEGY

The walls of Eamhain Mhacha became visible as Killeran led his weary troop along the dirt road that paralleled the Corazon River. He had thought of taking a boat. That was the easiest way to get from the east to the seat of the High King, ruler of Armagh. But it was not always the fastest depending on the time of year, nor the most covert. After his meeting with Chertney, he had left the Highlands immediately. The discovery he had made about his fellow conspirator unsettled him. Sane men did not willingly make deals with a master such as Chertney's, yet Killeran's current ally had.

Killeran pushed those thoughts from his mind as he surveyed the fortress sitting atop a massive cliff. The palace of the High King rose above the city and overlooked the Heartland Lake, while the city itself had its own wall that continued along the road leading to the fortress, protecting anyone making the journey between the two. The port jutted out into a small bay, with the city on one end and the cliff on the other. A sea wall ran the length of the bay, except for a small opening that allowed ships to pass through. An additional section of the sea wall could be swung in place to close the opening, effectively sealing the port and fortress from attack.

The citadel towered over the bay. The cliff rose five hundred feet from base to top. The walls of the fortress added several hundred feet more. In the shape of a perfect circle, three concentric walls protected the main portion of the castle. The first outer curtain stood a hundred feet tall, with the second and third of the same height behind it. If invaders actually made it past the first wall a grass-covered space between that and the second wall awaited them, and again between the second and third. The children living in the bastion often played games there, unaware of the land's true purpose. The soldiers of Armagh had dubbed the immaculately groomed lawns the Killing Fields. Killeran knew the name was well deserved.

He had forced his personal guard to ride hard. The Council of the Kingdoms would begin in two days. Most of the rulers of the various lands would gather to discuss everything from trade agreements to border disputes, and Killeran had to meet with the High King before then. Otherwise they would not be able to take advantage of their success in the Highlands. Yet that success would have been even greater if not for Chertney's failure. Killeran cursed his ill luck. No matter. At least the Kestrels were dead, and if the boy still survived, he would not be alive much longer. Killeran had no doubt regarding the Nightstalker's deadly skills. As to Chertney's inability to destroy the Marchers, when Killeran returned to the Highlands he would see to it himself. Once the mining operation was in place and running smoothly, he would not have much else to do. Hunting the last of the Marchers would provide him with a little sport.

As the gates of the city wall took shape in the distance, Chertney directed his soldiers off the road toward the forest a half-mile away. He wanted to avoid any prying eyes when he entered the city. It had been a hard ride, but he smiled nonetheless. He didn't care that the many days in the saddle had forced the aches and pains of the road into his bones. The fun was just beginning, and soon, very soon, Killeran would have all the wealth and power he could imagine. Then, perhaps, he could achieve the station in life he so richly deserved.

CHAPTER TWELVE

UNFINISHED PLANS

I t was a room designed to intimidate. Everything in it had been built with that purpose in mind. The large, stained-glass windows depicting battles throughout the ages that ran along the length of the eastern and western walls captured the sunlight, throwing schemes of dazzling colors along the white marble floor. The walls were also made of white marble, brought all the way from the Distant Islands. On the wall above the dais hung a huge tapestry, threaded with the image of Ollav Fola, the first High King, right after he had consolidated the other Kingdoms under his own rule. Some said that Ollav Fola once sat on the very same throne, though it had never been proven. Carved from a block of black granite, the ancient chair stood out starkly against the rest of the room.

Everything about the chamber spoke of power, except for the man sitting on the throne of Eamhain Mhacha. The Council of the Kingdoms was to begin the next day, and most of those expected to attend had already arrived. But Rodric Tessaril, High King of Armagh, did not care about the other kings and lords. He wanted to see just one then, and his impatience was getting the better of him. The delay was necessary, of course. He knew that. He just didn't like it. And when things didn't work out the way he liked, he became irritable, more like a petulant child rather than the ruler of the most powerful of all the Kingdoms.

He was not a tall man, nor was his frame very imposing. That's why ceremony and protocol were so important to him. He did not look like a king, and he knew it. Therefore, he made sure that everyone remembered exactly who he was at all times. The dark purple cape he wore over his blue breeches and snow-white shirt concealed his gaunt frame, but it could not hide the feverish gleam of his eyes. With his coarse black hair and ruddy complexion, his features could only be described as plain, and some thought even that was too generous. No one would ever voice their opinions out loud, of course. If overheard, the consequences would be severe, probably deadly.

Rodric glanced out the windows for the hundredth time, noting the position of the sun and growing even more impatient. His visitor should have arrived by now. Getting someone covertly into the Palace, as he liked to call his fortress, was not a difficult task, it just took time. Finally, after what seemed an unbearably long wait, the large oak doors opened to admit a tall man in a gleaming silver breastplate and snowy white cloak. Rodric smirked. Killeran's overlarge nose preceded him into the room, yet the Dunmoorian lord didn't seem to care.

Killeran strode through the chamber as if he ruled it, stopping at the first step leading up to the throne and bowing perfunctorily. Rodric watched him carefully. The bow had been correct, though perhaps a bit too brief. A sign of disrespect, or something else? Rodric always latched on to the details — the little actions that gave away a person's thoughts. From them he could often guess the person's intentions, a skill that had proven useful upon assuming the Armaghian throne.

"All went well I trust?" asked Rodric, shifting uneasily on his throne. The chair certainly added to his sense of authority, but the hard stone did not make for a very comfortable seat. A cushion would have been a sign of weakness, however.

"Well, indeed, my lord," replied Killeran, unable to keep the nervousness from his voice. Killeran viewed Rodric as a weak man, but Rodric still held all the strings. Until Killeran could cut them, he would have to watch his step. It was well known how the High King liked to dispense his peculiar, and often indiscriminate, form of justice.

"Then the Highlands are mine," said Rodric, clapping his hands in pleasure. His excitement prevented him from catching the uncertainty evident in Killeran's voice. His thoughts had already moved to the future. Rodric abruptly stood and began to pace along the edge of the dais, his robe dragging along behind him. "Then the first step is complete. With the Highlands conquered, I have removed a thorn from my side. And once I have the riches hidden in that uninhabitable land, I can take control of the Eastern Kingdoms. After that, putting the Western Kingdoms in my pocket will be an easy task. You have done well, Killeran. I will not forget this. With the Marchers out of the way, no one will be able to stop me."

Rodric would have continued, but a quick glance at Killeran's jittery movements told him that the

Dunmoorian had held something back. Rodric stopped in his tracks. "What aren't you telling me, Killeran?"

"Nothing to dampen your plans, my lord. Only that Chertney wasn't as successful as he promised to be." Killeran hoped that if he phrased it right, the blame would fall squarely at his competitor's feet.

"What do you mean?" Killeran saw the vein bulging in Rodric's forehead. He reminded himself to tread carefully. No one was immune to the High King's displeasure, not even his children.

"Well, my king," he began, taking his time to ensure the words came out properly. "The Crag has fallen, that much is true. Nevertheless, not all of the Marchers were there at the time of the attack. As a result, some escaped to the higher passes."

"How many escaped?"

"It's hard to say exactly, my lord." Killeran saw that his answer was not satisfactory. "More than half, milord."

"More than half," repeated Rodric angrily. "You allowed more than five thousand Marchers to escape?"

"No, my lord," said Rodric. "Chertney did."

"Chertney. Yes, Chertney." Rodric smiled as he began pacing once more. He was not as easily fooled as some believed. "And you, Killeran? Where were you when this happened? Chertney may have led the attack, but you had the final say in things. Why did you allow this?"

"Well, my lord," said Killeran. "I did the best I could. But the Ogren follow Chertney. There was not much I could do." Rodric stared at Killeran, the vein in his forehead close to bursting. The feverish light in his eyes had turned ice cold.

"Perhaps," allowed Rodric. "Perhaps that was the case. With more than half the Marchers still free in the Highlands, taking control of that wretched land will be that much more difficult. But it will be accomplished nonetheless. You will not fail me in this. Will you, Killeran?" The question held an edge of menace. Killeran nodded quickly.

"No, milord. Have no fear of that."

"Good," said Rodric. "The Marchers may remain, but they will have a hard time putting up any organized resistance with the Kestrels eliminated. That was accomplished, was it not?"

"Yes, milord," said Killeran. A thin layer of sweat had formed on his forehead. Many of those who had brought bad news to the High King had never emerged from this chamber alive. Killeran had the feeling that he was very close to joining them. He had weighed withholding this last bit of news, and finally decided that it would do him more harm to hold it back. "For the most part."

"For the most part. For the most part! What do you mean, 'For the most part'?" The vein in Rodric's forehead threatened to explode as his face turned an angry red.

"Well, milord," answered Killeran, searching desperately for a good way to explain. He finally decided to blurt it out. "Talyn Kestrel and Benlorin Kestrel are both dead. That's been confirmed. But the grandson, Thomas, has not been found. We've searched the Highlands and haven't found him. Again, Chertney has failed you."

"Allowing a boy to escape is one thing," said Rodric heatedly. "That simply shows incompetence. But allowing this particular boy to escape, a boy who has a claim to the Highland throne, is a true sign of stupidity. He can ruin everything. I can't afford to have stupid people working for me, Killeran!" The threat in the High King's words was crystal clear.

"I understand, my lord. But you have nothing to fear. As I said, he is only a boy. Most likely he is already dead. We simply haven't found his body. Just in case, though, the reivers are still combing the Highlands for him, and we know for a fact that he went in a different direction than the Marchers during his escape. So you see, milord, it's just a matter of time. It won't be long before Chertney's mistake is corrected." He had not actually lied, though he hadn't been entirely truthful. Still, the facts were on his side. The boy probably was dead, or would be dead very shortly. Highlander or no, he could not have survived on his own for more than a few days. And if by some miracle he had, the Nightstalker would finish the job. Killeran knew that Rodric was thinking much the same thing, which made him breathe a little easier. The vein in his forehead was no longer throbbing as violently as before.

"Knowing for a fact that the Kestrel line had been eradicated would make my life much easier. But there might be a way to get around this remaining difficulty. I assume that Chertney will continue to hunt the boy until this task is complete?"

"Yes, milord. That's been arranged."

"Excellent. The other rulers have not yet heard of the attack on the Crag, though they will become suspicious when Talyn Kestrel does not arrive for the

Council. The less they know beforehand the better it is for us. If they don't find out about the boy, then I can still get what I want from them. Does anyone but you know that the boy might be alive?"

"Just a few of my soldiers," said Killeran. "But they won't talk."

"See that they don't," said Rodric. "If they do, I will hold you personally responsible. Is there anything else that you're forgetting to tell me, Killeran?" His voice said clearly that there better not be.

"No, milord. If all goes well during the Council, at its conclusion I'll return to the Highlands as we agreed. We captured several hundred Highlanders during the attack. They are all more than willing to help with our project."

Rodric imagined just how willing the Highlanders were, but it was better than ending up tied to a spit while being slowly turned over an Ogren cook fire.

"Good," said Rodric. "I'm glad to see that all was not lost. You may go."

"Yes, milord," said Killeran, bowing as before and walking quickly to the door, glad to be out of the room.

Sitting again on the hard, black granite throne, Rodric's mind remained on the Highlands and the missing Kestrel. He had a nagging suspicion that this boy would continue to be a problem. And he didn't like problems. Not at all.

CHAPTER THIRTEEN

STYMIED

G regory Carlomin, King of Fal Carrach, hated coming to the Council of the Kingdoms. Most of the time, you were stuck in a stuffy room for days, arguing over table scraps that had little or no importance. But appearances had to be kept up.

The Council met every two years. During that time all the rulers of the different Kingdoms gathered to discuss trade agreements, settle border disputes, arrange marriages and handle any other necessary tasks. It did prove useful, though. It was the easiest way to get things done. Otherwise, a task such as putting a trade agreement in place could take months to accomplish. Messengers had to be sent back and forth after each change was proposed to make sure both parties agreed, and that added a huge amount of wasted time to a process that should take a few hours at the most. But he still didn't want to be here.

Gregory was a large man, both tall and broad, and his years of handling a sword were evident. It was on the battlefield that he felt most comfortable, not in a room full of courtiers and diplomats. His short beard, once black and now speckled with a few salty whiskers, complemented his curly, black hair. Years before he had looked like a rogue, his eyes always smiling and open. That's what his wife had told him. Now his eyes were sad. His wife had died the year before, and though he had gotten over it — at least he told himself that — his daughter Kaylie had not.

Before her death, Kaylie followed her mother wherever she went, always trying to emulate her. Now that she was gone, Kaylie wanted to go exploring or learn how to handle a bow — anything that was different from what she had done before. Gregory had, for the most part, left the raising of his daughter to his wife, while he ruled Fal Carrach. He had both responsibilities now, and he had quickly discovered that raising a girl without her mother was a much harder job than ruling a kingdom. He wished he were back in Ballinasloe, spending time with her now. He did not like being away from her so soon after her mother's passing. He promised himself that he would make it up to her when he got back.

As Gregory looked around the High King's throne room, he saw many of the same faces, and a few new ones. Loris, King of Dunmoor, conversed with Rodric, which made Gregory nervous. A month didn't seem to go by without Fal Carrach's soldiers skirmishing on the border with some of Loris' thieves as they tried to sneak across and steal his cattle.

Loris' beard still looked scraggly. He had grown it as a boy to hide a scar he had gotten when he had raided Fal Carrach, wanting to make a name for himself before assuming the throne. Yet, it could do nothing for the weak chin or dull eyes.

Gregory watched the people walking past him, many of whom he nodded a greeting to, even sparing a kind word, but he quickly grew bored. Normally, he spent most of his time at the Council speaking with Talyn Kestrel. They'd been friends since childhood and had many common interests, besides the fact that their kingdoms bordered one another. But Talyn hadn't arrived yet, which was strange. It was not like him to be so late to the Council, even though Talyn hated these gatherings as much as he did.

Across the room, Gregory caught the eye of Rendael, King of Kenmare, and his wife Lorena. Both he and his wife waved, and Gregory returned it gladly. Of all the kings, Rendael had ruled the longest, though his age hadn't slowed his step. In fact, the only sign of his many years was his white hair. Gregory was certain that he had gotten most of it because of Lorena. She grew bored easily, and when that happened she liked to meddle in Rendael's affairs.

Gregory realized that Lorena was coming in his direction now that her husband was occupied with someone else. He knew exactly what she wanted to talk about. Lorena was renowned for her matchmaking. Her first words would be, "You've mourned long enough, Gregory. A year shows the proper respect. You shouldn't be alone, and I just happen to know the right person." Once Lorena got started, it was very hard to make her stop. And he really didn't want to talk with her at the moment. Turning quickly, Gregory looked for a way to escape. Instead, he nearly knocked over a beautiful young woman standing behind him.

Gregory quickly reached out his hand and caught her by the arm to prevent her from falling. Taking a closer look, full red lips and a dangerously low-cut green dress made Gregory's heart quicken a beat. He thought he could drown in the dark green pools of color that formed her eyes. He wouldn't have minded that at all.

The woman steadied herself. Gregory realized he no longer had to support her, but he was reluctant to let go. His mind was still caught up in the woman's green eyes. Green eyes. Green eyes and a green dress. There was someone he had heard of who preferred green dresses that matched her eyes. Who was that? It suddenly came to him, and he removed his hand.

"I'm sorry, Sarelle," apologized Gregory. "I didn't see you there."

"Quite all right, Gregory," said Sarelle Makarin, Queen of Benewyn. "No damage done, and I saw the reason for it. Lorena seems to be up to her old tricks again." Sarelle had taken the throne of Benewyn less than a year before. Her sister had died from a wasting sickness. Unlike the other Kingdoms, only a queen may rule Benewyn. If the ruling monarch died without a daughter to rule after her, then a sister wore the crown next.

"Yes, she is," replied Gregory. "But now that you're here as well, perhaps she'll turn her attention to you rather than me."

"Thank you, but no," said Sarelle. "I'm not ready for marriage. I haven't found the right husband." Gregory found that surprising. Sarelle was a remarkably beautiful woman, and he was certain she had a constant stream of suitors. He reminded himself to be very careful if he discussed any trade agreements with her. The traders of Benewyn were the most ruthless negotiators in the Kingdoms. They had to be, since their country depended on commerce to survive. Gregory had no doubts that Sarelle could hold her own in any situation. If he didn't pay attention to what was going on, he'd lose his Kingdom to her before he knew it. And in the end, he'd probably not even be bothered by it if he could gaze into her eyes just one more time.

"That makes two of us, then," said Gregory. He would have liked to say more, but Rodric now stood on the dais at the end of the room.

"My lords, would you please take your seats. The Council will begin."

Gregory offered his arm to Sarelle, which she cheerfully accepted with a smile. If he thought those eyes were difficult to ignore, the smile made her almost irresistible. Escorting her to her chair, he quickly took his own, one seat removed from Rodric.

A space had been cleared in the middle of the throne room with ten highback chairs of equal height placed in a semicircle. Rodric took the one in the center, with the other rulers sitting to his right or left. The High Kingship was an honorary title. Rodric was indeed the King of Armagh, but he certainly did not exercise the power of the High King such as Ollav Fola did when he had conquered the entire continent a thousand and more years before. The first High King knew that he could not effectively govern such a large empire, so he had allowed the defeated rulers to keep their thrones, so long as they swore fealty to him. As the years passed, others less skillful than Ollav Fola followed him to the throne, and the individual Kingdoms slowly regained their autonomy. Rodric was simply responsible for maintaining some semblance of order during the Council. That would change, Rodric promised himself. And very soon.

All the other rulers took their seats. Even a representative from Inishmore had arrived, though Gregory couldn't remember the man's name. Ten years before a group of lords had assassinated the legitimate king of Inishmore. Since then, rival factions had fought for the throne. None had been able to hold it for very long. Gregory saw that all the chairs were taken, except for the one between him and Rodric. Talyn's chair was conspicuously absent. Something was wrong. Gregory could feel it.

"My friends," said Rodric, rising from his chair and sweeping his eyes over each ruler. "Before we begin, I have difficult, unexpected news to report that I have only just received. News that cannot wait." The High King's eyes were filled with sadness, his voice laced with grief. It was an altogether convincing performance. Rodric sighed heavily before continuing. "The Crag has been destroyed. Even more terrible, Talyn Kestrel, Lord of the Highlands, and his son Benlorin, have been murdered."

Gasps of shock and shouts of anger rang throughout the room. Many looked at Rodric in disbelief. Though each of the rulers might have their differences, most did not like to see one of their own murdered. For Gregory, the news was like a physical blow. Talyn was his best friend, and though Rodric offered no proof, he was certain that he would not make a statement like that unless it was true. Talyn dead? It was unthinkable. His wife and now his best friend. Did life only get worse?

"Talyn was a good man, as was his son, and I promise that this evil deed won't go unpunished." Gregory looked at Rodric. The man's attempts at sadness and grief were fairly convincing. But his eyes sparkled with delight. Rodric had much to gain with the Kestrels gone.

In the last few years, Rodric had continually pushed to increase his power as High King, but the other rulers had resisted. It was always little things. Only a few months before, Rodric had asked to establish a small garrison in Ballinasloe to protect Armagh traders from the pirates in the Sea of Mist. Gregory had refused. There were no pirates in the Sea of Mist. He had seen to that. And if there were, they were Armaghian. It was really a very simple stratagem that Rodric employed. Any increase in power for Armagh came at the expense of the other Kingdoms, and Armagh already had the largest army in all the Kingdoms. No one wanted to make life any easier for Rodric. Things were going far too well for him as it was.

"We do not know yet who was responsible, but they will be found. Initial reports are that a group of Highlanders wished for a new Lord and decided to take matters into their own hands."

Gregory thought that highly unlikely. If the Crag actually had been conquered, there must have been a traitor involved. That's the only way it could have happened. Rebellions did not take place in the Highlands. The Marchers wouldn't allow it. Anyone could challenge the Lord of the Highlands at any time, with the victor taking the throne. Highlanders saw revolts as trickery; something only attempted by cowards.

He had been to the Crag many times before. In fact, as a young man he had been over every inch of the fortress. The only way to conquer it was from the inside. If the Crag had fallen, someone had betrayed the Marchers.

Besides, becoming Lord of the Highlands was not an easy thing to accomplish. Succession to the Highland throne was not like any of the other Kingdoms, where members of the same family usually followed after one another. True, the Kestrels had ruled as Lord of the Highlands for centuries, but there was a reason for that. They had passed the tests to become the Highland Lord and defeated any challengers. Rodric's story, though plausible, was very unlikely. Looking across the room, Gregory saw that Sarelle was having a hard time believing it, as were many of the other rulers. Except for Loris. At least one other ruler had tied his fortunes to Rodric. Gregory immediately knew what was coming next.

"I would be remiss in my duties as High King if I did not take action against those who committed this heinous act," continued Rodric. "As the law requires, since there is no heir, I will assume control of the Highlands until I can fairly determine who should rule there. Not wanting to burden you and your Kingdoms with the cost of a military expedition, I will send troops there immediately to bring those who committed this wicked deed to justice and to restore order."

Gregory's face resembled a thundercloud. Rodric wanted the Highlands for himself. If he got them, Fal Carrach would probably be next on his list, with Benewyn not far behind. Gregory glanced at Sarelle and saw that she had already reached to the same conclusion.

"What about the grandson?" asked Gregory harshly. "Did he survive?"

Rodric's eyes glittered darkly, his anger almost breaking through his façade. The High King waited a few moments before answering, weighing his options. He could lie and say the boy was, in fact, dead. But Killeran had shaved away part of his confidence in Chertney. Lying would be dangerous. If the boy suddenly appeared, Rodric could always fault his source of information, but it could also implicate him.

"The grandson?" said Rodric, feigning ignorance.

"Yes, there is a grandson," said Gregory, his anger rising. He knew Rodric was lying, but he couldn't do anything about it. "Your offer to aid the Highlands is certainly a noble gesture, but it is a moot point if Talyn's grandson survived."

"I don't know. I didn't know Talyn had a grandson," said Rodric, trying to control his anger. He should have known that Gregory would be the one to hinder him. He had been a friend of Talyn's. "The bodies of Talyn and Benlorin Kestrel were recovered, but the grandson was never found." Rodric almost ground his teeth to the bone having to say that. Incompetence! How was he supposed to succeed with so many fools surrounding him?

"Then according to the law," said Gregory, "a regent may rule for ten years or until such time as the legitimate heir is found or the heir's death is confirmed. Until that time, no one shall rule the Highlands in name except for the blood of the Kestrels."

"You know the law very well," replied Rodric in a tight voice. "As you say, King Gregory, we shall appoint a regent — perhaps a lord from another Kingdom — and hope for the boy's safe return. I promise that I will do everything in my power to make sure Talyn's grandson is found and given his proper place."

The menace in Rodric's eyes and tone confirmed it. Gregory knew exactly what Rodric considered Thomas' proper place to be — a hole in the ground next to his father and grandfather.

CHAPTER FOURTEEN

A SIGN

C atal Huyuk had experienced an uneasy feeling, as if something was wrong or out of place, since coming down out of the Western Highlands a few leagues from the Breaker. He was walking on a little-used trail that led to where the Clanwar Desert met Kenmare. The slant of the land was evening out and the forest was becoming thinner. Maybe it was because he was closer to civilization, as he had never felt comfortable in the places where people herded together behind stone walls. He knew he was wrong before he even thought it.

He stood a head taller than most men, and his dark brown face disguised his age. The leathery skin showed him to be a man who had spent most of his life outside. And the long black hair held back from his face by a knot of leather at the base of his neck affirmed that he wasted little time in towns or cities. Dressed like a woodsman, the huge sword and the wickedly curved axe strapped to his waist looked out of place. Most would have expected a bow and a quiver of arrows.

The land showed a more cultivated appearance here at the base of the Highlands, with sheep busily munching on the long grass of the many knolls. His feeling of something being out of place grew stronger. His hand drifted closer to the haft of his axe, his eyes constantly searching the trees for danger. It was not until he had walked a few more miles that he noticed the smoke rising over the next hill.

Axe now in hand, he moved more quickly down the trail, guessing that it would pass close by the source of the smoke. One end of the axe was a steel half-crescent while the other ended in a length of sharp steel a foot long. Catal Huyuk had ended several fights before they even began by simply pulling his axe from his belt.

The feeling continued to grow stronger, and he now recognized it. He had felt it many times before, and each time it made him scowl in disgust. Through the thin cover of the forest buildings appeared just ahead. Slowing to a walk, Catal Huyuk listened for any movement in the forest around him. Seeing and hearing nothing, he silently stepped to the edge of the tree line. A large farm stood before him, stretching for several acres on both sides of a small stream that ran right in front of the main farmhouse.

Normally, Catal Huyuk would have expected the sounds of children playing, dogs barking and men and women working. The old adage that a farmer's work was never done was all too true. But here there was nothing. Even the forest around him was silent.

Stepping out quietly from between the trees, he walked around to the front of the main farmhouse. About a dozen smaller houses and barns ran in a line next to it. At least, that's what he should have seen. Instead, all the other buildings had burned to the ground. Remarkably, the main farmhouse had withstood the fire, though smoke still rose from several places. The beams supporting the second floor were charred black and sagged dangerously. The only sound came from a gate to a small corral, which swung against a post at the whim of the wind. The feeling of evil remained.

He looked down into the dirt, confirming his suspicions. Footprints three times the size of a man's ran in every direction. He fingered his axe hopefully, but knew it was not to be. The Ogren had come and gone. Trying to catch them would be a waste of time. And he doubted there would be any survivors. Ogren ate their victims.

He was a little surprised, though. Ogren usually didn't travel beyond the Breaker. Normally they'd hunt in the Northern Highlands, even though the Marchers were very good at making sure they did not stay there long. The beasts were growing bolder, and that worried him. He'd have to send a note to the Isle of Mist. Someone else needed to know what was going on and help spread the word among those charged with doing something about it.

CHAPTER FIFTEEN

SOMETHING NEW

The Isle of Mist sat only a mile from the eastern shore of the Highlands, yet most men considered the shallow barrier of water to be several leagues wide and avoided the island at any cost. As with any culture based on an oral custom, where history largely survived because of the efforts of the taletellers, legend, rumor, and the truth often became mixed into one. So much so that even the taletellers didn't know if the stories they recited were truth or fiction.

Though each taleteller offered a distinct version of the same legend, they all agreed on one thing. Those unwise enough to venture onto the Isle of Mist usually did not return. Pirates used to prowl the Sea of Mist, and legend said that the Isle was their sanctuary. This, of course, drew the stout-hearted in search of fortune, but no gold or other riches were ever found, only hideous creatures and spirits waiting to feast on the unwary adventurer. As a result, most believed the island cursed, haunted by the spirits of the dead pirates protecting their hidden treasure.

Thomas had heard the tales as a child and believed them. When Rya had told him that that's where they were taking him the day after their first meeting, he tried to escape the following night, but Rynlin caught him. Now, after five years on the island, he was beginning to hope that there might be some truth to the stories that Rynlin had fabricated to keep people away from his home. He could do for a little excitement.

It truly was a beautiful island. A handful of large mountains dominated the landscape, and heart trees covered its expanse from one tip to the other. He enjoyed running beneath and leaping over their roots. Also, the rough bark offered excellent handholds, and Thomas found that he could pull himself up fairly easily. He climbed to the top of several, enjoying the view across the sea to the east or into the Highlands to the west, all the while holding on tight as the uppermost branches swayed in the wind.

Thomas had just finished his lessons with Rynlin and he looked forward to having some time to himself this afternoon. This morning he'd gotten out of his studies without any extra work, so he'd gone to one of his favorite places, a small cove along the western shore of the island. Beluil went with him. Though Beluil liked to wander the island every day, he never stayed away from Thomas for very long. On cold nights, Beluil liked to curl up by Thomas' feet as he read a book in front of the fireplace, though the large wolf, almost the size of a pony, always made sure that he was closest to the fire.

Sometimes Thomas stood on the beach and watched the waves as they crashed against the shore. It was a very peaceful place, Shark Cove. He had swum out past the rocks once, trying for the deep water. He had learned very quickly how the cove had gained its name. Before he had gone very far, two very large fins broke the surface of the water, headed in his direction.

Luckily, he had not yet swum past where the seafloor dropped off at a steep angle, so the sharks couldn't reach him. Rynlin had spoken of the sharks during one of their lessons soon after that frightening experience. Great Sharks, they were named. Thomas could understand why. The two he had seen must have been at least forty feet long and could have easily swallowed him whole. The grey-blue skin perfectly matched the color of the water. Their long, pointed snouts with large, triangular, serrated teeth, some four or five inches long, had sent a chill down his spine. Since then, Thomas stayed close to the shore.

From where he stood in the sand, Thomas observed the Highlands reaching for the sky just across the channel. He missed his grandfather, the passing time failing to heal the wound. Sometimes when he was asleep he dreamed of the night that had changed his life so dramatically.

"As a man, as a Kestrel Highlander, I give you these charges," his grandfather, Talyn Kestrel, had said solemnly. "This is the sword of the Kestrels. I charge you to bring it to safety and to guard it with your life. When the time comes for you to be Lord of the Highlands, you will have this sword."

When he becomes Lord of the Highlands. It didn't seem likely at the moment.

"My second charge is for you to remember who are," said Talyn. "You are Thomas Kestrel, Lord of the Highlands, and I charge you to remember that, and to make sure that others remember it as well."

And then the final scene, with him standing in the darkness yelling, "I am Thomas Kestrel, Lord of the Highlands. The Highlands will not be forgotten." His grandfather shouted in return, "For the Highlands," before enclosing him in darkness.

He thought about the tasks his grandfather had given him almost every day. They were a heavy burden to bear, and he knew that he would have to deal with those responsibilities soon. He just wasn't sure how to go about it. His mind turned to his morning lessons and afternoon chores. Why was it so important that he be able to recite some ancient code of laws from memory, when the laws weren't even used anymore? Or the dancing. Why was Rya so insistent that he learn a dance hundreds of years old? How could any of this possibly help him in the future? Thomas shook his head in frustration. Sometimes he just didn't understand his grandparents.

Both Rya and Rynlin were very good at keeping him busy. That's why he had left the house as soon as he could after finishing his chores. Whenever Rynlin was his teacher, there was always one subject that proved difficult. And Thomas never knew which one it would be. One morning it could be history. The next, geography. Or maybe woodlore. Both loved to test him with questions. In Thomas' opinion, these questions only confirmed that they took a particular delight in making his life difficult.

Rynlin and Rya always expected him to know the answers to whatever questions they might ask him about that day's lessons, even if they hadn't told him beforehand what the lessons were going to be! How was he supposed to know the answers if he didn't know what he was supposed to study? He had asked Rya the same question not long after beginning his studies, thinking he could avoid Rynlin's likely caustic response. But she had simply ignored him. At the end of each morning's lessons, Rya or Rynlin would always say, "Now for the test." Thomas dreaded those words more than anything else. If you didn't know the answer, it meant more work. Much more. Enough to keep you occupied until dinner.

Today, Thomas had finally turned the tables. Rynlin had asked him the name of an obscure group of warriors, and Thomas knew the answer. Even before Rynlin had finished asking the question, Thomas replied, "The Sylvana." Thomas thought Rynlin's jaw was going to fall off. Rynlin had actually started to say you're wrong before he caught himself.

"They were also known as the Sylvan Warriors," Thomas had said. "They are a small group of men and women who have fought the Shadow Lord since he first threatened the Kingdoms. The stories say that the Sylvana live in the more uninhabitable parts of the Kingdoms, preferring to stay away from cities and civilization, guarding the Kingdoms until it is time to fight again." It was the first time he had gotten the right answer in five years. Better yet, it was the first time he had actually seen Rynlin surprised. It really did look like Rynlin's eyes were going to pop out of his head. But Thomas didn't stay to see if that actually happened. He had hopped off his stool and ran out the door as fast as he could.

Thomas sighed as he turned away from the waves. Beluil hadn't moved from where he had lain down when they first arrived, having found a comfortable place on a soft bed of moss at the edge of the small beach. Beluil was full grown now, but Thomas had never guessed on that day so long ago, when he had carried the little wolf pup in his arms, that his friend would grow to be so large. Admittedly, Thomas was not very tall. Still, Beluil's head easily reached above Thomas' chest.

Beluil appeared to be napping. Thomas knew better. As soon as Thomas walked by on his way back up the trail leading to the mountains, Beluil was at his heels.

"Enjoy your nap?" asked Thomas derisively.

Beluil just looked at him with an impudent grin. Upon seeing those sharp teeth, anyone not familiar with Beluil would have been halfway up the nearest tree. Thomas had taken only a few more steps before he felt his foot catch on something. Stumbling, Thomas caught himself just before he fell flat on his face. He looked back to see Beluil sitting on his haunches in the middle of the trail, trying to appear innocent, and failing miserably. He could feel his friend's soft laughter in the back of his mind. Thomas promised himself that he'd get even as he continued back along the trail.

CHAPTER SIXTEEN

A New Friend

Although the evening was cool, the fireplace warmed the downstairs floor. Unfortunately, it was getting a little too hot, so Rya left the window over the sink open to let in the night breeze. As soon as Rya had opened the window, the delicious smell of the stew wafted outside and drew Thomas inside. Venison stew. His favorite. He didn't know what he liked best — the stew itself, or the rye bread Rya baked to go with it.

"So where were you this afternoon?" asked Rya. "Rynlin told me that you answered his question correctly."

"Down at Shark Cove," he said with some difficulty, as he tried to speak and eat at the same time.

"It was a lucky guess," said Rynlin, still slightly annoyed that Thomas had gotten the right answer. He didn't like it when people knew the answers to his questions. It just didn't seem right.

"What were you doing down there?"

"Just thinking," replied Thomas, this time remembering his manners and waiting to finish a bite of stew before responding.

"How did you learn about the Sylvana?" asked Rynlin, an intent look on his face. Glancing at his grandfather, Thomas sensed that this was more than just a casual question. Rynlin was too interested in his response.

"I read about them in a book," said Thomas, not offering more than just the necessary information. Rynlin waited for more of an answer, but soon decided that he wasn't going to get a better explanation. Thomas certainly didn't mince words, which Rynlin approved of. There was no need to say more than was necessary. But when you're trying to get to the bottom of something, it could become an extremely frustrating exercise. Rya simply shrugged her shoulders and passed him a slice of bread.

Thomas kept his head down and focused on eating his stew. He didn't want to talk too much about this subject. Yes, he had read a book about the Sylvana, and he was interested in learning more about them.

But the main reason thoughts of the Sylvana remained in his mind were the dreams. For the last few months, he had dreamed about the Sylvana. Or at least he thought he did. The book hadn't been very specific about what the Sylvana looked like as people, but it had explained in detail how Sylvan Warriors rode unicorns into battle. Unicorns no longer lived in the Kingdoms, at least not that he knew of. But that didn't mean that there weren't some unicorns still around somewhere. The book implied that the Sylvana were really just a myth. Thomas wasn't so sure. Many people tended to believe in only what they could see or touch, but that did not necessarily mean that a thing or a person didn't actually exist.

At first, he thought his dreams resulted from the book, his brain still holding the images he had created while reading. But this had been going on for several weeks now, and each night the dream came it was the same. He would be standing in a grassy field, with the tallest mountains he had ever seen in the background. A black unicorn would walk toward him. Thomas would reach out his hand and touch the unicorn's horn, and then he would wake up. He never knew how the dream ended.

Many times the images seemed like more than a dream, and lately he had woken up with the urge to go off and find this valley, though he had no idea where it was located. All in all, he thought it was extremely strange. If he told Rya and Rynlin, it would probably sound even stranger. So he decided that the wisest course was simply to keep his mouth shut. Maybe he could change the subject. Looking out the window, he found a way to do so.

A large raccoon sat on the windowsill gazing intently at their meal. Extending his senses, Thomas reached out to the raccoon with his mind.

"Rynlin," said Thomas. "I was wondering if you might be able to spare some bread."

Rynlin gave Thomas a perplexed look. He normally didn't like to share his food, and he had assumed that Thomas was done with his meal. He decided to be generous.

"You want a piece, then?" he asked, beginning to tear a smaller chunk from his own slice.

"No, not me," said Thomas.

"Then why do you want it?" he asked, somewhat confused.

"I don't want the bread," Thomas said. "I was hoping you could spare some for my new friend."

"What new friend?" interrupted Rya, now just as thoroughly confused as Rynlin.

Thomas nodded toward the open window.

Both Rynlin and Rya saw the raccoon sitting calmly on the windowsill waiting to see what would happen.

"How do you know this, Thomas?" asked Rya, still not understanding.

"I just know," said Thomas. Though he had been on the island for five years now, he still didn't feel right calling Rynlin grandfather or Rya grandmother. The only person he had called grandfather had died, and a small part of him thought that he would betray his grandfather's memory if he called someone else by that term. Thomas knew that such a thought was ridiculous, but he still couldn't bring himself to call Rynlin and Rya by anything but their given names.

"You can speak to raccoons?" asked Rynlin, unable to keep the surprise from his voice.

"Yes. No. Well, yes, I guess," said Thomas. The frowns on Rynlin and Rya's faces grew deeper as he tried to explain. "I can talk to raccoons, but not just to them. I can communicate with any animal in the forest I want to, as long as the animal allows it."

Absently, Rynlin finished tearing off a large chunk of bread, then handed it up to the raccoon on the windowsill. The raccoon took a quick bite, then grabbing hold of the bread, leapt down from the windowsill with its prize and raced away.

"How long have you been doing this?" asked Rya. Her keen interest had replaced her initial surprise.

"I don't know," said Thomas, leaning back on his stool, but not so far that he would tip over. He had done that once, and the back of his head had hurt for days. "Since before I came here."

Rynlin and Rya exchanged a knowing look. A handful of people in the past few centuries had been able to communicate with animals, though it wasn't normally discussed. Most people saw it as something that was evil, but those who knew more about such things saw it for what it truly was — a gift.

Nevertheless, the people with this particular skill had only been able to speak with animals on a very limited basis and communicated through a few basic concepts. Thomas didn't seem to have any of these restrictions. More shocking, Thomas had kept this unique skill hidden from them for five years. They had always assumed that all those times Thomas and Beluil knew what each other was thinking came from their closeness as friends. Now they saw that they had been mistaken.

"What are you two thinking?" asked Thomas in a worried voice. He didn't like it when Rynlin and Rya had those expressions on their faces. It usually meant more lessons or work.

Rynlin and Rya eyed Thomas. They knew that their grandson was a unique child, they just hadn't realized how unique he might actually be.

CHAPTER SEVENTEEN

NEW SKILL

"So what exactly can you do?" asked Rynlin. After dinner, he led Thomas outside, wanting to explore his grandson's unique ability.

"It's kind of hard to explain," replied Thomas nervously. He had always viewed this skill as a secret and had planned to keep it that way.

"Let's start with your speaking to the raccoon," said Rynlin.

Thomas thought for a moment, struggling to find the best way to talk about it. Actually communicating with an animal was simple, at least when he did it, but explaining it was another matter entirely.

"I guess you could say I—," he began, seeking the right words. Rynlin waited for him to continue, demonstrating a patience usually reserved only for his dealings with Rya. His grandson was obviously uncomfortable, so he took a more reserved approach.

"Don't worry, Thomas. I'm not going to rush you like I do during your lessons." Rynlin smiled at Thomas' obvious relief. Normally, when Rynlin asked a question, he expected an immediate answer.

"When I was younger," said Thomas, "I spent as much time as possible outside of the Crag. I didn't like being inside the walls. Sometimes it felt like I was in a dungeon. But when I was in the forest, I knew I belonged there." His grandfather nodded in understanding. He didn't like being cooped up behind stone walls either. It dampened his awareness of what was going on in the natural world, and that made him uncomfortable. Seeing his grandfather's nod, Thomas plunged ahead with more confidence.

"One time, when I was sitting in one of the glades at the base of the Crag, I kept hearing this noise, but I didn't know where it was coming from. It was very faint, almost like the sound of light, misty rain hitting a tree's leaves.

"I got up and walked around the glade searching for the source. At first, I thought it might have been an animal or a bird, but it wasn't. So I went back to the tree and I heard the sound again — a slow, misty rain falling on a tree's leaves. That's when I focused on the tree I had been leaning against. It was a clear, sunny day, so it definitely wasn't rain. The only other explanation I could think of was that the sound came from the tree, from the inside.

"I put my hand on its bark, getting a feel for its roughness. Then I concentrated on the tree. I didn't really know what I was doing, but I stayed like that — kneeling in front of the tree, my hand against its bark — for more than an hour. No matter what I did, I wasn't getting anywhere. I could still hear that sound, but I couldn't find the source."

"What did you do next?" asked Rynlin, captured by the story.

"It was getting dark, and I had to get back to the Crag, so I decided to try one last time. I closed out everything that was going on around me — the breeze pushing against the branches and leaves, the sounds of evening in the forest — and focused completely on the tree. Everything else disappeared. I kept pushing out with my mind, trying to force it into the tree. I guess that's the best way to explain it." Thomas shrugged his shoulders. He had never had to discuss this before, and he was still having a hard time with it. Rynlin gave him a nod of encouragement, so he continued.

"It was like trying to shove a huge rock up a hill, and every time you got it to roll forward, your feet would give way and you'd slide a little farther down the slope, so you actually weren't making any progress at all. I was about to give up since it was so frustrating. I think that's what did it."

"What did it?"

"The frustration. I was getting irritated because I could still hear the sound, however faint, and nothing was working, so I poured every bit of energy I had into what I was doing. And then it happened." The look of wonder on Thomas' face spoke volumes.

"I could feel everything there was to feel about the tree, not just its rough exterior against my hand, but the tree growing, stretching for the sun, and so much else. I knew that tree as well as I knew myself."

"And the sound?" asked Rynlin.

"The sap," replied Thomas. "That was the sound. The sap running through the tree. Anyway, after awhile, instead of focusing on a single tree, I concentrated on several. It still took some time, but it got easier since I had already done it once. And it worked. I could feel the trees, and even more than that. I knew there was a redbreast in one of the trees, guarding three small eggs until they hatched. And the squirrels. There must have been several dozen just in that small area. "The more I did it, the easier it became, and the farther I could extend my senses. Now I don't know how far I can go."

"The island?" asked Rynlin. "Can you extend your senses all the way around the island?"

"Yes," said Thomas, "I know that for sure. I think I can actually go farther, maybe as far as the western edge of the Highlands. I just haven't tried it yet."

"And the animals?" asked Rynlin.

"That started when I first met Beluil," said Thomas. "His mother had been killed and I needed to speak with him. But I don't communicate with animals in words. Maybe it's because they can't actually say words. I don't know for sure. When I communicate with animals, it's all based on emotions that I translate into images in my mind. At least that's the only way I can explain it." Thomas shook his head in frustration. Though he could do it, he wasn't quite sure how he did it.

"The hard part is translating the emotions. For example, the raccoon on the windowsill. I had never met him before, so when I entered his mind the first time I had a hard time figuring out what he was trying to say because I was unfamiliar with the images passing through my mind. It didn't take long though before I got it. I translated his primary emotion into hunger, and from there it was simple. With Beluil, it's a little different because I know him so well. The more time I spend with a particular animal, the easier it is to communicate with them. I'm sorry I can't explain it any better than that, Rynlin. All I know for sure is that I can do it."

"That's all right, Thomas," said Rynlin, knowing how hard this must have been for him. A fair comparison would be trying to grab hold of the fog. "That's enough questions for now. Let's see just how far you can extend your senses."

"All right," agreed Thomas with some enthusiasm. Thomas turned away from Rynlin and focused on the surrounding forest, seeing the individual trees clearly in the darkness. He closed his mind to everything else around him.

Though his eyes were still open, he really couldn't see anything now, not even the trees. Instead, the surrounding forest appeared in his mind. One tree became several, which then became even more, until he glimpsed leagues and leagues of heart trees running along both sides of the mountainous spine of the Isle of Mist. Not too far away, he found a raptor reveling in the strong breezes coursing off the cliff faces and a bear waiting patiently at the shore of a river for a fish to come within reach.

Whenever he extended his senses, it felt like his spirit had left his body. He could look down and see himself standing there, as well as Rynlin, and now Rya, who watched from her seat on one of the roots of a heart tree. Though most of his awareness was focused on the forest, a detached part of his mind remained with his body, and that part heard someone talking to him. It was Rynlin.

PETER WACHT

"Now I'm going to do something so I can see what you're seeing," he said. "Don't worry about me, just stay focused on your task." At first, nothing changed. Gradually, though, Thomas sensed that he was not alone as he looked down at the Isle of Mist. Rynlin. It felt as if Rynlin was riding along on his shoulder.

"Go as far as you can, Thomas," ordered Rynlin.

Taking one final look at the Isle of Mist, he pushed his senses out slowly, reaching for the Highlands and beyond. He imagined he was a raptor soaring through the sky. The rush of speed thrilled him as he flew through the Highlands and quickly arrived at the Crag. He picked out the remains of the once formidable fortress, the forest having already reclaimed some sections of it. Though that terrible event had taken place only five years before, the grass and moss that had found a home on what had once been the walls of the stronghold appeared to have been there for centuries. With a sense of loss now weighing down his heart, Thomas continued to push his senses outward. The feeling of Rynlin sitting on his shoulder remained.

Viewing the Crag depressed him, so rather than take his time as he viewed the Highlands, he moved as fast as he could toward the western boundary, skimming over the tops of mountains. Certain peaks — with clouds ringing their slopes like a crown on a king or queen's head — he circled around because of their tremendous height. Reaching their summits would have wasted both time and energy.

In a matter of seconds he came to the edge of the Western Highlands. The Breaker was visible to the northeast. This was the farthest he had ever gone before.

"Can you go farther?" asked Rynlin, his question a small voice within Thomas' mind. Not bothering to answer, Thomas extended his senses to the west, pushing into the Clanwar Desert. He marveled at the endless sand flowing beneath him and running far to the west. A dark patch appeared within view far off in the distance. Curious, he rushed forward. Suddenly, swirling sound clouded his vision. He realized he had flown into a sandstorm and was amazed at just how quickly it had engulfed him. One moment the sun was shining brightly, the next he was in darkness and in danger of becoming disoriented. Rising above the storm, he continued his journey to the west, now angling to the south as well. Sand was definitely not the most exciting thing to look at, and he had just found out how dangerous it could be.

As Thomas pushed his senses farther to the southwest, he felt his body back on the Isle of Mist begin to sweat. The strain of extending himself so far was beginning to affect him physically, and his attempts to go even farther took more of his strength. Gritting his teeth, he tried one final push. As his energy dissipated, he passed over the border of the desert, where sand fought with grass for dominance. The grass soon rushed beneath him as he headed south, the strain of his efforts forcing him to fight harder and harder to maintain his concentration.

He knew that he was close to his limit. Finally, he stopped at a large river that sliced across the land. The Corazon River. He was close to Armagh, halfway across the continent. His efforts had strained his strength and exhaustion was quickly consuming his body. Thomas decided it was time to return home. At least he didn't have to follow his trail all the way back to the island. Relaxing his concentration, he was back on the Isle of Mist instantly. Rynlin now stood next to him in case Thomas needed support, a look of concern on his face. Rya perched on her rock, worried as well.

He couldn't understand why until it hit him as to just how tired he felt. Rynlin hovered at his side as he walked unsteadily to the heart tree and sat down next to Rya.

"Not many can do that, Thomas," began Rynlin, adopting the scholarly tone he favored when explaining something. Rya smiled at Thomas. For both of them, it was a common occurrence. "In fact, I don't think there are any who can go as far as you can. Years ago, some could, but they're gone now. Rya and I are about the same in terms of strength regarding your particular skill, what we'll call searching. It's also known as wandering, or traveling, but I think searching will do just fine for now as a definition. Anyway, both of us can only search as far as the western edge of the Highlands, and even then it places a great deal of strain on us. If we tried to go any farther, we'd soon feel the same way you do now."

Thomas had listened with one ear, much like he did during his lessons with Rynlin. He was exhausted and almost completely spent. His mind quickly latched onto what Rynlin had just said. If he had heard Rynlin correctly, that meant Thomas had searched several hundred leagues farther than either of his grandparents ever could.

"You mean I can search farther than you can?" he asked. "How is that possible?"

"Well, Thomas," said Rya, cutting in before her husband could reply. "It's much like anything else in life. A jeweler has a particular skill in shaping gold or silver into intricate designs, while a blacksmith can do much the same with steel when making a sword. You, too, have a particular skill with searching. Both Rynlin and I can do it, but it's not one of our primary abilities. It stands to reason, then, that you should be able to do more with it than we can."

"And that ability will only grow stronger as you get older and become more experienced in it," interrupted Rynlin. "Within the next few years you'll probably be able to search on the other side of the Heartland Lake, maybe even to the western shore of Kashel."

"You think so?" asked Thomas excitedly. It didn't seem possible to go that far, but then again, he had just gone farther than he thought he could. He smiled at the idea of seeing the Western Ocean while standing on the Isle of Mist. That would indeed be a remarkable achievement. His grandfather, Talyn, had once told him about his mother's ability to do very much the same thing he had just accomplished, though he had called it by a different name. The people living in the Crag called her a witch because of it, but his grandfather had simply said that she could do something that others could not, and that it was a gift to perform magic of that sort.

Magic. Many people in the Kingdoms spitted the word out as if it were a curse. Dark Magic. Black Magic. He had never thought that searching or communicating with animals was magic. But maybe it was. Then again everyone said, including the taletellers, that magic no longer existed in the Kingdoms.

The most common story involved the Sylvana. Though the Sylvana had practiced magic for millennia, after the Great War the Sylvana left the Kingdoms and took the magic with them. Therefore, anyone who could still perform magic was automatically associated with Dark Magic — and the Shadow Lord.

When Thomas asked Talyn whether there were people still alive in the Kingdoms who could perform magic, he had answered yes. Thomas didn't know anyone in particular, except perhaps for his mother, but that didn't mean there weren't any left. He could almost feel the wheels churning in his head as the logic worked itself out. If his mother had performed magic, it stood to reason that he could. Perhaps he could do other things with this magic. But first, he wanted to confirm a few things.

"Rya?"

"Yes, Thomas?"

"My mother, was she able to perform magic?"

The question hung in the air for a few moments, as Rya looked to Rynlin for help. He shrugged his shoulders in response. A great help he was. Always willing to answer the easy questions, but never the hard ones. She didn't know how she was supposed to answer, and she didn't want to lie. Thomas was only fifteen. Then again, she had been about the same age when she learned about some of her special abilities.

"In a sense, yes, she could."

"And she could do what I just did? Search, I mean?"

"Yes, Thomas," Rya replied. She knew the next question.

"So that means I can perform magic, as well?"

"Yes, you can, Thomas." The look of realization on his face spread. He had held his breath in anticipation.

"Then both you and Rynlin can perform magic, too?"

"Wait a moment," said Rynlin, sighing in exasperation. "Before we start this discussion, let's get a few things straight. First, it's not magic. That's not the right term. We call it the Talent. Second, yes, Thomas. Both Rya and I have the Talent, but that's really not the right way to explain it. And searching is only a small part of it. Again, it all goes back to an individual's particular abilities. For you, searching is one of your strengths, while you might not be able to do something else as well as I can, or as Rya can.

"And we're not really *performing* magic, as those charlatans do at the annual fairs and festivals. You know what I mean. Making a rabbit disappear and such. That's sleight of hand, not magic. So don't say perform magic. Say use the Talent, or harness the Talent, or apply the Talent. Make sure you know what you're talking about."

Thomas took in everything Rynlin said in rapt attention. This was much more interesting than his normal lessons. Rynlin again adopted the pedantic tone he preferred when imparting knowledge.

"What you're really doing is harnessing power."

"Power from where?" asked Thomas.

"Where do you think?" countered Rynlin. He'd rather have Thomas figure it out for himself. It was the best way to learn.

Thomas thought about what he had just done. When he searched, he had always been outside. And he didn't like being within stone walls for too long a time. It made him feel as if he were locked away from something. Once he was free of the walls, though, he could hear better, see better, he even had a sharper sense of smell. Put simply, he felt more alive.

"From the forest?"

"Yes," said Rynlin, patting Thomas' shoulder, pleased with his response. "From the forest. That's a part of it, though that's not the actual source."

"Then what is it?" he asked.

"What is the forest a part of, Thomas?" asked Rya. Now she was answering him with questions as well. Thomas forced down his growing irritation. Patience was something he had not yet mastered.

"Nature."

"Right," said Rynlin, clapping his hands with pleasure. "You're exactly right. When you search, you're harnessing a power, and that power is nature. That's why you feel more comfortable outside than in. You can sense the power of nature, and you don't like to be away from it. That's the main difference between sorcerers or sorceresses — that's what we like to call ourselves — and those people who can't use the Talent. We can get closer to nature. We can actually feel it within our blood. When it's taken away from us, we hunger for it. Other people, they can *see* nature — the trees, the bushes, the water in the stream, the birds, the animals, the mountains — but that's all they can do. They can't *feel* the life around them.

"Because we can feel nature in a much more direct and intimate way, we can also harness its power. When I asked you earlier how you searched with your mind, you said it's mainly your ability to concentrate. You can close out everything around you, and focus specifically on the trees, then the mountains, then whatever comes next. When you're concentrating like that, you're actually pulling in the power that exists in nature. You're pulling in the power of the heart trees, and the rivers, and the mountains, and redirecting it. You're taking in the energy, and then using your own strength to make use of it in some fashion."

"So that's why I can only reach the border of Armagh when I search," said Thomas. "If I understand correctly what you're saying, I'm not actually using my own strength to go there with my mind. I'm using nature's strength, whatever it might be — the rocks, the trees, the bushes. It doesn't matter. The only thing that's holding me back from going farther is my ability to make use of the strength that nature gives me, because that's what's maintaining control of the energy, or power, that I'm using."

"That's right," said Rya with a smile, pleased that he had caught on so quickly. She remembered that it had been much more difficult teaching this to Marya.

"So in order for me to push my senses all the way to the coast of Kashel, I have to become more experienced in searching so I can control a larger amount of the energy I'm taking from nature."

"Exactly," said Rynlin. He too smiled. He liked it when Thomas got something right on the first try. It helped to puff up his ego as a teacher.

"Then I guess for me to learn how to do something else with the Talent," trying the word out for size, "I need to learn how to redirect the power of nature in a certain way."

"Again, you're right, Thomas," said Rynlin. "All you have to do is take in the power that exists around you — which you have already mastered — and then focus it in a specific way."

"But not tonight," said Rya. "It's almost midnight, and it's time for bed. We can continue this discussion tomorrow morning." She had seen the look on Thomas' face, and she knew what he was going to ask next. He wanted to learn what else he could do. But it was getting late, and he needed his sleep, especially since Rynlin had asked him to see how far he could go. The test had actually served an altogether different purpose. Yes, Rynlin was curious about how far Thomas could search, but he also wanted to know just how strong he was, and how much of the natural power he could handle at one time. Thomas was only fifteen years old, yet his strength was staggering. He was already stronger than Rya and was just a few notches below Rynlin. And Rynlin was one of the most powerful sorcerers in all the Kingdoms.

Thomas nodded his acquiescence. Lifting himself off the rock, he stumbled more than walked as he headed to the house, and was thankful that the stairs leading up to his room had a banister. Otherwise he wouldn't have made it. Too tired to take his clothes off, he flopped down onto his bed and was asleep in seconds.

Nevertheless, the exhaustion he felt didn't keep him from dreaming. Again, he swept out over the Sea of Mist and into the Highlands, moving at a blinding speed. Abruptly he came to a stop. Looking down he recognized the Crag. This time, instead of seeing the grass and moss that covered the once formidable walls, he viewed them as they were after the attack — blackened and charred, with monstrous holes blown into the fortifications. *Five years, five years, five years* kept playing through his mind. He had left the Highlands five years before. He knew now with a certainty that he would never be able to escape from his responsibility. He could delay. But even then the time would come when he couldn't even do that anymore.

CHAPTER EIGHTEEN

THE TALENT

The next morning, Thomas awoke to rays of early morning sunshine streaming into his small room. Besides a bed, a chest for his clothes, a washstand and piles of books, he did not have much of anything else. That might have bothered some, but not him. In his opinion, he had everything he needed.

In the bottom of the chest, covered by his clothes, lay the Sword of the Highlands wrapped in an oiled cloth. Rynlin had professed not to know how to use a sword. It was one of the first things Thomas had asked when he arrived on the Isle of Mist. If he ever ran into those reivers again, he wanted to be able to defend himself and exact some revenge. Rynlin had said that when the time was right, Thomas would learn how to use the blade. Thomas promised himself that he would not remove the sword from the chest until it was time. So far, the time had not yet come.

As he washed his face, he looked in the mirror. More soft whiskers. He might have to start shaving soon. And the red in his eyes was unmistakable. He had slept like a log, but it certainly didn't look like it had helped. Running a hand through his short hair, even now curling around his ears and in the back, he wetted the comb that lay beside the porcelain bowl and brought some semblance of order to his hair. Then, after scrubbing his teeth with soda, he put on a clean white shirt, brown breeks, and tugged on his boots. The smells of fresh bread and porridge topped with cinnamon and apples greeted him as he sauntered down the stairs.

Mumbling a greeting to Rya and Rynlin, who had already begun to break their fasts, he dug into the bowl that was placed before him. He was famished. Before either of his grandparents had gotten halfway through their porridge, he had refilled his bowl and eaten half a loaf of bread.

"Hungry, Thomas?" asked Rya with some amusement.

He could only nod, since he had just stuffed another spoonful of porridge into his mouth.

"Then you've learned the first of your lessons for today," said Rynlin, leaning forward to make sure that Thomas understood the importance of what he was about to say. "When you use the Talent, the more you try to do, the more of your own strength it requires. That's why you slept so deeply, and that's why you're still tired this morning. Your body is not used to what you put it through last night."

Thomas put down his spoon, having finished his second bowl of porridge. He thought about having another, but decided instead to finish the loaf of bread. Rya had poured honey over the top of it, knowing he had a sweet tooth. Between bites of his bread, he asked a few questions.

"So my ability to use the Talent depends on my own strength?" Rynlin leaned back in his chair, nodding, glad to see that Thomas was listening so early in the morning. He had a tendency not to. "Does it depend solely on my physical strength?"

"That's a good question," said Rya, grinning at Rynlin. It was always a pleasure to tease her husband so early in the morning. "Rynlin didn't explain everything that he should have. Yes, it will depend on your physical strength. The stronger you are physically, the more you can do with the Talent. You will be able to control a greater amount of the power you derive from nature, which will allow you to do more difficult things. But it does not rely solely on your physical strength. It also depends on your will." Thomas was getting confused. What did his will have to do with it? "In fact, your will is more important than your physical strength. I've known sorcerers who were no more than skin and bones, yet they were more powerful than sorcerers who appeared to be carved from granite. Why? Because they had a stronger will."

"That's what we need to practice," said Rynlin, cutting in on Rya's explanation, and earning a sour expression from her for it. "In terms of your physical strength, that will obviously increase as you get older and continue to grow. But as Rya explained, you do not have to be solid muscle to be strong in the Talent. That's why we have to work on your will, and I don't mean the fact that you can be extremely stubborn and hard-nosed." Thomas grinned. He had long since decided that stubbornness was a hereditary trait, though he chose to keep that belief to himself.

"No, what I mean," continued Rynlin, "is that you have to learn how to control your will and use the strength of your purpose to accomplish what you want with the Talent."

"Almost like when Rya pulls a hot apple pie from the oven and puts it in front of me on the table," said Thomas, trying to understand what Rynlin was saying by putting it into his own words. "She expects me not to eat it, though she knows it's one of my favorites. I have to show some willpower in not taking a slice."

"Yes," said Rya, this time interrupting her husband. She also earned a sour expression for it. Rynlin didn't like to be cut off. "The better you can learn to master your will, the better you will be able to use the Talent. There are many reasons why you need to have excellent control in the future. The primary one is that you will have to use your Talent when you have very little time to think. Your will could determine whether or not you live or die in that and other situations."

A sobering thought, indeed. It reinforced Thomas' belief that no one was invincible, even someone strong in the Talent.

"So what I can do with the Talent will be determined by how well I can control it?"

"Yes," said Rya.

"What if I try to do something for which I'm not strong enough, or I don't have the necessary control?"

"Then you will die," said Rynlin. Thomas gulped at the finality of his words.

"You don't have to say it so harshly," said Rya, giving her husband a withering look. This time, it did not faze him.

"Yes I do. Harsh words or not, it's the truth," answered Rynlin, ignoring his wife. "Thomas has to know what he's getting himself into." Rynlin turned his gaze to his grandson. "This isn't a game, Thomas. This is very serious business. Are you ready to learn more of what you can do with the Talent? Are you ready to risk the possibility that if you don't do it right, you will die?"

Thomas looked from Rynlin to Rya, then back again. He had never been faced with a decision like this before, where something he chose to do could lead to his death. Strangely, he didn't think it would be the last time.

"Yes, I'm ready," he replied in a firm voice, doing his best to hide his nervousness.

"Good," said Rynlin. "Then let's begin. Both Rya and I will be teaching you in the morning how to use the Talent, and we will continue with your current lessons. In the afternoon, you will be learning another new skill as well, but we'll discuss that after lunch. We have too much to do now as it is."

Thomas wondered what that new skill might be. He didn't have time to dwell on it, though.

"Before we get started there are a few things we need to discuss. First, you must promise not to use the Talent unless Rya or I are there to help you." Rynlin raised his hands to ward off Thomas' attempted objections. "I know that there is much you can already do, and for that reason, we'll take searching off the list, as long as you don't go so far as to tax your strength too much. But what Rya and I teach you, until we give you permission to do it on your own, must only be attempted while we are present. You must promise to obey us in this."

144

Thomas didn't really see it as much of a choice. "I agree."

"Good," said Rya. "Now, for your second lesson, let's discuss the Talent." Thomas settled more comfortably onto his stool. He sensed it was going to be a long discussion.

"The Talent, as was explained yesterday evening, comes from nature. There are certain people in the Kingdoms who are closer to nature than others, and it is they who have the Talent. Their ability, of course, depends on their strength and their will. When we use the Talent, we link ourselves to nature, using its strength and redirecting it in a way that meets our desired objective. Let me show you." Rya adopted a look of intense concentration as she gazed directly at Thomas. He wondered what she was doing.

"Hey," he said in surprise, as he was lifted several feet off the ground, stool and all.

"Let me explain how I did that, Thomas," said Rya, as she gently lowered him to the floor. "As you do when you're searching, I opened myself to the Talent — that's another way to describe linking to the power of nature — and then used my will to redirect that power so I could lift you off the ground. This might help you understand a little better. I opened myself to the Talent, and then in my mind I looked at you and the stool and thought 'Rise.' By thinking that thought and directing the Talent with my will, I was able to do it.

"You'll be able to give it a try in just a moment, but there are a few more things you need to know. One is that there are actually two forms of the Talent. The first is one that both Rynlin and I practice, in which we derive our power from nature. There is another type that does much the same, though with far darker purposes. The best way to describe it is to simply call it Dark Magic, since it doesn't really involve the Talent at all. Dark Magic is practiced by warlocks, men and women who have sold their souls to the Shadow Lord in return for some skill in this cursed art."

The Shadow Lord! While growing up at the Crag, he had been told that the Shadow Lord was dead, destroyed in the Great War two hundred years before. But Rya had talked of the Shadow Lord as if he were still alive.

"What's the difference between the two?" he asked.

"Not much in the way they are practiced," answered Rya, "but certainly in the way they are applied. There is an evil that comes from Dark Magic. It changes those who use it, and not for the good."

"Most of the people who have turned to Dark Magic did so for a reason," said Rynlin. "They wanted power or wealth or revenge — you name it. It could be anything. But they all felt that the only way to get what they wanted was to sell their souls for it. That is the greatest mistake you can ever make. When you're dealing with the Shadow Lord, you don't know the cost of doing business until it's too late."

"What is the cost?" asked Thomas.

"It depends," said Rynlin. "The Shadow Lord is a hard master. Though we call those who have gained some ability in Dark Magic warlocks, which connotes strength or power in battle, if you look back into history the word has an older, mostly forgotten meaning — oathbreaker, or betrayer of covenants. In a literal sense, these people have betrayed nature, since the true enemy of nature is the Shadow Lord. They are nothing more than servants. They do what he wishes, and if they don't, they die — or worse. He doesn't have to worry too much about not having enough servants to perform his given tasks. There are always plenty of people who desire something and will go to great lengths to get it. In reality, they are weak people, and you need to remember that. If you ever come up against one, you can use that to your advantage, much like the Shadow Lord already has."

"I think we've traveled far enough away from the subject for now," interrupted Rya, moving back to her lesson.

"What about spells?" asked Thomas. "All the books speak about using them to perform magic. Does the same apply for the Talent?"

"Thank you, Thomas. You've brought me to my next point. You're right, many books speak of spells. But there is no such thing as a spell. Do you remember from last night what Rynlin was saying about prestidigitators?"

"About what?" asked Thomas, thoroughly confused.

"Sorry," said Rya. "Prestidigitators are those people who say they can perform magic, but really can't. It's all just sleight of hand. The disappearing bunny and all at the country fair?"

Thomas nodded in understanding.

"They say that the power to perform their magic comes from the spells they repeat when they are standing on the platform. They're lying. It's just a way for them to maintain the crowd's interest, and it adds to the mystique. But believe me, Rynlin was right. It truly isn't magic. And you definitely don't want to confuse tricks like those with the Talent. There is more to handling the Talent than trickery.

"True sorcerers don't learn tricks; they learn control. That's the hard part. If you can't control what you're doing, you can kill yourself and others. That brings me to my last point. When you use the Talent you have to be very careful. As Rynlin and I explained before, the more of the Talent you use, the weaker you become. It doesn't matter how strong you are, or how good your control is, it happens to everyone. When you're weak, you're vulnerable. That's why you should only use the Talent when absolutely necessary."

"Now it's my turn to give you an example," said Rynlin. He had a very hard time not adding a word or two to a conversation about a topic he knew something about. "Let's say you're using the Talent to fight someone skilled in Dark Magic." Rya threw her husband a black look, her face resembling a thunder-cloud. She certainly didn't approve of his example. "You defeat the warlock — man or woman, it really doesn't matter, since it could be both. It was a long battle, and it took a lot of energy. What happens if right after your victory another warlock appears? The warlock might not be as strong as you in the Talent, but if you're in a weakened condition, that really won't matter. What happens then?"

"I die," said Thomas with a cold certainty.

"Most likely, yes," said Rynlin.

"If you're done scaring the boy," said Rya, "perhaps I could continue?"

"Certainly, my love," said Rynlin, giving his wife his best, and hopefully most disarming, smile.

Sighing in exasperation, Rya took up where he left off. "Though Rynlin did not choose the best possible example, he did, in a way, explain what I was going to say next." She again shot Rynlin a withering look, just to make sure he knew she wasn't very happy with him. "When you use the Talent, you will be vulnerable if you weaken yourself too much. And just like anyone else, an arrow or a sword can kill you just as easily as a warlock. Now, when you use the Talent, it marks you."

"What do you mean 'marks me'?"

"I mean that since you are using the power that resides in nature, you are shaping it in a way that differs from its intended purpose. That will be obvious to those with the Talent. And perhaps even more important, it will also be obvious to those skilled in Dark Magic. They will know where you are as a result. Which, I must admit, makes Rynlin's example somewhat relevant. There are ways to get places very quickly with the Talent, or Dark Magic, and because of that your vulnerability increases."

"So anytime I use the Talent, others who can use it as well will know?"

"Not exactly," said Rya. "It will depend on how strong they are in the Talent. Some might only feel you using the Talent if they're within a mile of you. Some may be hundreds of miles away, yet they'll still be able to mark exactly where you are, and be there in a matter of minutes, or perhaps even faster, if they have the skill."

"Let me get this straight. If I use the Talent, you're saying I need to be careful because I could die if I don't do it right, and I could also become a target for someone else skilled in the Talent, or more likely Dark Magic?"

"Rya, I think he's got it," said Rynlin, with a touch of misplaced humor.

"I believe you're right," she replied.

"The Talent certainly isn't what I thought it was," said Thomas. "I always thought those who could use it were all powerful, at least that's what all the books say."

"And that," said Rynlin, "is just another reason why you should take everything you read from a book with a grain of salt. When something is written in a book, it doesn't necessarily mean it's true."

"I'll have to remember that," said Thomas, promising himself that he would be more skeptical in the future.

"Good," said Rya. "Then it's time for you to learn what you can do with the Talent."

Thomas instantly sat up straight on his stool. He'd been waiting for this since last night, though he did have to admit he wasn't as eager as he was earlier. His grandparents had certainly done a good job of deadening his excitement with their somber attitudes and stories.

Both Rynlin and Rya stood, and Thomas did the same. He stepped out of the way as they pushed the table against the far wall.

"Now," said Rynlin, standing next to Thomas, "I want you to pick up that chest over there." He pointed to the chest that sat next to the door against the wall.

Rynlin kept extra pieces of firewood in it so he wouldn't have to go outside on a cold night. Made from an old piece of oak and several inches thick all the way around, it also happened to be very heavy.

"You want me to move that?" Thomas asked, waving at the chest with his hand in skepticism.

"Yes," said Rynlin. He then hooked his thumbs in his belt and waited.

Thomas looked at the chest, weighing it with his eyes. He had tried to move it by himself once. Rya had given him a leather ball as a gift and it had fallen behind the chest. He couldn't reach the ball, so he tried to move the chest out of the way. That had been a losing struggle on his part, and it took the combined efforts of him, Rynlin and Rya to move it just a few inches. This was definitely not going to be easy. Well, if he could search all the way to the border of Armagh, he should be able to do this.

Taking a deep breath, Thomas focused his attention on the chest, closing out everything around him. There was nothing else in the room except for the chest. Almost immediately he felt the Talent surge within him. Now that he thought about it, it did, in fact, have the feel of nature. If he really concentrated on it, he could sense the soft caress of the wind, the taste of dew in the morning and so much more. Thomas pushed away those thoughts. He had to focus on his task.

When he searched, he pushed the power of nature out in front of him. He wasn't really sure how he did it, but if he directed the power a certain way, he could search. Now, he did much the same thing, taking the energy he had gathered within himself and directing it toward the chest. But nothing happened. Instead of moving the chest, the power simply hit it and flowed around it. He pulled in more power, filling himself to the point of bursting, but to no avail. The chest would not budge. He was about to try one last time when his concentration wavered. He could hear something. What was it? It was an extremely annoying sound, and it was bothering—

Thomas shook his head and rubbed his eyes, having lost control of the Talent. He had a splitting headache as a result. Rya was standing a few steps behind him, just smiling. Rynlin was still standing next to him, but he was whistling. That's what had broken his concentration. He's trying to master the Talent and Rynlin's whistling?

"What are you doing that for?" demanded Thomas angrily.

"What?" replied Rynlin innocently.

"That whistling. Why were you whistling?"

"Did it bother you?" asked Rynlin, feigning shock.

"Yes, it bothered me. It broke my concentration." Thomas was going to say more, but Rynlin's expression changed from wide-eyed innocence, which in fact looked rather comical on him, to anger.

"Well, don't yell at me then. Losing your concentration was your own fault." Rynlin removed his thumbs from his belt and crossed his arms. "Do you think you're always going to have the time and the best possible environment to use the Talent?" Rynlin plowed on, not letting Thomas answer. "Don't count on it. When you use the Talent you will most likely be under a great deal of stress. For example, a man with a very large knife might be trying to stick it between your ribs. So you have to be able to do this anytime, anyplace, regardless of the circumstances. Letting my whistling stop you was foolish, so don't let it happen again."

Slightly ashamed, Thomas nodded mutely. He had failed on his first try. Rynlin was right. He couldn't afford to let that happen in the future.

"Thomas, remember what I said," interrupted Rya. "You were doing it right, but you forgot to visualize in your mind what you wanted the Talent to do for you. You had plenty of power, you simply weren't directing it correctly."

Thomas turned back to the chest. The headache had subsided somewhat. Now it was only a dull thumping behind his eyes. Rynlin began whistling again, and even moved closer to him. Doing his best to ignore it, he focused on the chest, blocking out everything else. Quicker than before he felt the power of nature flow within him. This time, instead of throwing it out toward the chest, he concentrated it even more. He imagined the energy within his grasp moving in a single direction for a single purpose. Feeling himself gain control, he pictured in his mind what he wanted to do. He visualized the chest rising up off the ground.

Directing the energy he had gathered toward the chest, gradually he released more and more, making sure he maintained his control. Thomas turned his head away for a moment. The whistling in his ear had stopped. Rynlin wasn't looking at him any more, but at the chest, and he had a large smile on his face. Thomas looked as well. The chest was slowly rising in the air. Thomas grinned. He knew he could do this. It just took a little practice. As the chest rose higher off the ground, it became heavier, so he released more of the power he had gathered. Suddenly, the chest slammed against the ceiling, the bang reverberating throughout the room.

Thomas looked at Rynlin with an apologetic grin. "Sorry, I put a little too much into that last bit."

"Yes, you did," he said, "Perhaps you could let go of the chest before you put it through the ceiling."

Shrugging his shoulders, Thomas released the Talent completely. Before the chest slammed against the floor, Rynlin caught it with the Talent with just a few inches to spare, then eased it down gently.

"Thomas, I told you—"

"Rynlin," cut in Rya, "you can't blame Thomas. You told him to let go of the chest, and he did."

"That's right, Rynlin. I was just doing as you said." Thomas smiled innocently, but Rynlin knew better.

"All right. All right. Let's go outside where the chances of your damaging anything are less."

They both headed out the door. Rya stayed behind, deciding that this was Rynlin's lesson.

"You did a good job with that chest," Rynlin said, as he guided Thomas toward a small glade just through the heart trees. It had rained the night before, and Thomas saw from the tracks in the mud that Beluil had left early in the morning on one of his forays. "But you need control. You can hurt yourself and others if you can't control your Talent, and we can't allow that. That's the hard part, learning control."

Reaching the glade, the warmth of the sun caressed Thomas' face, filling him with confidence. "You have a tremendous potential in this," continued Rynlin.

"Someday, you might even be stronger than me in the Talent, and I'm one of the strongest in all the Kingdoms." That got Thomas' attention. Stronger than Rynlin. That would indeed be quite an accomplishment.

"But it's useless if you don't learn to master it."

Rynlin bent down and picked up a large nut that had fallen from one of the heart trees ringing the glade. Showing it to Thomas, he dropped it a few feet in front of him. "Now we're going to practice control. I want you to grow a heart tree."

Several hours later, with the sun directly above the glade, Thomas trudged wearily next to Rynlin as they made their way back to the cottage for lunch. Behind him stood a half-grown heart tree, right in the center of the glade. Thomas couldn't believe using the Talent took so much energy out of you. The headache had returned, and this time it felt like his head was going to explode. At least Rynlin had been right about one thing: The more you use the Talent, the easier it becomes. More than anything else, Thomas wanted to go up to his room and sleep for a day. He was absolutely exhausted. But Rynlin had said that was only one of the new things he would be learning today. He couldn't wait to see what he would be doing next.

CHAPTER NINETEEN

STEEL DREAMS

A short rest after lunch from his morning's lesson soothed Thomas' aching head. Walking through the Shadowwood with Rynlin helped as well. Rynlin had named the forest on the Isle of Mist years before, using the huge shadows formed by the heart trees to create a perception of fear. It had worked, adding to the legend of the island and keeping away most unwanted visitors.

After lunch, Thomas was shocked when Rynlin told him to get his sword. He had waited five years for this. Running up to his room, he dug into his chest and pulled out the Sword of the Highlands. Throwing his clothes onto the floor, he lay the sword on his bed and carefully unwrapped the oiled cloth. Even after five years, the blade shined brilliantly. There was no evidence of rust, and it looked as if it had been newly sharpened.

Thomas had seen many different blades before, especially in the books he had read. All the swords that kings or lords wore at their sides had magnificent jewels in the hilt that sometimes ran halfway up the blade. But his grandfather's sword — he corrected himself — *his* claymore was different. In fact, it looked just like any other claymore that a Marcher might own. The long, double-edged blade held an air of menace. The hilt was wrapped in soft leather so his hand wouldn't slip. The symbol of the Kestrels — a raptor streaking down from the sky, claws outstretched to grasp its prey — was carved into both sides of the blade and at the pommel and was the only form of ostentation. The blade was still heavy in his hand, though it was much easier to control than it had been when he had first received it. That would change as his arms, hands and wrists grew stronger with practice.

"This'll do," said Rynlin as he led Thomas into a small glade. He walked around its edge as if he were looking for something. "No more than ten feet in either direction from the center of the glade. That'll do just fine for your training."

"But, Rynlin. You said you didn't know how to use a sword. How am I supposed to learn?"

"That will be taken care of shortly," replied Rynlin. "But first, there is something you must understand before we begin." Thomas hoped this wasn't going to become a lecture. Rynlin had that tone in his voice. "As the next Lord of the Highlands, you are in a position to do both good and bad. If you rule as I know you will, with a fair and even hand, the Highlands and its people will prosper and remain safe. If you do not rule well, you can cause more hurt than you could ever possibly imagine."

Once again Rynlin managed to surprise him. He had never expected this discussion, as Rynlin had never before said anything about him ruling the Highlands.

"There will come a time when you will have to fight to defend the Highlands. When that time comes, you must do so wisely. Your decisions will lead to the deaths of men who are fighting because they believe in you and in the Highlands. That is a power not to be treated lightly. If you let your desire to rule, and to have power, become your main priority, you will be sending men needlessly to their deaths, all because of your whims and fancies. Do you understand what I'm saying?"

"Yes, Rynlin," said Thomas, nodding soberly. "You're saying that war is a terrible thing and should only be seen as a remedy to a situation when all other remedies have failed."

"Good. I'm glad you're listening. Also, keep in mind that fighting is to be avoided as much as possible, but sometimes it's required. When you must fight, you fight to kill, because the other person surely will. When you're looking across a field at someone with a bared blade, you don't have time for compassion."

Rynlin waited to see if Thomas understood, and with a slight nod from his grandson, he began the lesson. "Give me your sword." Thomas handed it to his grandfather. "Let me show you your first opponent." Thomas watched in awe as a man coalesced out of the air right in front of him. A man, remarkably, who stood almost a head taller than Rynlin, with a spear of the same height. Perhaps even more remarkable, the man was naked.

"As I said before, Thomas, I don't fight with blades."

"Rynlin?"

"Yes," he replied, perturbed at being interrupted.

"The man's naked."

"Naked?" Rynlin looked at what he had just brought forth. His face turned a faint red as he realized that Thomas was right. With a quick gesture the man wore leather armor tanned black.

"Sorry about that. I forgot who I had summoned. Now where was I? Oh, yes. From now on every afternoon, you will come here after lunch before doing your chores, and you will learn how to fight by following the instructions of the spirit you find here."

"A spirit?"

"Yes, a spirit," explained Rynlin. "A three-dimensional image of someone who, when alive, was a legendary warrior. I can't teach you how to fight with a blade, but I can, in a sense, bring back to life someone who can."

Suddenly, a spear about the same height as himself was in Rynlin's hands. He handed it to Thomas. It was a real spear, he discovered, as he hefted it, getting a feel for its balance. He stuck the spear out toward the warrior and was amazed when the man didn't flinch or move away. Instead, he stepped forward, seemingly impaling himself on the sharp point. But it passed right through him. Thomas couldn't believe it. Rynlin just smiled. Thomas told himself that he definitely had to learn how to do this. Touching the blade of the spear with a finger, he pulled it back with a yelp. It was also incredibly sharp. He placed his forefinger in his mouth to stop the bleeding.

"That will teach you to be more careful with your weapons and to listen to what your instructor," pointing to the tall spearman, "has to say. Today you will begin with the spear, and on other days you will learn how to fight with a sword, mace, axe, knives, hands and bow, though Rya seems to think you're already pretty good with the last one."

Thomas grimaced. He thought Rya had kept that a secret. The Marchers at the Crag had, in addition to their swords, carried bows. Because he wasn't allowed to learn how to use a sword when he arrived on the island, he decided to try his hand at the bow since that was not specifically prohibited. So he had found a book that explained how to make a bow. He had had a difficult time with it, but in the end succeeded. It wasn't the most impressive looking bow in the world, but it worked. Occasionally, when he was practicing, an arrow might miss the target he aimed for, usually because of a gust of wind, he liked to tell himself. One time, it had struck the back of the house, much to the displeasure of Rya, and he had promised never to do it again. Rya had made him dig all the rocks out of her garden because of it; then when he was done, she made him put them all back.

"As you've discovered, there really isn't much to our spearman there, so any time you strike him with your blade it won't matter. I doubt that will be a concern, however. In a moment, you'll see that there's more to this spirit than meets the eye. Although when he lived he spoke an ancient language no longer heard in the Kingdoms, he will be speaking in our language today, and he will instruct you on how to use the spear. Make sure you pay attention. Are you ready?"

Thomas nodded, not knowing what to expect. Rynlin nodded as well. Thomas barely had time to comprehend that the spearman ran directly at him, spear pointed right at his chest.

Moving instinctively, Thomas dropped his spear and ducked to his left, rolling on his shoulder and avoiding the spearman's charge. Thomas didn't have time to think. Before he had his feet under him, the spearman again charged forward relentlessly, having changed direction incredibly fast. The man was clearly too big for Thomas to fight one on one, so he'd have to stay out of his attacker's way and hope for a mistake. This time, he rolled to the right, but rather than avoiding the spearman altogether, he shot out his left leg, trying to trip him.

Unfortunately, it didn't work as he had expected. His leg never made contact with the spearman's shin. Instead, the man stopped his charge, caught Thomas by the leg and with one arm hoisted him up off the ground. All Thomas could see was the grass beneath him and the man's chest before him. Spirit or not, the tight grip the man had on his ankle hurt. What happened next, though, made Thomas forget the pain.

"Your first attempt to get away, by rolling to your left, was a good idea," said the tall spearman in a hollow voice. Thomas thought it sounded like a voice from the grave, cold and uncaring. "You should have kicked out with your leg then. Trying the same move twice in a row was foolish. If you do that in a real combat, you will die."

With that, the spearman dropped him, and Thomas saw the grass rush up to meet him. The fall knocked the wind out of him for a few moments. The spearman towered over him as he tried to catch his breath.

"Your instincts were right to escape my charge," said the spearman. "But never drop your spear. In my country, doing something like that in battle brands you a coward, and you are banished forever from the empire. Never drop your spear. Coward or no, you will always have need of a weapon."

Slowly, Thomas got to his feet and picked up the spear, not bothering to wipe the dirt from his clothes. He had a feeling things were just beginning.

"Good," said the spearman, pleased that Thomas now had his spear. The spearman gathered from the look on the boy's face that the only way Thomas was going to let go again was if it was pulled from his dead fingers. Even then, the spearman wasn't too sure. He had been less than pleased when Rynlin had woken him from his slumber. Yet, the boy showed promise. Besides, it was good to do something that he enjoyed. Thousands of years before he had spent his time teaching the young men in his homeland how to fight. He had missed that more than anything since he had died. Perhaps Rynlin had done him a favor, rather than cursed him as he had first thought. "I am Antonin, First Spear of the Carthanians. I will teach you to use the spear. You will do as I say, when I say."

Thomas nodded his agreement, seeing life behind those dead eyes for the first time.

"Who stands before me?" asked Antonin, shouting the words. He already knew, but he wanted to see how the boy would respond.

"I am Thomas," he replied in a quiet voice.

"Bah," said the spearman, waving his hand in disgust. "That is not how you respond to a question like that. You are marked on the forearm, so you are a warrior, and as a warrior you must be confident in your abilities. Otherwise, the men you are fighting with, the men you are leading, will have no confidence in you.

Many men are arrogant and like to brag of their supposed abilities, but the only thing that matters are your actions. Do not confuse arrogance for confidence. Arrogance will kill you. Confidence will keep you alive. In my country, we say who we are when that question is asked in such a way. Now, who stands before me?"

"I am Thomas," he shouted, after glancing at his right forearm. The raptor. A hunter. It was time to become one himself.

"Better," said Antonin. "But not good enough. This will be your final chance. Who stands before me?" The shout echoed through the mountains of the small island.

Thomas didn't want to find out what would happen if he failed this time. "I am Thomas Kestrel, Lord of the Highlands!" His shout wasn't as loud as Antonin's, but he thought he could hear a faint echo in the mountains as well. It brought a smile to Antonin's face, again giving him a lifelike quality.

"That is the way it is done, Thomas Kestrel, Lord of the Highlands. Do not be afraid of who you are. Use it to your advantage. When you fight, you will use everything you can to win. The ground you are standing on; if it is dry, you can fling the dirt into your opponent's eyes. If you see your opponent is slow to protect a certain part of his body, you attack there. If the sun is in your eyes, get around your opponent so he has the sun in his eyes. Is that understood Thomas Kestrel, Lord of the Highlands?"

"Yes."

"Good," said Antonin. Seeing an eager pupil before him warmed his cold heart. "There are some who say that you must follow rules during a combat. But there is only one rule: If you don't kill your opponent, your opponent will kill you."

Thomas nodded soberly. He understood that all too well.

"You will do whatever is necessary to survive," said Antonin, "and what I am about to show you will help you do that. We will begin with the correct way to hold the spear."

Antonin stepped forward and moved Thomas' hands on the weapon, so his right hand was about a third of the way down the shaft of the spear from the blade, and his left hand a third of the way below his right hand.

"This is what we call the turtle — the primary defensive posture. It is also how you hold the spear if you wish to attack with the haft. For example, if you want to capture your opponent by disarming him." Antonin moved Thomas into a position where his feet were spread apart for balance with the spear parallel to the ground and level with his chest. From that point on, the day passed in a blur as Antonin walked Thomas through the basics of using the spear — how to hold it when defending, when attacking, even when traveling so you can make the best possible speed. Then came more defensive postures, and then more offensive postures.

After practicing everything he had learned — Antonin believed that repetition made fighting instinctual rather than thoughtful — Thomas matched himself against the Spearmaster. He thought that he would never stand a chance against someone of Antonin's size because of his shortcoming in that respect. But he didn't give up hope, learning that if you were better trained than your opponent, if you worked harder, you could win.

Thomas knew he had a long way to go before he would even come close to beating Antonin. The man's spear was a blur. During the end of the session, when the sun was beginning to set, rather than actually seeing where Antonin's spear was going, Thomas had to guess because it was moving so fast. He hoped this wasn't the way it was always going to be. Thomas came away with a large bruise over one eye and sore ribs. He would have to talk to Rynlin about that. Thomas' spear had passed right through Antonin when the tall spearman had first appeared in the glade. How was it possible that Antonin's spear could be real now? Antonin had let Thomas attack for a while, turning away his thrusts and jabs with ease. But soon he grew bored and began his attack. It was all Thomas could do just to survive. Whenever Antonin slipped his spear through Thomas' defenses, the spearman gave him a hard whack on the ribs. Each time he did, Antonin would say, "Remember that. Remember that." Thomas knew that he would. It was a hard thing to forget.

As the sun slowly sank behind the mountains to the west, Antonin again stood in front of Thomas, looking down at his pupil with cold, dead eyes. Yet, this time, Thomas thought he saw a small spark of life somewhere deep within those black depths.

"You have done well for your first lesson," said Antonin. Thomas smiled at the compliment. "But this is just the beginning Thomas Kestrel, Lord of the Highlands. I promise you that in the future I will not be as lenient as I was today."

Thomas gulped. If this was Antonin's idea of an easy lesson, he was in for a lot more aches and bruises.

"In my country, there is something that is said by those who have tested their abilities against each other. The saying ends the combat, whether for training or a more serious purpose." Antonin stepped backwards.

"You may leave the ring," said Antonin, bowing his head slightly toward Thomas.

"You may leave the ring," repeated Thomas, bowing his head in return. With that, Antonin disappeared, going back to what had served as his home for more than a thousand years. He already longed to return for another lesson with Thomas. It was good to feel alive again.

Turning toward the cottage, Thomas saw Rynlin sitting comfortably on a large root, leaning back against one of the heart trees and finishing what looked to have once been a juicy apple. It made Thomas' stomach growl plaintively. The lesson had taken a lot out of him, and his desire for some food was now his main concern. When the Spearmaster disappeared, so did the spear.

Rynlin jumped down from the root, tossing the apple core into the trees. "A good fight there at the end." He handed Thomas his sword.

"How did you do that?" asked Thomas as he walked with his grandfather through the Shadowwood. He hoped Rya had already started to make dinner. He was starving.

"Do what?"

"Where did Antonin come from, exactly?"

"Well, Thomas," he began, searching for the right words, "there are some people who say that when you

166

die, when your body dies, there is nothing left. I don't agree with that. Yes, when you die the body dies too, but you," motioning to Thomas, and pointing to his chest, "what you are on the inside, what some would call the spirit, doesn't die. It simply returns to nature, from whence it came."

"So you brought back Antonin's spirit?"

"That's the best way to describe it, I guess. If I tried to explain it to you exactly, we'd be here all night."

"Oh," he said, taking a moment to think. "Is that something that I can do?"

Rynlin looked down at his grandson, seeing the desire to learn, to know everything. Thomas had a craving for knowledge, whether it concerned history or the Talent or anything else, like learning to fight with a spear. He tried to be the best he could be in everything. That could be a dangerous thing, but as long as Thomas realized he wasn't perfect, he'd be fine. Otherwise he might drive himself, and those around him, crazy. Rynlin could understand Thomas' desire, though. He thought he knew the source of his intensity.

"In time, yes, you will be able to do that. But pulling someone out of the spirit world is not something to be taken lightly. If you don't do it correctly, you may free the spirit completely and be forced to take its place. You definitely don't want to do that."

"I can see why," said Thomas. "Antonin's a good teacher. Who was he? I remember reading about Carthania a little bit in one of the history books Rya gave me. It was to the west and was one of the two empires that shared the continent long before the different kingdoms took shape."

"I'm glad to see that Rya and I aren't wasting our efforts."

"Very funny, Rynlin. I try to ask a simple question, and I get a—"

"All right, all right," said Rynlin. "Enough." Thomas smiled to himself. He had found that setting Rynlin off was a very easy thing to accomplish, and could actually be a lot of fun, as long as you didn't push too far.

"Antonin, First Spear of the Carthanians, was perhaps the greatest warrior of his time. He was also known as Antonin the Blade. I'm sure after today you can understand why. At that time, the two empires were battling one another for dominance.

"From what I remember, serving as First Spear was very much like being a country's champion," he continued. "Battles between armies were commonplace, but smaller disputes that led to bloodshed as well were more so. So the two empires, rather than wasting their armies on petty differences, used champions to settle these disputes. That way, only one man would die, rather than thousands. All in all, it was rather civilized."

"How long was he the First Spear?" asked Thomas, caught up in Rynlin's story.

"For a quarter century," said Rynlin in admiration. Thomas was impressed. Rynlin normally didn't speak so highly of warriors. "I think he was only a few years older than you when he was named First Spear, having earned that distinction by besting the man who was First Spear before him. Anyway, from that point forward, he fought for Carthania."

"How many men did he defeat?"

"Defeat isn't the proper term, at least not in his eyes," said Rynlin, the respect evident in his voice.

"What do you mean?" asked Thomas, a little confused. It was now full dark, but Thomas didn't have a problem walking though the forest. He easily avoided the roots that tried to trip him thanks to his sharp eyesight.

"At that time, when champions met in the Ring, there could only be one result. It was called a kill. During those twenty-five years Antonin earned more than two thousand kills."

The magnitude of that number settled in the pit of Thomas' stomach. Two thousand kills. Two thousand people killed. He wasn't very hungry any more. How could anyone kill two thousand people? Thomas felt sick to his stomach. Rynlin saw how Thomas had processed what he had just told him. He was actually glad for the result. He didn't want his grandson to enjoy killing. It was often necessary, but never to be done for sport.

"Antonin had much the same reaction as you're having right now when he thought about his life during his twenty-fifth year of service to the Carthanian Empire. Abruptly he resigned his title and left the Empire, taking ship toward the North Sea and up the coast. Some said he fled his past, others that he was a coward. But they were wrong. He became human again. At that time, the Empire was a very harsh place to live and was spartan in terms of its social arrangements. All the women, along with the men, were trained to fight. Babes were given knives in the crib in the place of rattles. Consequently, I would imagine that in a situation like that, you would lose some part of your humanity. I think Antonin found his again. No one saw him, at least in his homeland, ever again."

Thomas contemplated what Rynlin had just told him. He wondered what it would be like to live in a society like that, when there is nothing but fighting. It made life simpler in a way, and in another more complex. There has to be more to life than that in order to really live. Doesn't there?

"Why was he naked?"

Rynlin chuckled. "I was waiting for that question. The spearmen of Carthania believed that the human body invoked a magical protection against death."

"Did it?"

"No, it didn't. Eventually they started to wear clothes like everyone else."

"Why did they do that? I would think that your opponent might be at a disadvantage."

"Yes, I guess he would be," agreed Rynlin. "I imagine it was quite a startling sight to see thousands of naked men and women charging toward you."

"Then why did they change?"

"I'm not really sure, Thomas. I guess they saw their friends dying, and fighting naked really didn't give them any protection. They must have decided that if they were going to die, they might as well do it with their pants on."

Leave it to his grandfather to make a joke out of something like that.

CHAPTER TWENTY

Useful Encounters

"Thank you for meeting with me. I hope the arrangements that were made weren't a bother."

"Not at all," lied Norin Dinnegan, still irritated by the strict guidelines he had been forced to follow in order to gain this audience. He had left his home three days before, traveling on what had to be the foulest-smelling ship in all the kingdoms. Still, he was where he wanted to be.

He looked around the plush room he had just entered. A thick carpet covered the floor and magnificent tapestries hung from the ceiling. Gold and silver keepsakes and statues shined brightly in the sunlight that streamed through the many portholes lining the cabin walls. Very impressive. Very impressive indeed. Such an open display of wealth normally did not have much of an effect on a man such as Norin Dinnegan, if in part because he was the richest man in all the Kingdoms. But it seemed to fit the High King's personality perfectly. Norin had done quite a bit of research before meeting with Rodric Tessaril, learning the man's strengths — and many weaknesses. Judging from the appearance of the room, his information was correct.

Norin stretched out his long frame in the chair offered to him by Rodric, memorizing every line in the High King's face. Vanity showed there. As did arrogance. Yet there was something else as well. Something darker, almost sinister. He would have to watch his step carefully with this one.

When one of his agents had broached the possibility to the High King of working together to achieve their mutual goals, Norin had not expected such a quick response. Less than a week had gone by before he had received instructions to meet with Rodric aboard his flagship, the *Throne*, which was now anchored a few leagues from the eastern shore of Heartland Lake. Rodric had demanded the utmost secrecy, which Norin also preferred under the circumstances. It wasn't often that a man in his position chose to follow a course of action that could lead to the loss of his life — and his fortune. Yet, it was the only way to gain what he truly wanted.

"Your offer was intriguing," began Rodric, pouring a cool glass of wine for himself and his guest. Although it was a fall day, the warm sun beat down on the ship. Without the breeze that wafted through the cabin, the chamber would have been stiflingly hot. "I had not considered that a man such as you would go to such lengths to achieve something like this." He took a sip from the wine, then placed the glass on a table, instantly forgotten. Rodric stared at Dinnegan shrewdly, judging the man's mettle and trying to determine the validity of his intentions. "Why risk so much for a thing such as this? Outside of Fal Carrach, you wield more power than he does?"

Norin drank deeply from the wine. It was not a vintage that he would serve to even his lowest guest, but then again, he and the High King obviously had different tastes. "But that is the point, Rodric." The High King's brow tensed slightly, irritation flashing across his face at being addressed in such a familiar manner. He let it pass. There was too much at stake for him as well. "I do not have Fal Carrach, even though it is my home."

Rodric chuckled softly, amazed by the man's greed. To have so much in the world, yet to want even more. Then again, he was much the same. "And if I agree to support you in this endeavor, when will those funds be made available?"

"Immediately. The ship I took to meet you here contains a million gold pieces. It's yours within the hour, with more to come as is required." Norin watched the High King's eyes light up at the mention of such a vast sum. He knew in that instant that his plan would work.

"Then you have a deal, Dinnegan. I will have my chamberlain draw it up within the hour."

Norin frowned. "Are you sure that's wise, Rodric. Having such an agreement in writing—"

"Not to worry, Dinnegan. Not to worry. The agreement won't see the light of day. It is simply for my sake, to ensure my peace of mind, if you wish. Without it, we have no deal."

Dinnegan considered quickly, despite his misgivings. "As you wish."

"Good," said Rodric. "Very good."

"And how soon before the plan is set in motion?"

"Soon, Dinnegan. It will be taken care of very soon."

CHAPTER TWENTY ONE

A STIRRING

C atal Huyuk tore the blade of his massive axe from the neck of the Shade in which he had embedded it just seconds before, gore and blood flying through the air. He swung the weapon behind him in a backhanded stroke. The steel tip disappeared into the chest of the Shade that had tried to attack him from behind. The creature slumped to the ground, a gaping hole in its chest. He spun around, scanning the rocky enclosure. Another Shade stood at the far end, but made no move to attack. Instead, he motioned behind him. Two Ogren stepped around the Shade, brandishing their axes with glee. The two beasts howled with pleasure, saliva dripping from their sharp tusks. They saw an easy kill standing before them.

The tall warrior cursed his luck as he stepped around the bodies of the two Shades to meet the inevitable charge of his new adversaries. Where was Daran? This was supposed to be a simple task of surveillance. Follow one of the Ogren raiding parties plaguing the western Highlands near the Breaker and find out what was going on in the Charnel Mountains. Everything had gone as planned until Catal Huyuk had woken up just a few minutes before to find a Shade about to slit his throat and his friend nowhere to be found. The fight had been furious and fast, as Catal Huyuk surprised his attacker. Leaping from his blankets with his weapon already coming down toward the creature's neck, the Shade didn't stand a chance.

Now, it seemed as if Catal Huyuk didn't stand a chance. The Ogren approached slowly, moving to opposite sides so they could attack from two different directions. Catal Huyuk didn't allow them to follow their strategy. In a burst of speed, he was on the Ogren to his left before the beast knew what was going on. His axe slashed across the Ogren's leg. The creature dropped to ground screaming in pain, his leg collapsing beneath him. He quickly drove the steel tip through the beast's skull and turned to face the other Ogren.

Not wanting to give the Shade time to call for reinforcements, he was about to charge toward the other Ogren in an effort to end the skirmish as quickly as possible. Instead he dove to the ground, seeing the orange flame blazing toward him from the corner of his eye. The heat of the fireball passed over him, singeing his hair. The ball of fire crashed into the Ogren, consuming the creature in flames. Catal Huyuk didn't know what was worse, the Ogren's scream of anguish or the stench as the blackened corpse disintegrated into ash before his eyes. When he rose to his feet, he realized the Shade had disappeared.

"Where have you been?" he demanded angrily, turning to face his rescuer.

Daran Sharban jumped down from the rock overlooking the tiny battlefield to stand before his friend, a grin on his face. "I can't leave you alone for a minute, can I?" The red-haired man's eyes twinkled with glee as he surveyed his friend's handiwork. "The call of nature, but I had not expected this."

Catal Huyuk spit in disgust. "Never mind. Gather your things. We need to get out of these mountains. Your using the Talent here will probably draw every warlock within a hundred leagues." The tall warrior immediately began rolling up his blankets after wiping the blade of his axe on the cloth of one of the Shade's garments.

"What, no thank you?" asked Daran in mock anger. He was going to say more, but recognized the serious expression on his friend's face. His humor would have to wait. "Ah, well. You're probably right. We've learned more than enough already."

Indeed they had, thought Catal Huyuk, as he cinched his pack together. He saw that Daran was already set to go, so they immediately trotted off to the south. They had been in the Charnel Mountains for two days, and at that only along the edges, yet they could feel the wrongness. Something stirred in the Charnel Mountains. An evil long dormant was awakening, and woe to any who stood in its way.

CHAPTER TWENTY TWO

LEGACIES

Rya was cleaning the dishes when Rynlin walked in with some firewood, placing it by the wood chest. He smelled the frost in the air. It was only early fall, yet it felt much colder. Although winter had come early before, this time it felt different. This fall had the feel of another he had experienced many, many years before. You would think that after so long a time, the mind would forget such things. But not that autumn. Better to remember. It had started at much the same time then too, the early chill in the air, summer only a few weeks past. It had quickly grown worse during the next few years, with a cold settling over the land that was unforgettable and terrifying. For the cold brought more than frost and ice and snow. An evil followed in the cold's footsteps, an evil—

Rynlin cleared his head of the dark thoughts, settling into his chair by the fire. It was too soon to know if he was right. But a small part of him worried, and he knew that Rya worried too.

"What's troubling you, my love?"

"Nothing," she replied in a quiet voice, wiping her wet hands on her apron and sitting down in a chair across from her husband. She was not very good at hiding things from him, not after being married to him for so long.

"Rya," Rynlin chided. She waited a few minutes before answering, but Rynlin knew that she would.

"I'm worried about Thomas." Thomas had nearly fallen asleep in his chair during dinner, his mind and body tired from the day's activities. And this was just the beginning. He had dragged himself up to bed soon afterward, his sword hanging in its scabbard from a bedpost.

"How so?"

"He's a boy, Ryn, but you're pushing him hard."

"He's not a boy, Rya," countered Rynlin, leaning forward in his chair, his sinewy forearms resting on his knees. "He's never been a boy. Ever since he joined us here, he's been a man. He couldn't be anything else after growing up in the Crag the way he did, and then having to escape from it."

"Maybe so, Ryn. But in many ways he's still a boy," said Rya, her voice firm, unwilling to concede the point. "You pushed him hard today."

Rynlin flopped back in his chair, arms dangling over the rests. A sigh of resignation escaped from his lips. He should have expected this.

"Of course I pushed him hard, and I'm going to push him even harder tomorrow, and the next day, and the next …" Rya shushed him. Rynlin's voice was getting louder with each word, and she didn't want him to wake Thomas.

"But you don't have to push him so hard. Thomas is not Marya. You don't have to take your anger out on him. He's not going to run off and marry a Highlander like she did."

"Take my anger out on him? Take my anger out on him?" His voice rose in irritation. When Rynlin had been instructing Thomas during the day, he had never been angry. He had been proud. But now he was angry. "I did no such thing. There's no reason to bring Marya into this. My anger is long gone from that, and it left me completely when I saw Thomas for the first time. Fine, I didn't handle it well when she left. I've come to terms with it now. I know I made a mistake. You don't have to keep reminding me."

They were quiet for a few moments, both letting their emotions drop from a boil to a simmer.

"I'm sorry," said Rya. "That was uncalled for." Rynlin still glared at her. She knew she was only taking her anger out on him as a way to deal with the uneasy feeling she was having now, the feeling that had stayed with her for a few days.

"You felt it, too," said Rynlin. "You felt it in the wind this evening, like before, when darkness marched from the north." The anger drained away, replaced by calm and purpose.

"Yes," said Rya. "I felt it. I think I've been sensing it for the last few days; this evening for sure. It's starting all over again."

"Yes, but this time we might be able to end it once and for all," said Rynlin, holding his wife's eyes with his own.

"You think Thomas—"

"Yes, I do. Ever since he got here I've been reading, and rereading, the prophecies. I always come back to that one passage." Rynlin sat up in his chair and held out his hands before him. "I know, Rya. I know," he said, cutting off her protests before she could voice them. "I know every line of the prophecies has more than one meaning, and that there are always two or more courses of action whenever the prophecies come to a time for decision. As murky and obscure as the prophecies may be, I think it all fits."

"He has much to worry about already, Rynlin. He's Lord of the Highlands, in name anyway. If what you say is true, this new legacy may be more of a curse than a blessing."

"That's why I'm pushing him, Rya. That's why I have to push him. I hope we're both wrong. I hope we're just two old codgers afraid of the wind. But—"

"But you don't think we are."

"No, I don't. I think we're right. And I'm sure some of our friends, and enemies, are coming to the same conclusion. That's why I pushed Thomas so hard today and will push even harder tomorrow. I hope we're wrong. I really do. But we can't afford to take that chance. That's why he has to be ready. He has much to do in his life, and he needs to be prepared. I won't let my grandson, my only grandson, die. That's why I think it's time he learned about some of the things we've been keeping from him."

"I know," said Rya. "I agree with you." Rya had listened to her husband intently, seeing the same fire in his eyes that had attracted her to him. He had always believed in what he was doing with a passion, but when Marya ran away, that fire had died down, as if he had lost some of his purpose in life. Everyone had a purpose in life, some more than others, even if they didn't realize it. For some that purpose meant working as a blacksmith or jeweler or cobbler. For others it meant something else. She and Rynlin, along with a few select others, had perhaps the most important purpose of any in the Kingdoms. She stared deeply into her husband's piercing green eyes. The fire had returned. It was raging within him, looking for a way to escape its bonds.

Rising from her chair, she sat down on Rynlin's lap, slipping her arm around her husband's neck and laying her head on his chest. She felt Rynlin's arms, the strength still there after all those years, hug her to him. They stayed like that well into the night. A time of change was coming. For better or worse, they didn't know. In their hearts, even if they didn't want to believe it, they knew their grandson was in the center of it all.

CHAPTER TWENTY THREE

DARK AND LIGHT

T he next day was very much like the last for Thomas, though this time Rya instructed him in the Talent instead of Rynlin. He learned that she had a great ability with the weather. He marveled at the storm clouds she created on what was a sunny day, and the rain that fell where she directed. Again, it was a struggle in the beginning, but by the end of the lesson he had achieved a better understanding of what he was doing. He had even succeeded in controlling his own storm cloud, though it was much smaller than Rya's. That afternoon, Rynlin again brought him down to the glade, which he now called the Ring, for another training session. This time, he found himself facing a different spirit, a young fellow named Ari. He soon found that his other name, the one used most often in the history books, was The Archer. Thomas quickly learned why.

The Archer laughed at first upon seeing his new pupil, throwing a large bow into his hands. Ari himself stood almost seven feet tall, with a bow slightly larger. His opinion changed rapidly. Thomas' skill with the bow was obvious from the start, so much so that the bow appeared to be a normal extension of his arm.

Nevertheless, Thomas found that he still had much to learn from Ari, and that like fighting with Antonin, the physical abilities of a warrior played only a small part. Mental strength and determination were required as well.

After two hours of shooting the bow, he spent the rest of the afternoon practicing his concentration with the Archer. At the end of the session Ari had him cut down a sapling growing not far from the Ring so Thomas could make a new bow. Then, much to his surprise, and displeasure, when he got back to the house in the late afternoon, his other lessons and chores still waited for him. Thomas quickly realized that his life was becoming much more difficult, and there was nothing he could do about it.

That evening Thomas rushed through his meal, using the last of his bread to capture the rich gravy of that night's stew. He still had some firewood to chop, and he couldn't get to work on his bow until he had finished. Ari had shown him the first steps in shaping a bow from a length of wood, and he wanted to get at it right away. He was halfway out of his chair when he discovered that other plans had been made for him.

"Don't worry about the firewood, Thomas," said Rya. "I think we've got plenty for tonight."

Thomas stopped in his tracks, one leg toward the door, the other still under the table. They had never let him escape his chores before, even when he was sick. In fact, even if he was so ill he could barely stand up, they'd still send him out for pieces of wood in a driving rainstorm, telling him, "It builds character." Sitting back down, he looked warily at Rynlin, then Rya.

"Why not?" he asked suspiciously. He didn't like surprises. They usually included unpleasant consequences.

"Don't worry, Thomas," said Rya. "We just wanted to talk to you about something that we both think you should know. You're growing up very quickly, faster than we realized in fact." Thomas had absolutely no idea where this conversation was going. He liked that even less.

Rynlin leaned forward, crossing his arms and resting them on the table.

"You look like a cornered rabbit, Thomas. Relax. There's nothing to worry about."

"Thomas," cut in Rya, "we were wondering. You've picked up the skills we've shown you regarding the Talent very quickly. How do you do it?" She and Rynlin had discussed this earlier in the day. They wanted to approach their real topic for the evening carefully, and they thought this would be the perfect avenue.

"How do I use the Talent?"

"Yes."

"I imagine the same way the both of you do."

"Well, actually," broke in Rynlin, "everyone does it a little differently." They both looked at him with the sharp eyes of two raptors. He felt like a cornered deer.

"I don't know," he said, again having a hard time explaining something that seemed so much a part of him. Trying to describe it exactly was impossible, so he thought of an analogy instead. "I guess you could say it's like opening a door that was blocked from the outside. At first, when I was very young, I'd push on the door as hard as I could, struggling to force it open. But I couldn't. Then, with time, I was able to nudge it just a little, then a little more. Now, with the lessons that you and Rya have given me, I've been able to push it open even farther. It's still a struggle, but it's much easier than before. "I don't know exactly why that is. I assume it's because I'm learning how to use the Talent. I do know one thing. The more I open the door, the closer I feel to nature." Thomas crinkled his nose for a moment. That wasn't quite right.

"I feel as if I'm more a part of nature, as if I belong there. I can't really describe it. It just feels right. I feel more alive, and more at peace too. It's just—"

"Thomas, you don't have to explain anymore," said Rya. "I think Rynlin and I understand quite well."

Thomas relaxed visibly, slouching back in his chair, shoulders bent. This one time, Rya let him get away with it. She always told him that standing and sitting up straight added inches to his frame. He'd need that in the future. He wasn't very tall and knew that wasn't going to change.

"You see," continued Rya, "Rynlin and I do much the same thing when we use the Talent. The difference, though, is that we know our limits. We can open the door only so far. But you, Thomas, you're different. You don't know it yet, but we do. One day you'll be able to open the door all the way."

Thomas stiffened and moved his eyes over to Rya, and then Rynlin.

"Yes, Thomas," said Rynlin, seeing the recognition. "You are stronger than us, or rather will be. You simply haven't learned as much as we have. But with time—"

Rynlin trailed off, shrugging his shoulders and himself leaning back in his chair.

"But you and Rya are two of the strongest in the Talent," he protested. "Two of the strongest in all the Kingdoms."

"Yes, we are," said Rynlin. "And some day you will be stronger than us."

Before Thomas could really sink his teeth into that admission, Rya jumped in. Now was the time. She hoped it wouldn't be too much of a shock.

"Thomas, there are a few who are as strong as us in the Talent, or if they don't have the Talent, have achieved a closeness to nature that cannot be matched by others. They form a special group, and Rynlin and I are part of this group."

"The Sylvana," he whispered, his mind working furiously.

"Yes, the Sylvana," confirmed Rynlin.

"Thomas," said Rya, drawing his eyes. She wanted to make sure that he understood what she was going to say next. "As I said, only a few are members of the Sylvana, because of that closeness to nature. You have that closeness to nature, a closeness greater than any we know."

Thomas couldn't tear his eyes away from Rya. It felt as if the pieces of the puzzle were slowly coming together in the back of his mind. His skill with the Talent. His friendship with Beluil. The feeling of comfort he enjoyed while in the forest. Still, it was almost too much for him to comprehend.

"Then you're saying I could be a member of the Sylvana, too."

"Yes, Thomas, you could," said Rynlin, leaning forward. "In time, if you so choose, and you overcome the challenges, then you may join us." Reaching into his shirt, Rynlin pulled out his necklace, the silver amulet catching the light of the fire. Rya pulled out hers as well. "You see, this necklace is more than just a remembrance of the Keldragan family. It is also given to each member of the Sylvana. You wear your mother's now, more a keepsake than anything else, but you know the power it contains."

Thomas' hand automatically went to his chest, feeling the gritty texture of the unicorn's horn beneath his shirt. He nodded. The amulet had brought him to safety while escaping the Crag.

"If you join the Sylvana," continued Rynlin, "you will receive your own necklace. In a way it will tie you to us. You'll find that out when you join us."

Thomas knew with a certainty that Rynlin had not spoken mistakenly. *When you join us.* Rynlin was expecting him to become a member of the Sylvana, and from the look on Rya's face, she expected it as well. It was an exciting possibility. Rynlin knew that Thomas had read about the Sylvana before. That had been the only time Thomas had answered one of his dreaded questions correctly. The Sylvana, or Sylvan Warriors as they were also known, protected the Kingdoms and nature from the Shadow Lord. They had last ridden forth during the Great War, when they stood at the Breaker against the hordes of Ogren, Shades, warlocks and other hideous beasts that had come from the north.

"The Sylvan Warriors," he said. Legends come to life. Two were his grandparents, and he could be one as well. "Neither of you carry any weapons. Do the other Sylvana?"

"Some do," said Rynlin. "Others don't. It really depends on their abilities. It doesn't matter how we fight the Shadow Lord, it simply matters that we do." At the mention of the Shadow Lord, a chill ran through Thomas' body, as if he had been touched by ice. Instinctively, he looked to the north. He felt drawn there, as if that was where he was supposed to be. Not now. No, not yet. But at some time in the future. A future that didn't feel very far away.

Rynlin continued, "As I said, some Sylvan Warriors have the Talent; others don't. That's not what determines their worth as a Sylvan Warrior. Rather, it is their closeness to nature. As you already know, there are other ways to fight than just with metal."

In a flash, a small ball of fire appeared in Rynlin's hand, less than a fingerbreadth from his palm. Thomas was mesmerized by it, as he watched the orange flame turn white hot, then back again, in a never-ending process.

"Remember that Thomas. Remember what Ari explained to you earlier today. Strength plays a part in any fight, whether with the Talent or steel, but it's what's in here," said Rynlin, pointing to his head and his heart, "that will determine the victor."

"This," continued Rynlin, grabbing hold of the sword propped against the table, "is easy to fight with, but this," the ball of fire grew rapidly in size, outgrowing Rynlin's palm, "requires a bit more skill."

Thomas sat back in his chair, impressed by Rynlin's display.

"Stop that, Rynlin," snapped Rya. "Your showing off is not helping matters any. Let's get back to what we were discussing." The ball of fire disappeared in a wisp of smoke. Rynlin huffed in indignation, but Rya ignored it. When she had something to do, she did it, and she wouldn't let anything, or anyone, get in her way.

A scratch at the door interrupted the conversation. Thomas rose and opened it. Beluil sat there on his haunches, waiting patiently. In his mind he formed a greeting, which was returned by the large black wolf as he padded silently to the fireplace and lay down on his favorite rug. It would be a cold night. As confirmation, a strong gust of wind rustled the leaves of their home and gusted through the door. Thomas quickly pushed the door closed and moved his chair closer to the fireplace.

"We have told you some of this before, but not all of it," she said. "As you know from your readings, the Sylvan Warriors are a small group of women and men dedicated to perhaps the most important task in all the world. "The stories say that we, the Sylvana, are the guardians of the forest. In a sense, that is true. But it is not completely accurate. Rather, we are the guardians of nature. As a result, one of our primary duties is to protect the forests and the creatures that live within them, for the forests are the focal points of nature. They are the greatest and most prominent example of nature's power, and its goodness—"

"You see, Thomas," said Rynlin, "it is because of the forests that there is life. It's what sustains us. Thousands of years ago there was a specific sect of people known as druids, who supposedly gained mystical powers from the forests and in return cared for the trees. A tree can provide many things. Shade for the weary. Food for the hungry. Protection from the elements. Without trees, life would end."

"And that's why we do what we do," interrupted Rya. "We keep the forest healthy and strong."

"You care for the trees?" asked Thomas, slightly confused.

"No, not in the way you mean," said Rya. "The trees of the forest are a part of nature, and they will live or die as nature desires, according to the basic rules of life. For example, the tree that stands closer to the sun has a better chance of survival than one that is shielded from it. Nature does not play favorites. Instead, we protect the forests, and nature, from what it cannot fight back against. We protect the forests from what can kill it."

"You mean like a fire?"

"That's a good question, Thomas. But you've confused things somewhat. Fire is a part of nature. Even after a fire, the forest rejuvenates. Life returns. You know of Ogren and Fearhounds and Shades, yes?"

Thomas nodded. His desire for revenge on those who had destroyed the Crag had not diminished with time.

"Those creatures are normally found in the Charnel Mountains, and they form the bulk of the Shadow Lord's army." Without thinking, Thomas looked to the north again, then turned quickly back to Rya. He couldn't help it. Every time he heard that name, he felt a small tug at his heart.

But Rynlin hadn't missed the movement, and he stared at his grandson with a curious look. In the last few days, his thoughts had headed down a particular path. One that he hoped would be avoided. Lately, though, little things, like Thomas' quick glance to the north, twice now, confirmed his suspicions even more.

"Why do you think the Charnel Mountains are sooty, almost black?"

"I don't know," replied Thomas.

"The Shadow Lord has lived for thousands of years, but there was a time when he did not exist. No one is sure exactly where he came from. Anyway, before the Shadow Lord came to be, the Charnel Mountains looked very much like the Highlands, with the hidden valleys and lakes, the wind-swept peaks, lush trees and vegetation. When the Shadow Lord took up residence there, and began creating his servants — the Ogren, Shades, Fearhounds, as well as other things now thankfully hunted to extinction — those mountains slowly transformed into what they are today.

"You see, Thomas," said Rya, leaning forward, now less than a foot away from her grandson, "the Shadow Lord and his creatures kill nature simply by walking within it. They are an evil so great, they kill whatever they touch."

"So if a Shade stepped on a blade of grass, that blade of grass would die immediately?"

"Not immediately, but it would, in time, if that blade of grass was in a land ruled by creatures of the Dark Horde. The land itself would begin to change, resembling the Charnel Mountains — a land of sooty, black soil in which nothing grows. A dead land. That's what happened to the Charnel Mountains. The Northern Steppes, again before the time of the Shadow Lord, used to be farmland. It was the primary source of wines and fruits for all the other Kingdoms, but no more. Because of its proximity to Blackstone, the land is covered by a dry, withered grass.

"However, the Northern Steppes should teach you something else, Thomas. The evil of the Shadow Lord is very strong, which is why nothing else can grow on the Northern Steppes, but that territory is not his. Nature is still fighting there and trying to live. If the creatures of the Shadow Lord continue to use it as an avenue for their raids into the Highlands, nature will eventually lose the battle. All of the creatures of the Shadow Lord enjoy only one thing, and that is to kill. "

"Can the Breaker hold back the Shadow Lord's evil?" If the creatures of the Shadow Lord were killing the Northern Steppes as they marched across to the Highlands, then they must be having the same effect on the Highlands, though at a slower pace. Worry grew in his heart. Talyn had said the Highlands were his responsibility.

"To an extent," replied Rynlin, again earning a sharp glare from his wife. No matter how hard he tried, he couldn't keep his mouth shut when there was a story to tell. "The evil of the Shadow Lord is actually carried within his scions. In a very real sense, they are vessels of evil. It is through them that he increases his power. Those creatures are an abomination, an affront to nature. Everything created by nature was done so for a purpose. For example, Beluil," he motioned to the wolf, now lying half-asleep in front of the warm blaze, "hunts deer and other animals, but only enough to eat. If he sees two deer he can bring down, he will only kill one. That's all he needs to survive. But Ogren and Shades and Fearhounds, they kill simply because they can. That's why we fight them. As the guardians of nature, Sylvan Warriors have a natural ability to sense the evil of the Shadow Lord, and the evil within his creatures. When they enter our territory, that's when it's our turn to hunt."

There was a wicked gleam in Rynlin's eyes. He obviously enjoyed fulfilling that obligation. "You can do it as well, you know. You said before that when the Crag fell, you had a bad feeling, as if there was something wrong in the surrounding forest."

"Yes," said Thomas, remembering that day vividly. He had, indeed, sensed that something was wrong within the Highlands. He just didn't know the cause.

"What you were feeling were the Ogren traveling through the forest toward the Crag." Rynlin saw Thomas bow his head and knew what he was doing. He reached toward his grandson, taking hold of his forearm and giving it a hard squeeze. "Don't blame yourself, Thomas. There was nothing you could do. You were a boy then, and you didn't know what you were feeling. Now you do. You can only blame yourself now if you fail to act."

Thomas nodded. Still, there was a nagging doubt. Perhaps there was something he could have done, should have done.

"The Breaker does hold back the Shadow Lord," said Rya, bringing the conversation back on track. "Guards used to stand atop that massive wall, especially after the Great War." Thomas tried to imagine what the Breaker looked like. He had read that it was three hundred feet tall and one hundred feet wide. He knew it was true, but he really wouldn't believe it until he saw it. "As time passed, the Kingdoms grew lax, and the number of soldiers who formed the First Guard — those waiting for the next attack by the Shadow Lord — dwindled in number. Now, no one waits, as most of the Western Kingdoms believe the Shadow Lord is dead or simply a myth. But the Breaker still stands, and I have a feeling it will be put to use once again." Rya exchanged a look with Rynlin. *Sooner than we know,* they both thought. *Before we, and perhaps you, Thomas, are ready.*

"We have been fighting that abomination for a long time," said Rya mournfully. "The Sylvana were first called together to fight an evil in the far north, which had entered the Charnel Mountains. At the time, those mountains were known as the Northern Peaks, and as I said before, they were a beautiful sight to behold. That was the first time the Shadow Lord tried to conquer the Kingdoms. In the beginning, the rulers of the different lands didn't see him as a serious threat, since it was far to the north and the Northern Steppes stood in the way. So only a few went into the Northern Peaks to fight. They did the best they could, but were heavily outnumbered by the Dark Horde. They fought valiantly, yet could only delay the inevitable advance and hope that help would come.

"The other Kingdoms soon realized the great danger they were in, but it would take weeks for them to call together their armies and march to the north. At that time, druids still held sway over the land, and often served as advisors in the courts of the different kings. The chief druid, a woman named Athala, suggested that the Kingdoms send their best warriors to her, and they would fight the Dark Horde until the massed armies of the Kingdoms could take the field.

"The other rulers thought it was an excellent idea, and the greatest warriors of that time met Athala on the Northern Steppes, for the Dark Horde was pushing hard for the south and would soon break out of the Northern Peaks. When that happened, the Kingdoms would have no chance to stop them. Athala called her small army of only several hundred Sylvan Warriors, naming it after a mythical band of soldiers who, the stories told, appeared in times of need and fought for those who had been wronged.

"The Sylvan Warriors met the Dark Horde at the edge of the Northern Peaks, and there they battled for three days and three nights. The Sylvana fought desperately to hold back the Shadow Lord's advance. In the end, they succeeded. They forced the Dark Horde to retreat. Before the Shadow Lord could recover, the armies of the Kingdoms arrived and pushed him even deeper into what was then already being described as the Charnel Mountains."

Thomas was captured by Rya's words, clinging to every one. Images of the battle came to life in his mind thanks to what was often described by his grandparents as his overactive imagination.

"But they couldn't destroy the Shadow Lord. They could only defeat him. So the rulers of the Kingdoms again followed the advice of Athala and made the Sylvan Warriors a permanent fighting force, with no ties of allegiance to any country. Their sole purpose was to fight the Shadow Lord, and they have done so ever since. That was the first time the Shadow Lord tried to conquer the Kingdoms, but not the last. He continues to attack, and we continue to defeat him. Yet, he grows stronger each time, and it becomes more difficult for us to hold him back.

"Many great men and women have been members of the Sylvana. Rynlin's family used to rule a kingdom larger than Fal Carrach and the Highlands combined, but the Keldragans prided themselves more on being part of that original group to fight the Shadow Lord. Ollav Fola, the first High King, was a Sylvan Warrior before assuming his throne. Yet even when he ruled as High King, he could not break his ties fully with us. They were too strong."

"Why was that?" asked Thomas. He had listened in rapt attention to Rya's story. Some of what she talked of was discussed in the history books he had read, but much of it, in fact most of it, was not mentioned.

"When you join the Sylvana, Thomas," said Rynlin, "you are marked." Rya had been waiting to see when Rynlin was going to interrupt her again. She was amazed he had not done so earlier. Since he had behaved himself for so long she decided she would permit this one transgression, adopting the pose of an indulgent schoolteacher allowing her favorite student to speak. She knew that Rynlin found that posture extremely irritating, and he confirmed it with his brief scowl. How easy it was to play with her husband's mind. Rynlin again pulled out his necklace to make his point.

"You are bound to nature for the rest of your life. That is the purpose of your life, to protect nature and those who live within nature's touch — people, animals, trees, life in general — from the evil of the Shadow Lord. It is not a decision to be made lightly."

Thomas took in Rynlin's words and wondered if he would some day have the opportunity to join the Sylvana. One day perhaps he would. But he had a promise to keep to his grandfather and the Highlands. Would that interfere?

"The Sylvana held the Shadow Lord at the edge of the Charnel Mountains?" asked Thomas for clarification. They both nodded. "Then why was the Breaker built?" He had wondered about that. He knew the obvious reason: to hold back the Shadow Lord. But he wondered why that would be necessary if the Shadow Lord could not extend his power outside of the Charnel Mountains.

"Because there used to be hundreds of Sylvan Warriors," said Rynlin in a sad tone, the sorrow readily apparent in his face. "As the years passed and the number of battles grew, our numbers have decreased. Now there are no more than a hundred. Because there are so few of us left, the Breaker is our last defense. If the Shadow Lord attacks, and breaches the Breaker, the Kingdoms will fall, and with them nature itself."

"You don't have to worry about that," said Rya, seeing Thomas' concern. "There are still enough of us left to defeat the Shadow Lord, and he hasn't stirred for more than two hundred years, since the Great War."

"So where are your unicorns? I thought unicorns were the steeds of Sylvan Warriors." Both Rynlin and

Rya stared at him in surprise. They were both taken off-guard by the question. Rynlin decided to give him the truth. Thomas usually smelled a lie from a mile away.

"They live in the Valley of the Unicorns and come out into the world when there is a need." Thomas had been curious about that since he had first learned that Rynlin and Rya were both members of the Sylvana. He knew from the history books that the Sylvan Warriors did not ride horses. Instead they rode unicorns into battle, but it was always very vague as to why that was the case.

"Are unicorns only white, or can they be different colors?" Again, the history books only spoke of white unicorns, but Thomas doubted their accuracy.

"Why do you ask, Thomas?" Rya sensed that Thomas was asking these questions out of more than basic curiosity.

"No reason."

"Thomas." He had heard that unyielding tone of voice from Rya many times before. Holding back information now was not a good idea. He had hoped to get answers to his questions in a roundabout way. He now saw that it would be impossible.

"Because I keep seeing unicorns in my dreams," he replied. Both Rynlin and Rya leaned forward, gazing at him intently, but for some reason were not surprised. Thomas cleared his throat, somewhat nervous under their close scrutiny. He decided to tell his grandparents everything. "Recently I've been having the same dream, where a black unicorn stands before me in a huge valley of green. Then the unicorn approaches me. He bends his head and touches my palm with his horn and I wake up."

"How often do you have this dream, Thomas?" Rya asked the question calmly, but on the inside she was having a hard time controlling her emotions.

"When I first had it a few months ago, maybe once a week at most. Now it's several times a week. Is that a problem? The books that I've read only speak of white unicorns, not black ones."

"No, not at all," said Rya. "Unicorns can be many different colors."

Rynlin had been following Thomas and Rya's conversation only partially. Since Thomas had arrived on the island, he had delved deeply into the ancient prophecies, trying to find a hint as to what would come next in their battle against the Shadow Lord. Though each of the different prophecies was obscure and difficult to understand, they all came to a single conclusion — at a certain point in time one person would fight against the Shadow Lord in Blackstone, or rather Shadow's Reach as it was known when the prophecies were written. The fate of the world hinged on that single battle. If the challenger survived, the world would live. If the Shadow Lord won, the world as they knew it would die. All of the prophecies agreed on this, but none ever explained who the challenger would be. They simply gave the person a name — the Defender of the Light — and only one prophecy offered any hint as to whom that person might be.

CHAPTER TWENTY FOUR

A PROPHECY

When Rynlin had seen Thomas for the first time, in that glade in the Highlands, he had appeared to be nothing more than a small, frightened boy. But something had been jarred loose from his memory then, and he had gone back to the prophecies for an answer. Now, with the weather changing, and harkening back to that dire time two hundred years before, his search through the prophecies had moved at a faster pace. He had found what he had been looking for just the other day — that one prophecy's explanation, vague as it was, as to whom exactly would be the Defender of the Light. Those lines of the prophecy passed through Rynlin's head:

> *When a child of life and death,*
> *Stands on high,*
> *Drawn by faith,*
> *He shall hold the key to victory in his hand.*
>
> *Swords of fire echo in the burned rock*
> *Balancing the future on their blades.*

Light dances with dark,
Green fire burns in the night,
Hopes and dreams follow the wind,
To fall in black or white.

Rynlin thought that the first few lines of the prophecy applied to Thomas. For example, when Thomas had been born, his mother had died — *When a child of life and death.* Thomas was, or rather would be, the Lord of the Highlands. And now it seemed as if he was destined to become a member of the Sylvana as well. When you became the Lord of the Highlands, according to custom, it was known as *standing on high.* When you joined the Sylvana, you actually *stood on high*, atop a rock that was thought to be the highest point in all the Kingdoms, so that requirement would be doubly met. These coincidences further confirmed Rynlin's suspicions.

The other lines were still a problem. Rynlin hadn't been able to figure them out yet. He had an inkling about a few. Such as the one *Light dances with dark.* He had concluded that it simply referred to the battle between the Defender of the Light and the Shadow Lord. In ancient times, dancing was another term for fighting because many of the movements were similar. And *Green fire burns in the night.* That could be a reference to Thomas' eyes, since they glowed brightly when he was angry or feeling some other strong emotion. Admittedly, it was not much to go on. But it was a start.

Though Rynlin thought he was right only time would allow him to prove it, and time was running out. As a result, he had no choice but to assume that he was right and prepare Thomas accordingly. Then, if he was wrong, nothing would be lost. But if he was right, he could honestly say that he had done everything possible to ensure Thomas was prepared. He considered broaching the topic with Thomas then, but decided against it. The dreams were not coming every night yet. When they did, though, he'd no longer be able to avoid the topic. Rynlin was drawn back into the conversation by Thomas' next question.

"What happened exactly during the Great War? All the history books say it was a victory for the armies of the Kingdoms, but from what I can tell only the armies of Fal Carrach, the Highlands and the desert clans were there."

"You're absolutely correct in questioning that, Thomas," said Rynlin, now on one of his favorite topics. Rya sat back in her chair. She knew it would take a while for him to tell the story just the way he liked to. "There were only a few armies there, and Fal Carrach and the Highlands, along with the desert clans, played a large part in our victory. The Great War is a bit of a misnomer, though, for it was actually a single battle fought at the Breaker.

"The Shadow Lord had assassinated Deric, then the High King, and there were two claimants for the throne, Rasen of Kashel and Keril of Dunmoor. As you probably know, the High Kingship is not an inherited position, passed from father to son. It is instead based on support by the rulers of the other Kingdoms. Once you are named High King, it's for life, unless all the other rulers unanimously vote for your removal.

"After Deric was assassinated, both Rasen and Keril claimed the throne and split the support of the other rulers. The Shadow Lord saw this as the perfect opportunity, as the Dark Horde again swept down from the Charnel Mountains onto the Northern Steppes.

"I always wondered about it myself, but then I finally saw the logic. Deric was a weak High King, perhaps the weakest ever. Nevertheless, as High King, he could, in theory anyway, marshal the forces of the different Kingdoms and march northward to stand against the invader. Then, the Shadow Lord would have to fight a single opponent, which with the Breaker, would have ensured defeat. He needed some confusion, and that's what Rasen and Keril unknowingly, or perhaps uncaringly, provided for him. Those two were so concerned about who would succeed to the throne of the High King that they ignored the warnings from the east of the Shadow Lord rising once again. And, in fact, during the Great War, none of the armies of the Western Kingdoms made it to the Breaker.

"That's why only Fal Carrach, the Highlands and the clans stood with the Sylvana. It was truly a remarkable battle," said Rynlin, standing up and placing himself in front of the fire. Just as the flames warmed his body, so was he warming to his story. Thomas relaxed into the back of his chair. Rynlin knew how to tell a good story, and it was fun to watch him.

"We fought delaying tactics as the Dark Horde made its way out of the Charnel Mountains, and then again across the Northern Steppes. We weren't so much trying to slow them down as to decrease their numbers. When the Horde came out onto the Steppes, it was like a flood of darkness. For leagues around, you could see nothing but this seething mass of evil — thousands, nay, hundreds of thousands of Ogren, Shades, Fearhounds and other hideous monsters marching toward the south." Rynlin was very much into his story now, his eyes dancing with the flames of the fireplace and his arms conjuring up the different scenes.

"The Northern Steppes was littered with the bodies of dark creatures as they faced the might of the Sylvana. Fireballs and tornados and lightning strikes tore into the Shadow Lord's host. You could walk from the Breaker to the Charnel Mountains and not once set foot on grass, the bodies were so thick. But no matter. The Dark Horde continued its inexorable advance, and we had no choice but to retreat to the Breaker.

"We stood atop the wall, still early in the morning, watching as the light of day gradually disappeared. By noon, it was completely black, and we knew that the Shadow Lord had arrived on the field of battle. Only a few minutes passed before we heard the beating of swords and spears against shields and breastplates. Some of the Sylvana used the Talent to provide light over the Steppes in front of the Breaker. It only added to the eeriness of what was to come.

"The Dark Horde was coming forward, the Ogren in the lead, the Shades right behind, the Fearhounds held in reserve to exploit any gap in our defenses. We looked out over our enemy, our hearts filled with purpose knowing that if we failed, a never-ending darkness would settle over the Kingdoms."

Rya rolled her eyes. She had heard Rynlin tell this particular story several times. Each time, he twisted the facts ever so slightly. He called it artistic license and described it as a necessity in order to tell the story the right way. She simply laughed to herself. At least he was having a good time. Remarkably, Thomas was listening to him intently. She knew how hard it was for her grandson to sit still. There was always something he must do, and he wouldn't rest until he had done it. But Rynlin had succeeded in taking that impulse out of him, at least for the moment. Thomas hadn't moved in his chair since the story began, and his eyes were wide as Rynlin's theatrics played through his imagination.

"The first wave of Ogren smashed against the Breaker, and the Sylvana and the clans stood strong against the onslaught, each arrow finding an unwilling home, each rock sweeping two or more Ogren down from that great wall to fall on their brethren. You see, that was the danger. The Ogren, with their clawlike hands and specialized armor, could scale the Breaker without the need for ladders. If they gained the height, we were doomed. The battle raged for several leagues along the length of the Breaker, but at last, we swept that first wave from the wall and enjoyed a much-needed respite. It didn't last long unfortunately.

"The warlocks came forward next and tried to use their evil to blow holes into the wall. They were an easier foe to deal with, for none could match the power of the Sylvan Warriors skilled in the Talent. It was a quick fight, and when it was over, barely one in ten of the warlocks remained standing, the rest having been burned to a cinder. Even more important, the Shadow Lord was growing angry. He had a much larger army, but only a few thousand had stopped its progress. He continued to attack, driving his host forward mercilessly. With every

PETER WACHT

attack, we swept the Breaker clean of Ogren and other hideous beasts. For every attacker removed, three took its place. We held strong, though. By the end of the first day, the Breaker remained ours.

"And that was what led to his downfall. The Shadow Lord lost patience with the steady assault and ordered an all-out attack, sending forward the last of the Ogren, which still numbered well over a hundred thousand, and his Shades and Fearhounds. Most would have fled in terror from such an onslaught, but we didn't. Sylvan Warriors never show fear, and we stood there on the wall, bracing ourselves for what could be the final battle. Blood and gore flew through the air, the stench of charred flesh almost overpowered us. We were growing desperate, and the Shadow Lord smelled victory. That's when we unleashed our first surprise.

"The Shadow Lord had made a crucial mistake. He had assumed that he had created enough confusion in the Kingdoms so that no one else would come to defend against his attack except for those of us already atop the Breaker. He was wrong. That first day of battle had bought us enough time for the army of Fal Carrach and the Marchers to sneak through the Northern Highlands and come up behind the Dark Horde. As we impeded the Shadow Lord's advance from the front, the men of Fal Carrach and the Highland Marchers fell upon the Dark Horde, slaughtering thousands before the Shadow Lord discovered that he was under attack from behind. It was that initial surprise that brought us victory.

"The Dark Horde turned to face its new foe, forgetting the Breaker for a moment, thinking we were too weak to come out onto the steppe. Seeing our chance, we left the safety of the Breaker. With the Dark Horde's attention diverted, we left the great wall and gathered our mounts, then sallied forth and caught the Dark Horde in its left flank. We rode out in a wedge, swords dancing in the air, never failing to find an opponent, the power of those with the Talent cutting a wide swath through this wave of darkness. We charged forward until finally, after a full day's fighting, we met the Marchers and men of Fal Carrach in the middle of the foe, effectively cutting the Dark Horde in half. The Shadow Lord lost control of his host then. It was time to unleash our second surprise. The clansmen then rode forth and attacked those forces now separated from their master. It wasn't long before that half of the Dark Horde broke in fear, trying to escape to the north. But the clansmen pursued. They were in their natural element, riding their sturdy horses and cutting at their enemy's side, always cutting at the enemy's side and whittling them down creature by creature. We continued to push for the Shadow Lord himself as the resistance around him diminished. Victory was within our grasp. We only had to reach out and take it.

"We had fought those two days with barely any room to maneuver. It was like cutting down wheat with a scythe for the harvest. No matter where we turned there was an Ogren or a Shade or a Fearhound. Suddenly, a space opened up, and the pennant of the Shadow Lord hung limply before us, just a quarter mile ahead. Without thinking, we charged, knowing that if you cut off the head of even the largest snake, its body dies. But he saw us coming, and he knew that his army, now just a fraction of its original size, was defeated. So he ran. One moment he was there, the next he was gone. We had lost our chance, and there was no way to pursue him. Nevertheless, when he disappeared, all resistance ended, and the once mighty Dark Horde was no more. Ogren, Shades and the other creatures began to fight among themselves as they looked for an avenue of escape. They did our work for us then. Still, they wouldn't get off easy. We harried them all the way back to the foothills of the Charnel Mountains, and we haven't seen the Dark Horde since. That, Thomas, is the true story of the Great War."

Rynlin sat back down, sweating heavily from his efforts. All told, he was pleased with the story — all of it true, if exaggerated just a bit. Rynlin's charisma had swept Thomas into the fabric he was weaving, so much so that images of the battle still danced in his head. Rya quickly extinguished them.

"The history books say that the combined armies of the Kingdoms led the way to victory, but most were not there. Remember that books tend to provide a slanted view of the facts, offering us a history as seen through the eyes of those writing it. Those people may not have actually been there, or they might be writing the book for a particular reason. Most of the books written about great battles are written by the victors. And as the years pass, people normally forget the actual events that took place, until there is nothing left but the books to guide us. But I was there, as was Rynlin, and we know what happened."

The images that Thomas had created as he listened to Rynlin's story continued to play in his mind, and he actually had to shake his head to clear them away. The vivid imagery of Rynlin's telling made Thomas feel like he had actually been there, fighting along the Breaker, pushing the Ogren away, and then charging through the evil mass before him toward the banner of the Shadow Lord. One detail plagued him, though, and he had to know the answer.

"You and Rya were there?"

"Yes."

"Then how old are you?"

"Thomas, that is not a polite question to ask a lady," said Rya in mock irritation. "Let's just say that because of who we are, because of our abilities, the laws of nature don't apply to us in exactly the same way as they do to others. The same goes for all of the Sylvana. That doesn't mean we can't be killed. We can. But because of our closeness to nature, we don't age as quickly as most everyone else."

"Sorry," said Thomas. He hadn't meant to pry, it was just that he was trying to learn more about his grandparents. He had known them for five years. Sometimes, though, it didn't seem like he knew them at all. It was all just a little unsettling to him. The oldest person he had known at the Crag was Wylee Cradon, the wife of a former Marcher, and she was said to be fast approaching a hundred when she died. Yet his grandparents were at least several hundred years old, probably more, and they didn't look any older than someone who had seen forty or fifty summers, if that.

"Maybe I can become one of the Sylvana," said Thomas. "I think I'd like that a lot."

"I'm sure you will, Thomas," said Rya. "I'm sure you will."

After Thomas had walked up the stairs to get some sleep, Rynlin and Rya sat with one another for a while, enjoying the quiet. The only noise came from Beluil, as he acted out some part in a dream. Probably chasing a buck, thought Rynlin, the way his paws were moving in his sleep.

"You know what this means, don't you, Rya?"

"Yes, I do. The burdens of his life only seem to be getting heavier."

"If he can survive them, he can survive anything."

"Yes, that's true. Of course, it only takes one to crush you."

CHAPTER TWENTY FIVE

TENUOUS ALLIES

Lord John Killeran was a man of power, a man accustomed to getting what he wanted. He was also a man of reputation, in that he was known throughout the Kingdoms for his ability with a sword. Whether actual or contrived really didn't matter from his point of view. And, he was a man of vanity. A single spot of dust on his cloak sent him into fits, and his body servant running for his life. Much to his displeasure, he was not a man of wealth. For centuries, his family had climbed the rungs of power and prestige, moving from farmer to merchant to noble. Yet, doing so, in turn, had cost a great deal of money, and none of his ancestors, particularly his father — curse the bastard — had ever thought to build the fortune required by a man in Killeran's position — Regent of the Highlands.

Perhaps that's why he was perpetually in a foul mood. A mood darkened by the meeting about to transpire. He didn't like dealing with people who had more than he, whether power or money or anything else. In just a few minutes, he would be meeting with the richest man in all the Kingdoms. A man whose fortune Killeran could not even begin to comprehend. A man Killeran desperately wanted to be.

"The party's been sighted, my lord," said Oclan, who galloped through the opened gates of the reivers' main camp. Killeran grimaced as he looked up at his second in command, as he always did. Oclan had lost an eye during a raid into the Highlands, and the man refused to wear an eye patch. The reiver viewed the wound as a badge of honor, as did his men. Yet, the gruesome display still could make a man with the strongest stomach retch.

Killeran turned around slowly, taking in everything around him. It wasn't the picture he had expected or wanted. He knew how dangerous the Marchers could be, and he remembered their tenacity when defending the Crag, even as it burned down around them. The Marchers may be defeated, but they had not been conquered. In fact, he doubted they ever would be. In his opinion, they could only be exterminated. So once he had been named Regent, he had found a promontory close to the mines in the lower Highlands and, before sending his men out after the remaining Highlanders, put them to work on a fortress from which Killeran could exercise his power.

The fortress had a rather simple design, with four corner towers made of stone connected to a thirty-foot-high wall constructed from the stoutest trees in the Highlands. A ditch filled with wooden spikes surrounded the fort, with just enough space between the two to allow his soldiers to shoot anyone foolish enough to come too close. Within the compound stood Killeran's private quarters, barracks for his soldiers and the slave pens.

"It's about time," said Killeran angrily. "What took you so long? The trip is no more than a day from the border."

"He was late arriving at the border, my lord," said Oclan, wary of Killeran's temper. Many had lost their heads during one of Killeran's moods, and Oclan did not want to join them.

"Late. Late! If that bastard thought to slight me by—" Killeran gained control of his anger. A tall man had just exited the forest, followed by half a dozen of his own men and twenty of Killeran's reivers. He rode on a tall, black horse with the confidence of someone accustomed to the saddle. For all his wealth, the man wore nondescript black riding leathers. The sharp eyes and intelligence could not be missed, though, and his baldness accentuated it. He resembled a hawk in search of prey.

"Good morning, Norin," said Killeran, putting on his most winning smile. "I trust your journey was comfortable?"

Norin Dinnegan looked down contemptuously at the man standing before him in gleaming silver armor, a white cloak draped from his shoulders. He had dealt with men like Johin Killeran before, men who craved what he had.

"Killeran," said Dinnegan, nodding perfunctorily. The tall man jumped down from his horse, then walked past Killeran and into the compound. "I don't have time for pleasantries. Let's get down to business."

Killeran trotted after Dinnegan, his face turning an angry red. The man had the nerve to upstage him in his own fortress? When Killeran caught up to Dinnegan, he turned him in the direction of his personal quarters, a large cabin set apart from the others. Killeran watched Dinnegan out of the corner of his eye, taking in everything he could. He took some satisfaction when Dinnegan slipped to one knee because of the mud that prevailed throughout the inner compound. With the number of men and horses traveling through the area, even in the dry season the mud survived. Killeran detested it. He did not belong in this outland fort. He belonged in a palace of his own.

As Dinnegan regained his feet with Killeran's help, ignoring the mud on his knee, he glimpsed a structure standing in the middle of the fort.

"What's that?"

"What?" asked Killeran, his attention diverted for a brief moment by the return of one of his raiding parties, again with little to show for it. The twenty reivers churned up the mud even more as they led their weary mounts to the stables. Once again, they had failed to bring in new workers. Those Highlanders were a slippery lot. You could be standing right next to one up in the higher passes, and you wouldn't even know it. He'd have to talk to Oclan about that. His supply of workers was getting low. If he didn't find some more soon, he'd have to cut his production. And that was something he couldn't afford to do.

"That, man! What is that?"

Killeran followed where Dinnegan pointed. "That is what happens when you try to escape from the mines." His tone was one of boredom. In the center of the compound stood a large wooden pole that rose thirty feet into the air. Another pole crossed at its top. A man hung from the structure by ropes attached at each end of the horizontal pole to his wrists. Dirt and grime covered his body, as well as blood. It did not look as if the Highlander had much longer to live, yet he still smiled. "He tried to escape a few days ago. He actually made it over the palisade, but he didn't go much further after a few arrows found him. It's rather common really, the Highlanders trying to escape. We string up anyone who tries, and it usually helps to cow them for a few days."

"And then?" Dinnegan was slightly sickened by the sight before him, yet a part of him was fascinated by it. He had ordered the murders of many of his competitors during the years. It was something that he had to do from time to time, viewing it as simply another aspect of doing business. At least that's how he saw it. His victims were nothing more than obstacles to be removed.

"Then they try again. They're a stubborn lot, these Highlanders. They don't learn very quickly."

Dinnegan mumbled noncommittally as he walked past Killeran into the large cabin. The door opened to an audience chamber. The remainder of the building was Killeran's personal quarters. A finely woven carpet of green covered the floor and a dozen colorful tapestries hung from the walls. Off in a corner was a small writing table and chair. In the middle of the room stood a large chair placed on a dais. Carved from oak, it resembled a throne. Another, smaller chair had been placed before it. If Killeran was going to have to spend ten years in these uncivilized hinterlands, why shouldn't he enjoy a taste of the luxury he so rightfully deserved?

215

Dinnegan took it all in with a single glance. His initial assessment about Killeran was right. He was out for himself first, regardless of his allies. That made him either a dangerous man or a very stupid one. You didn't play games with allies such as these.

Killeran motioned Dinnegan to the chair, then assumed his place on the throne. He enjoyed looking down on Dinnegan. It was something he could get used to.

"Why are you here, Norin?" So Killeran hadn't been told. He should have expected no less. The High King kept his own counsel and told his subordinates only what they needed to know.

"It's extremely risky for you to be here, as you well know. If Gregory found out about your part in all this, he'd have your head." Killeran smiled wickedly at the thought, obviously pleased by the possibility.

Dinnegan sensed that Killeran's words were more than a statement; they rung of a threat. He decided that he'd let Killeran enjoy himself for just a little longer.

"Gregory will not be a problem, at least not for much longer." Dinnegan settled himself into his chair. It had obviously not been selected for comfort.

Gregory will not be a problem, at least not for much longer? That had the ring of treason to it. Perhaps Killeran could take advantage of it in some way.

"Killeran, let me be brief," said Dinnegan. That smug look almost hidden by the large nose protruding from Killeran's face would soon disappear. "The High King is not happy with your efforts here in the Highlands. He needs more from the mines if he's to put his plans into motion. He can't afford any problems, yet that's all there seems to be — one problem after another. It took you two years to get the mining operation up to speed, a year longer than it should have, and you still haven't provided the amount of gold, silver and minerals required."

Killeran's confidence was replaced by worry. He should have known why Dinnegan had been sent here. He should have known!

"We're doing the best we can, Norin," he replied, his voice cracking with fear. "We don't have the best workers, and believe me, we do everything we can to convince them of the need to work hard for us. There's not much we can do, though. The Highlanders are a difficult people. They don't adapt well to enforced labor. No matter how many times you discipline them, they still don't listen. And the thought of being killed doesn't bother them. Worst of all, the Marchers are a continual problem. No matter how badly we outnumber them, they continue to harass us here and at our other guardposts."

"Enough with your excuses, Killeran. You sound like an old woman." Dinnegan had been in the same situation many times before. Someone he had hired had failed in what he was supposed to do and tried to remove himself from blame. Dinnegan didn't look kindly on people of that nature. He saw such people as obstacles. At least Killeran's smugness was gone, now replaced by fear. Good, he wasn't a total fool. The High King's allies had a harsher view of failure than Dinnegan did. Perhaps Killeran would learn before it was too late. Then again, perhaps not.

Dinnegan continued. "No more excuses. Is that understood?" Killeran nodded meekly, though his body told another story. Well, well, well. The snotty lord had some backbone in him after all. The anger that Killeran was trying so hard to hide was plain to Dinnegan.

"That's why I'm here. To fix things. The High King has made it clear that you will help me in this, doing everything you possibly can. Is that understood?" Killeran nodded again. It looked as if he had finally gotten control of his temper. Good. Maybe he wasn't completely useless. Regardless of how this worked out, Dinnegan planned to make sure that if this business venture fell apart, it would fall on someone else's head rather than his own. At the moment, Killeran was the likely candidate.

"Good. Now let's get started. How much have you been skimming off the top?"

"What?" demanded Killeran, his shock at the accusation obvious. "You accuse me of—"

"I will have none of this, Killeran," shouted Dinnegan, rising from his chair to tower over Killeran, who dug deeper into the throne as if the wood would protect him. "Don't make the mistake of thinking I'm a country bumpkin. I know exactly how much the mines can produce to the ingot, irrespective of the labor. Now how much have you been skimming? Twenty-five percent? Thirty?"

"Thirty," whispered Killeran. How could he have guessed? No one knew but himself and his most trusted men. Formerly most trusted men he corrected; soon to be dead men.

"Risky, Killeran. Very risky. If the High King had been paying more attention, he could have figured this out for himself. All right. Since he hasn't, we'll continue as before. From now on twenty-five percent goes to me, five percent to you." With that split, the income Dinnegan received from the mines would more than meet his financial commitment to Rodric. The deviousness of the arrangement pleased him.

"Twenty-five percent!" Killeran jumped up from his chair in protest. Just as quickly Dinnegan pushed him back down on his throne.

"Twenty-five, Killeran. You're not in a position to argue." Killeran nodded glumly, recognizing the futility of his position.

"Then how are we supposed to increase production?" he asked. "We're getting as much as we can as it is from the workers. I work them until they die. If I push them harder, they'll die faster. Then where will that leave us?"

"Well, if we can't get them to work any harder, we'll get more of them."

"How do you plan to do that?"

Dinnegan fixed Killeran with a cold stare. "I don't plan to do it at all. That part of this business is your responsibility. I don't care how it's done, Killeran. Redouble your efforts at enslaving the Highlanders or put your own men to work. I care only about profits. Push them harder. Let them die faster. Just make sure you find more workers."

"But, Norin. As I tried to explain before, the raiding parties have been less and less successful—" Killeran waved his arms futilely before him. Explaining

219

something to the man was like trying to walk through a brick wall. Couldn't Dinnegan understand? He'd tried everything, yet the Highlanders still escaped his traps.

"In the future, Killeran, for your sake, they better not be. Send more men out. Send more warlocks out. Make sure they succeed, Killeran. I don't want to have to come back here. If I do, you'll see the unpleasant side of doing business with Norin Dinnegan."

CHAPTER TWENTY SIX

SHADOW

A cold wind swept across the barren Northern Steppe, ruffling the tough brown grass. It was midday, yet a darkness had fallen across the plain, a darkness that stretched for leagues. Blackstone, the tallest peak in the Charnel Mountains, towered over the steppe, its shadow sweeping out over the wide expanse and placing the land under a coat of unnatural darkness. Minute by minute the shadow pushed farther to the south, inching closer and closer to the Breaker — and the Kingdoms beyond.

CHAPTER TWENTY SEVEN

FOGGY START

T he silky fog lay heavily on the bay as the first rays of sunlight brightened the sky. The sunrise in Ballinasloe never failed to lift Gregory's heart. Situated just a few leagues from the southern tip of the Highlands, Ballinasloe was the northernmost trading city on the eastern coast of the Kingdoms. That was both a blessing and a curse, making the city the center of trade and business for the eastern half of the Kingdoms, but only at particular times of the year. During the winter, ice floes came down from the north, sometimes closing the harbor until spring. It was shaping up to be that kind of year, Gregory thought, as he surveyed the dozens of ships lining the harbor docks from atop the battlements of the castle. It was cold this morning. Very cold for a late summer morning. Hopefully the sun would do away with the chill.

He took stock of the city spreading out before him as he walked along the parapet. Known as the Rock, the castle stood in the center of the circular harbor, built on a large rock in the center of the bay. The reefs that protected the city from winter storms provided a small opening through which ships could pass, while also offering an excellent natural defense. An attacking army had never conquered the imposing fortress in its thousand-year history. Because of the surrounding rocks, ships couldn't get close enough to unload soldiers. The only avenue for attack required traversing a bridge more than a half-mile long. The bridge connected the castle to the very center of Ballinasloe. Of course, because of the pins strategically placed throughout its length, which allowed sections to fall into the bay when pulled out, the bridge functioned more like a deathtrap than a causeway during an attack.

Gregory Carlomin, King of Fal Carrach, smiled as he thought of his defensive fortifications. A small part of him relished the prospect of repelling invaders, wishing for the excitement. A larger part of him, what he described as the more mature part — never old — recognized the folly of his hopes. He was thankful for the natural deterrents offered by the location of his city. It made governing much easier when you didn't have to worry about the constant threat of attack. Still, with the High King growing more ambitious by the day, the excitement he craved might come sooner than he thought.

Gregory wasn't a tall man, though he knew how to make it seem like he was. He wasn't really very old either. His years as a soldier and general could not be disguised, as his broad chest and thick arms testified. It was just that his daughter kept telling him that his flowing mustache and short hair, now speckled with gray, made him look old, and he had begun to believe her. Gregory pushed the depressing thoughts from his mind, not wanting such a beautiful morning to get off to a bad start. Though the sun was barely up, the sounds of life traveled across the bay to greet his ears — the yells of the longshoremen working on the docks, the teamsters readying their wagons, the merchants opening their stalls for the early-morning shoppers. And the smell of cinnamon buns wafting up from the castle's kitchen reminded him that he hadn't eaten breakfast yet.

But first he had to attend to his daughter. She and her friends were going on a day trip to Oakwood Forest. It was another one of Kaylie's ideas, and he didn't like it one bit. Having reached her sixteenth name day, according to the law she was an adult. More important, she could now assume the throne if anything happened to him. Unfortunately, legally being an adult did not mean you actually were one in terms of common sense and good judgment. His daughter had the spirit of a stallion, when she needed the demeanor of a mare; the courage of a lion, when she required the cunning of a fox. He would have sent guards out with her, but last night she had somehow gotten him to promise that she could go alone with her friends. Even worse, he didn't know how she had succeeded in winning that concession.

Looking down into the courtyard, his irritation melted away. Kaylie had just walked out of the castle. Her long, raven black hair flowing down her back and blue eyes the color of the sea reminded Gregory of her mother. A small smile from her could melt the heart of the stodgiest old man, and she knew it. She had the confidence of a princess in her step and a mischievous gleam in her eyes, which was why he worried so much.

Saying no to her had never been easy. On occasion he had, just so she knew he wasn't completely wrapped around her finger. He quickly considered several ways to have a troop of soldiers conveniently go in the same direction as his daughter's party, yet discarded them all. He needed to show that he trusted his daughter, especially now, and having her followed wasn't the way to do it. Gregory shook his head in bewilderment as he walked down the staircase. He had never thought that raising a daughter could be so much trouble. The challenges of ruling a kingdom paled in comparison.

CHAPTER TWENTY EIGHT

MISLED

G regory felt at home in the disorder of the courtyard. The blacksmith was already hard at work pounding on his anvil, his fire blazing strongly. His apprentices were repairing the nicks in the blades of several swords and spears. A squadron of soldiers had just returned and was leading their horses to the stables while another squadron trotted out under the portcullis. It looked like chaos, but he knew there was actually some organization to it all.

The one group who looked out of place had just exited the stables. Seeing her father, Kaylie rode toward him on Misty, a tall brown mare he had given her just a few weeks before. She had wanted, even demanded, a horse of her own for more than a year. He was still surprised that he had managed to hold out for so long against her ploys, which currently ranged from tantrums to presents to a cold gaze to absolute silence. The mare suited her — calm and placid to her fiery temper. Her friends headed for the gate, many barely awake in their saddles. They weren't used to getting up so early. Kaylie had wanted to be outside of the Rock before her father noticed so he couldn't change his mind. She hoped that failure wasn't a sign of the day to come.

"Good morning, father."

"Good morning, Kaylie. I didn't know you were getting such an early start this morning. It really isn't that far to Oakwood Forest."

"I know, father," she replied calmly, though her mind spun furiously, searching for a way to leave the courtyard as quickly as possible.

Her father had given her permission to travel to Oakwood Forest, but what was the fun of going there? There was no adventure in it. And that's what she wanted. She was a grown woman now, even if her father still didn't know it. But changing her father's perspective would be difficult at best. So, she had decided that it simply would be easier on everyone if she didn't tell him what she was going to do, or at least not all of it. Besides, they would be traveling through a part of Oakwood Forest. You had to go through Oakwood Forest to reach the Burren, so it wasn't a complete lie. Was it?

"We just wanted to get going since the light is fading so early now."

"Uh, huh." Gregory looked at his daughter doubt-fully. Kaylie normally didn't roll out of bed until late morning, and her friends were notoriously worse. He just couldn't imagine that Oakwood Forest held such an allure that she and her friends would so willingly rise at the crack of dawn. He had a feeling that his daughter wasn't telling him everything.

Kaylie maintained her smile. Her father's gaze made her nervous. It was the one he used on visiting emissaries who sought trade concessions. They rarely succeeded. She knew her father was recognized as a general. But most didn't realize he was a cunning negotiator as well. To get away from his gaze, she nudged her horse over toward her friends, biting down on her tongue as her father walked beside her. She had a tendency of chattering when she was nervous, a trait her father was well aware of.

"Good morning, my lord," said Maddan. The others members of the small group offered their greetings. Lissa, Nikola and Camilla had grown up with Kaylie, and also had quickly grown accustomed to having their needs taken care of. Lissa, tall and fair, had a pouty mouth that detracted from her beauty, though she thought it made her more attractive. Nikola was rather plain, but her wonderful smile made up for it. Camilla's high-pitched voice matched her sharp features. All three enjoyed ordering others about, and they happened to be very good at it. The boys were no better. At least Eric had the makings of a good soldier, or rather the body for it, if not the brains. Rohn, with his unkempt hair and pointed nose, had the look of a trickster, though he came from one of the most powerful families in the Kingdom.

Maddan, son of Noran Dinnegan, had always enjoyed the privileged life. When Maddan had begun his weapons training the year before, he had assumed that because of who he was, he would be given a sword and then that would be it. Kael had had a good laugh at that, and then told the boy to get in line with the other students with a sharp whack of his sword on the boy's rump. Nevertheless, he was still as arrogant as ever. He now fancied himself as the best swordsman in the Kingdoms. If Maddan wasn't careful, though, his sword would get the better of him. Lissa, Nikola and Camilla stayed by the gate, obviously half-asleep in the saddle. Eric stayed with them, flustered by the appearance of the king of Fal Carrach.

"Maddan," replied Gregory. "So where are you off to today?"

"To Oakwood Forest, my lord," piped in Rohn, moving his horse next to Maddan's. Gregory saw Maddan's face turn red with anger. Maddan didn't like to be upstaged. Rohn knew that as well, but it still didn't stop him. No matter how hard he tried, he could rarely keep his mouth shut. "On a picnic." He pointed to the food basket tied to the back of Eric's saddle. "And Eric, Maddan and I were going to practice our woodlore skills to be ready for the Swordmaster."

Gregory examined Rohn with a quizzical eye. Of all the young men, only Eric approached his training as a soldier seriously. Both Maddan and Rohn were known for their lackadaisical efforts. The idea of the two of them practicing on their own was preposterous. Gregory waited to see if Rohn would say more. The best lies were always the simplest. The more elaborate they became, the easier it was to make a mistake.

Kaylie tried to sit still on her horse, a look of alarm on her face. Why did men always think they had to handle things? She was doing just fine until these two oafs jumped in. She knew what her father was doing. She attempted to catch Rohn with her eyes, but he wasn't paying attention. Kaylie groaned inwardly. Rohn was opening his mouth to speak again. Luckily, Maddan saw her expression and nudged his horse to the left. It brushed against Rohn's dark grey steed, forcing him to steady the gelding. Annoyed by the disturbance, Rohn looked at Maddan in anger, who quickly motioned for him to stay silent. Seeing Kaylie's expression, he did.

"Well, we should really be going, father," said Kaylie, turning her horse toward the gate. Her friends followed after her.

Gregory smiled, shaking his head ruefully. Kaylie had hatched another scheme. Ah, well. Let her have her fun. If she could twist him around in so many directions he didn't know which way was up, just imagine what she would eventually do to her husband.

"Make sure you're back before dark," he called after them, receiving a wave from his daughter in return as the small party made its way out onto the bridge. Regardless of what she was up to, she couldn't get into too much trouble. Not in Oakwood Forest, anyway. Maybe her friends could offer some protection if need be. Gregory chuckled at the idea. None of them showed the mettle Kaylie had. He hoped her friends' attitudes didn't rub off on her. A future queen couldn't afford to have them.

As he watched the small group make its way toward the mainland, Kael Bellilil joined him. A head taller than Gregory, he had the grizzled expression of a veteran soldier, and the scars to prove it. Completely bald, and with a scar running across one half of his neck, the joke in the castle was that to win a combat Kael simply had to look at his opponent. A sword wasn't necessary with such a frightening countenance. No one would repeat such a joke to Kael, however. He was the best swordsman in Fal Carrach, which was why he was the Swordmaster. He had guarded Gregory's back for twenty years, and Gregory could not think of anyone else who could do a better job.

"Rohn, Maddan and Eric are going to Oakwood Forest to practice their woodlore."

"Are they now?" asked Kael in the lilting tone of a Highlander. His face crinkled in amusement, making him appear even more frightening. His father had been a Marcher; his mother a woman of Fal Carrach, who had returned to Ballinasloe when he was just a boy after his father was killed in the Northern Highlands fighting Ogren and Shades. Kael had never gone back to his birthplace, finding Fal Carrach more to his liking. "Eric, maybe. But the other two? I don't think so. They don't understand that if you want to be a soldier, you have to work at it. They're spoiled brats and nothing more."

"I agree, and that's what worries me." Kael knew Gregory was very protective of his daughter, probably more so than most since she was all he had. Kaylie's mother had died more than fifteen years before from a fever.

"You needn't worry over her. She's got spirit." For Kael, that was one of the highest compliments he could give, and he didn't offer many. He was an excellent judge of character, and an even better Swordmaster. After ten years of training Fal Carrach's soldiers, there was no danger in worrying over their ability. Only the Marchers could surpass the soldiers he trained. "You know, she wants to learn weapons herself. She asked me to teach her how to use a sword."

"And what did you say?" Gregory asked the question calmly, though his insides churned. First a horse and now weapons. How was he ever going to turn his daughter into a queen if she wanted to be a soldier?

"That I was busy training soldiers. I didn't have the time. Then she said she wanted to train with the soldiers. She said that just because she was a girl didn't mean she couldn't do as well as they."

"How did you handle that?" He envisioned exactly how she must have approached Kael — fists on hips, her face an angry red, standing right in front of him, a commanding tone. She just might make an excellent queen some day, if her friends didn't get in the way and she remembered what she learned.

"I told her she'd have to talk to you."

"Thanks for the warning. I'm sure it will be a fun conversation." Kaylie and her friends were barely visible now, so he turned toward the kitchen. Kael followed him.

"She does have spirit," said Gregory. "I just hope that when it gets her into trouble, it gets her out of it as well."

CHAPTER TWENTY NINE

AWARENESS

"Finally," said Thomas. "Finally I get out of here."
He and Beluil walked quickly down the trail
toward the western shore of the island. It was a beautiful
day, with the sun shining down warmly on his shoulders.
He couldn't remember the last time Rynlin and Rya had
let him have some time to himself, with no lessons of any
sort. And no chores. He hadn't bothered to ask why.
Instead, he left the house as fast as possible, having filled
a small bag with food and grabbed his sword, the bow he
had made with Ari's help and a sheath of arrows. The
bow was truly a massive thing, fully as long as he was tall.
Yet, he could pull the string back easily. The weapons
training had given him some additional muscle and
improved agility. Though he still wasn't very tall, he no
longer viewed that as a limitation.

When he had told Beluil where they were going, he
had gotten a sour look from his friend at first, which had
turned almost immediately to one of eagerness. He knew
the rule as well. Still, that wasn't going to stop them.
Thomas wasn't permitted off the island by himself.
Rynlin had taken him across to the Highlands a few
times in a small skiff, but only for a few hours. Today his
grandparents had said he could do whatever he wanted.

They liked Thomas to follow instructions to the letter, so he'd take that order literally. Besides, if he didn't get off the island, just for a little while, he'd go crazy.

Reaching the cove, Thomas pulled the small skiff down to the water, holding it steady so Beluil could jump in. He unraveled the sail and was about to push off when a voice behind him made him jump.

"Good, I'm glad to see that you're ready to go across," said Rynlin, walking down the path to the small beach. "Rya wants me to find some herbs and roots for her that only grow at the edge of the Burren. I could use an extra pair of hands." Rynlin walked past Thomas and stepped into the boat, sitting right behind Beluil. The wolf tried to appear innocent, but failed miserably.

Thomas couldn't believe it. His one chance for freedom, gone in the blink of an eye.

"Are you going to stand there all day with that thick expression on your face, or are we going across to the Highlands?"

His grandfather's words quickly set him in motion. It may not be the way he had planned, but at least he was getting off the island. In only a few moments they were gliding across the waves. He should have expected this. It had all been a little too easy. As they broke free of the cove into open water a gust of wind caught the sail. The small boat skimmed across the waves, pushed along by the strong current. Thomas sat back comfortably, barely having to move the rudder. Relishing the feel of the wind against his face, he watched the fins of the Great Sharks follow after the craft. Though the massive sharks could bite the skiff in half, he wasn't worried. In this part of the channel, the water was no more than three to five feet deep. If he ventured a hundred feet to either side, then he would have to worry.

Rynlin also ignored the sharks, unconcerned. He settled back in the boat and soaked in the sun, oblivious to the waves lapping against the skiff. The sharks swam as close to the boat as possible, then turned away.

Reaching the shore, Thomas turned south and followed the coast for an hour until Rynlin told him to beach the craft in a rocky cove where the Highlands met the Burren. After pulling the skiff far enough onto the beach so it wouldn't be caught by the tide, they hid it under some branches. Thomas decided that his escape had failed because his weapons had given him away. Next time, he'd be more careful. He'd leave his weapons outside the house and pick them up on his way.

As they walked away from the beach, Thomas and Beluil followed Rynlin into the forest, as he led them on a game trail that offered a quicker passage through the dense brush. By midday they reached the edge of the Burren. Thomas pulled out his bag of food for a quick meal of dried meat and cheese and passed some around to Rynlin and Beluil, who just wanted the meat.

"Now that we're here, it's time to start looking for those herbs that Rya wants," said Rynlin, rising from the rock that had served as his seat. He was dressed much like Thomas — green shirt, brown breeks and soft but thick leather boots, laced up to the knee. "It'll probably go faster if we split up, so why don't you and Beluil head in that direction, and I'll go in this one. We'll meet back here in three hours." Thomas looked the way Rynlin pointed. That direction would take Thomas deeper into the Burren, which surprised him. Thomas smiled.

"Thanks, Rynlin," said Thomas, as he and Beluil slipped between the trees.

Rynlin just nodded as he watched his grandson disappear in the thick foliage, the sun barely making its way through the branches. Thomas would be right at home. When his grandson had walked out the door with his weapons, Rynlin immediately knew where he was going. Rya wanted to stop him right there, but she held her temper after Rynlin promised that he would go with him.

He agreed with Rya that it was safer for the boy on the island. Unfortunately, you couldn't keep him there forever. He had to see the rest of the world some time, even if only a small part of it. Besides, Thomas was no longer a boy, and in Rynlin's opinion, never really was one. They'd have to begin treating him as a man at some point anyway. With Beluil around, Rynlin was certain Thomas wouldn't get into too much trouble.

After Thomas and Beluil had wandered off, Rynlin moved over to an inviting looking tree, its roots curving along the ground in a manner reminiscent of a bed. Sitting back comfortably against the bark, Rynlin closed his eyes. Yes, three hours would be just long enough for him to take a nap. The herbs could wait. He had more important things to attend to.

CHAPTER THIRTY

SENSE OF DARK

T homas took several deep breaths as he journeyed into the Burren. He wasn't sure what he enjoyed most: the smell of new surroundings or the taste of freedom. After six years on the island, the urge to explore, to see something new, almost overwhelmed him.

Picking up his pace, Thomas jogged beneath the trees sure-footedly, darting around the trunks and easily avoiding the roots and branches littering his path. One of his teachers, Fergus Steelheart —the captain of the Golden Blades, the legendary personal guard of Ollav Fola — was now instructing him in swordplay. The men who formed the Golden Blades were reportedly the best swordsmen in all the lands. When Fergus served as captain, he was considered the best of them all.

He had explained to Thomas that most soldiers wore their swords at their hips, which seemed like a good idea if you were marching into battle. However, running through the woods with your sword in that position would slow you down, and possibly even trip you. So Thomas preferred to hold his weapons in his hands when wandering about as Fergus had shown him; sword in one hand, bow in the other, quiver of arrows across his back.

Beluil loped along beside him, enjoying the game. Soon, both were running at full speed, racing to see who could best negotiate the obstacles of the forest. The excitement of the contest thrilled Thomas as he ducked under a low branch then leaped across a small stream. Sometimes he would lead, other times Beluil, yet neither gained more than a pace on the other. Though dead leaves and branches covered the floor of the forest, neither made a sound. The only evidence of their movement was the air they disturbed in their swift passage.

Thomas had just dodged around a huge rock when he skidded to a halt. It took Beluil a few moments to realize that his friend was no longer with him. Trotting back the way he had come, the large, black wolf found Thomas standing as still as a statue, a faraway look on his face. Beluil formed a question in his mind. In an instant, Thomas' eyes opened.

"Something doesn't feel right, Beluil," he said, breathing easily despite the exertion. "It's almost as if there is something in the Burren that doesn't belong here."

Again Beluil formed an image in his mind.

"No, I don't think it's a Mongrel, or Fearhounds. I'm not sure what it is." Thomas focused on the source of his unease. He could feel nature all around him, and the Burren in particular. In his mind he pictured the dense forest as an area of green on a large map. The wrongness cut a deep red swath into the green, killing it, burning a hole into this well of life. He had had a similar feeling before, this sense of evil. The memory came back in a rush. He would never mistake that feeling again.

238

Beluil looked at him expectantly. Thomas sent him an image of the wrongness — Ogren. Beluil howled with eagerness. It was time to hunt. Thomas recognized what Beluil intended, and it took only a moment for him to decide what to do. Rynlin was more than an hour behind him. By the time Thomas reached his grandfather, the feeling might disappear. And, even if the trail remained, Rynlin probably wouldn't let him pursue it. Beluil was right. He had wanted excitement, and now he had gotten it. It was time to hunt.

CHAPTER THIRTY ONE

HUNTING AGAIN

T he darkness in the cave was complete. Though the season had just turned to fall, the heat of the Clanwar Desert, only a mile or so away, could still become unbearable in the far western reaches of the Highlands, and its nights could be deathly cold. That worked to the bloodsnake's advantage. Its prey, the wild pigs and small deer that lived on the border of the sand, often escaped the heat by finding a cave for shelter along the foothills of the Highlands, where it was cooler. For these animals, the caves were sanctuaries. For the bloodsnake, they were feeding grounds.

The bloodsnake slid slowly up the rocky slope. Its body stretched for almost thirty feet, and its head held hundreds of sharp fangs, each one filled with lethal poison. Only one result came from the bite of a bloodsnake — a quick and painful death. The reptile took its name from its blood-red skin. Rumor had it that the blood of the snake's prey actually created the color. The darker the color, the more kills the snake had made. Bloodsnakes were one of the greatest dangers of the Clanwar Desert, for they had no natural predators. As a result, these creatures feared nothing, not even man. More than once unwary travelers had come upon one, much to their misfortune.

The snake moved silently into the darkness of the cave, its long body twisting and turning to propel it forward. A bloodsnake hunted its prey by sound. Once it found a target, it mimicked the motion of its prey so that the animal's own sounds hid the snake's approach, until it was close enough to strike. As the bloodsnake moved into the deeper recesses of the cave, it sensed a slight motion toward the back. It began its attack, slithering forward quietly, the sound of its scales scraping against the rocky floor masked by the movement of its prey. When the motion stopped, so did the snake. It was a time-consuming process, but the bloodsnake was patient. Its hunger would be abated soon. Though it couldn't see in the pitch black, it didn't matter. It didn't need its eyes to hunt.

Suddenly, the snake felt a claw grab hold of its neck. It tried desperately to break free, opening its mouth to bite at its attacker, but the grip around its head tightened. The bloodsnake was dragged easily into the light of the cave's entrance. The snake finally saw the arm of its captor, corded muscle rippling under a skin as dark as granite. For the first time in its life the bloodsnake knew fear. It writhed desperately, trying to break free. The claw tightened its grip once more, crushing the air from its body. The bloodsnake knew that it was going to die.

The Nightstalker looked at the bloodsnake contemptuously with its glowing red eyes. With a quick flick of its wrist, the Nightstalker broke the bloodsnake's neck, letting the lifeless body fall to the stony ground.

Finally, after all this time, it felt its prey again. It had never hunted for so long before. The Nightstalker had followed its prey for several days after receiving its task, only to have the feeling abruptly disappear. The Nightstalker had waited through the years for its prey to appear again, and now it finally did. It had sensed its prey briefly at times, yet only for a few fleeting moments, and never long enough to begin the hunt. Now, though, it knew for sure.

The Nightstalker spread its arms out wide, the muscles in its shoulders flexing, the wings on its back stretching to their full length. The hunt would finally begin again. Its master would be pleased.

CHAPTER THIRTY TWO

EGO RUN AMOK

When Kaylie first thought of sneaking into the Burren, it seemed like the perfect adventure and a chance for some freedom. As she grew older, the demands made on her as a princess were becoming more and more of a burden. Her lessons were one thing. She didn't mind learning history or arithmetic or statesmanship. But standing still for several hours because of some stupid ceremony was just a little too much. She wanted to have some fun for a change. Unfortunately, her adventure wasn't turning out as she had hoped.

How come your expectations never matched reality? It had begun at the very start. After going across the bridge and through Ballinasloe, they had turned north and entered Oakwood Forest. Maddan automatically took the lead, which greatly irritated Kaylie. The expedition was her idea. Therefore, she should be at the head of the group, so she had demanded to know what he was doing, using her most commanding voice. Maddan's answer, "Because a queen's champion always rides before her," soured her mood for the rest of the morning. Why did men always assume that women needed protection? Judging by Maddan's skill with weapons, she stood a better chance on her own.

What bothered her even more was Maddan's assumption that he was her champion. He was handsome she had to admit — blond hair, blue eyes, dazzling smile — and he had been paying a lot more attention to her in the past few weeks. More often than not, he'd come to her apartments after his weapons training to see if she'd like to go for a walk.

Yet, despite his good looks, and much to the consternation of her friends, she quickly had grown tired of him. He spent most of the time bragging about how good a fighter he was, even going so far as to say that when Kael Bellilil retired, he would become Swordmaster. In Kaylie's opinion that was a long shot at best. Maddan was like all the other boys at the Rock — full of themselves; confident to the point of arrogance primarily because of their family's wealth or status. Many of them conveniently forgot that the respect and courtesy with which they were treated had not been earned by them, but by their parents or grandparents or great-grandparents.

True, hearing how beautiful her eyes were, or how silky her hair, or how witty her tongue, had been nice at first. But the more the boys voiced it, the less she believed them. Now it was a nuisance. None of the boys she knew could get past the fact that she was a princess. In fact, that seemed to be all they saw, especially Maddan. If Maddan's father had already talked to her father about a possible marriage, she would not have been the least surprised.

Kaylie crinkled her nose in disgust. The thought of marriage almost made her gag. Her father had said she should think about it. Becoming an adult, if only in the eyes of the law, had made it all too apparent. But what if she wasn't ready? All the Kingdoms were ruled by kings, except for Benewyn. Why should she have to share Fal Carrach with a man, just because he was a man? It didn't seem right. In fact, it wasn't right. Why couldn't a woman rule Fal Carrach? She had the distinct feeling that all the books she had read during her classes about the proper etiquette of a dignified and noble woman had been written by men. Why couldn't she ride off to war at the head of her father's army? Just because it normally wasn't done didn't mean she couldn't do it. She shook her head in frustration.

Whoever she married would have to understand that she could take care of herself. Yet, if all her choices resembled Maddan in any way, she promised herself that she would die a spinster. In one of Kaylie's history lessons her teacher had explained that many times a princess married for the good of the kingdom, forsaking her own interests for those of her people. After hearing that, she stormed into her father's office and told him quite clearly that she would marry who she wanted, when she wanted, and that it would be for love and no other reason. He had laughed, amused by her set jaw and blazing eyes. Admittedly, looking back now it was kind of funny, since she had been ten years old at the time. But it didn't seem all that long ago now that she had to think about the real possibility of marriage. Kaylie was drawn from her thoughts by a scream. She reached for the dagger in her belt on impulse.

Looking behind her, she discovered that Lissa had almost been thrown from her saddle. A fox had shot between the legs of her horse and startled the animal.

Normally, it wouldn't have been a problem, as Lissa was an expert rider. But Kaylie knew better. Recently Lissa had been focusing more of her attention on Eric, whom she found remarkably handsome. So she went to great lengths to flirt with him. It was of little use. Though blessed with good looks, at times he could be a little dense. The only way she was going to get him interested was to be more direct. Lissa had gotten so caught up in her task that she hadn't paid attention to her riding. Thankfully, Eric reached back and took hold of the bridle, steadying Lissa's horse. She quickly regained her seat, though she had to drag herself halfway back up her horse's rump.

"Don't worry, my lady," said Eric with conviction. "I will protect you from the dangers of the forest."

Maybe Lissa was getting to Eric after all, Kaylie considered. He normally didn't say more than a few words at a time. In fact, his latest statement qualified as a speech.

Turning back around in her saddle, Kaylie realized they had reached their destination. With just a few more steps they broke through the trees and entered a large glade. At the far end a small waterfall fell fifteen feet into a large pool of water. They had traveled mostly in shadows to make it here, the dense foliage of the Burren blocking the sun. Though a thick mass of branches spread out over the lake, the sun broke through in several places. It was well past noon, so Kaylie and her friends set up a makeshift camp. Eric was even gallant enough to help Lissa down from her horse. When Maddan offered to do the same for her, grinning up at her insolently, Kaylie ignored him. Why did men always assume a woman needed help? If she needed assistance, she'd ask for it.

CHAPTER THIRTY THREE

CHANCE ENCOUNTER

Thomas and Beluil reached the glade just after Kaylie and her friends. He was above them, concealed by the rocks at the top of the waterfall with Beluil lying beside him. They had followed the trail of evil for almost an hour now. For some reason the Ogren had stopped, so he had stopped as well so he could study these strangers. Thomas adjusted the leather guard on his right forearm, making sure it covered his birthmark. He still remembered his grandfather's warning about the power of the image of the raptor and did not want to take any unnecessary chances.

He and Beluil had considered moving closer to their prey, but they had decided against it for now. The Ogren were still about a mile away, and if they remained where they were, the beasts would have more of a chance to discover Thomas and Beluil's approach. That's something he definitely didn't want. As long as the Ogren didn't move any closer to this group of travelers, it would be all right. Besides, they had captured his interest. This was the first time he had seen people his own age since he had escaped the Crag. Thomas looked down at the group, somewhat puzzled. Most people stayed out of the Burren unless they had a reason to be there, and a picnic wasn't a good reason.

He and Beluil had heard the group travel to the glade from a good distance away. Luckily for them, it appeared that the Ogren had not. These people obviously were more accustomed to life in the city. They probably didn't know how far their voices carried in the woods, as well as the sound of the horses' hooves crunching on the brush covering the forest floor.

Thomas was a quiet person by nature, yet these people were chatterboxes, particularly the small boy with the scraggly hair and three of the girls, one of whom was talking incessantly to a large boy with blond hair. Every so often she would touch his arm with her hand, or even leave it there for a moment. Thomas wondered what that meant, and why the boy allowed it. In just the few minutes he had watched her, Thomas had found the blonde girl with her constant babbling extremely annoying.

However, one girl, the one who sat on the other side of the camp away from the others, seemed different. She was mesmerizing. Her long, black hair and blue eyes gave her a beauty most could only dream of. Thomas couldn't take his eyes from her.

CHAPTER THIRTY FOUR

FALSE TALE

"It was just the other day, in fact, that I came within a whisker of beating Kael in the training circle," said Maddan, as he bit into a piece of chicken. He wiped the grease that dribbled down the side of his mouth on his sleeve before throwing the bone into the forest. Picking out another chicken leg, he lounged back against a tree. "It won't be long before I'm given a post in the army, and from there, well, who knows. Swordmaster, perhaps?"

"You almost beat Kael?" asked Camilla in a doubtful tone. "Kael is the best swordsman in Fal Carrach. Maybe in all the Kingdoms."

Maddan had hoped that Kaylie would be the one to ask, but she was sitting on the other side of the camp, closer to the trees than the lake. How was he supposed to impress her if she wasn't listening to him as she should? The thought that she might not want to listen to him never crossed his mind. His father was the richest, and most powerful man after Gregory, in all of Fal Carrach. Yet, instead of following in his footsteps, his father had other plans for him. A commission in the army was the first step, Swordmaster the next. And from there, well, who knew? As his father had explained to him several times in the last few months, the quickest way to the throne was through the princess.

"Yes, I almost beat Kael," Maddan said in a louder voice. Kaylie couldn't help but hear him now. "I was about to make the winning move when I had a bit of bad luck." Maddan shrugged his shoulders as if to say there was nothing he could have done about it. "Someone had left a scabbard in the circle that lay half concealed in the dust. When I made my thrust, my foot slipped on it. If not for that, I would have bested him for sure."

The girls listened to Maddan's story, not sure whether to believe him. Everything he said sounded plausible. For Kaylie there was no doubt. Maddan was lying. She had learned long before that boys liked to brag, thinking it impressed girls. Many times it worked, but not on her. Maddan misinterpreted Kaylie's smile of disbelief as permission to continue with his story. Standing up, he began to replay the struggle, mimicking his movements from the day before.

"It was an even fight in the beginning," he said. "We parried each others' attacks for several minutes." Maddan made several lunges with his blade and demonstrated a few defensive positions. The girls were entranced by his performance, so much so that even Lissa was watching him, Eric momentarily forgotten. "Then I saw the opening I wanted, and I took it."

Maddan lunged forward quickly, sword leveled at Nikola. He brought it to a stop just a foot from her face, earning a scream of fright followed by giggles for his efforts.

"I attacked swiftly, lunging to the left, then the right and finally swinging low for his legs. All Kael could do was go backward. I refused to give him room to escape." He was now jumping around the circle, caught up in his imaginary battle.

"I knew I had him, so I continued to attack. I lunged forward, ready to deliver the killing blow, but the scabbard got in the way, and though I tried to recover, Kael took advantage of my misstep and won the duel. If not for that scabbard, I would have won easily."

Nikola and Camilla beamed at Maddan in admiration as he stood there posing after his almost-certain victory. They both looked at Kaylie, who was obviously not paying attention, in bewilderment. How could she not be interested in Maddan? He was so dashing, and so handsome.

"Tripped on your own two feet, rather," said Rohn, his mind elsewhere as he gnawed on a chicken leg. "Wasn't a scabbard within thirty feet of the circle."

"What did you say?" said Maddan, turning an angry glare on his friend. His face was beet red, from embarrassment or fury Kaylie couldn't tell.

"I said you tripped over your own two feet. There wasn't a scabbard anywhere near—"

Maddan moved closer to Rohn, his sword still in his hand. Rohn gulped as his friend approached, and immediately decided that prudence should win out over the truth.

"Ah, sorry. I was mistaken. As you said, you tripped over a scabbard. I was there. I saw it. You tripped over a scabbard. No two ways about it." Rohn had a hard time staying quiet. As a result, he had learned quickly that disagreeing with Maddan wasn't always a good idea even if you were his friend, so he had perfected the art of backtracking.

Maddan nodded, satisfied. He sat down again, biting into his unfinished piece of chicken. He glanced quickly at Kaylie and saw that she was looking into the trees. He wondered why. His story had the desired effect on Nikola and Camilla. Why not her as well?

"I hope we don't get lost," said Nikola, shuddering at the possibility. "I don't like forests, and I've heard of evil things lurking in the Burren. Monsters that walk the woods during the night."

"Not to worry," said Maddan, seeing another opportunity to improve his chances with Kaylie. "There is absolutely no way we can get lost."

"And why is that?" asked Rohn.

If nothing else, his help in allowing Maddan to brag would make up for Rohn's earlier indiscretion. Besides, he was curious as to what Maddan was going to come up with next. His lie about going to Oakwood Forest to practice their woodlore was exactly that — a lie. The three had spent all of their lives in the city. The closest they had been to nature, until now, was at the various fairs that took place outside the city's walls.

"I'm glad you asked that, Rohn," replied Maddan, adopting a knowledgeable tone. "You see, there is a very simple way to find your way out of any forest."

"You're right, Maddan," interrupted Eric. "That's easy enough. You just keep walking until there aren't any more trees." Eric laughed at his joke, as did Lissa, perhaps louder than necessary. Lissa was obviously having an effect on Eric for him to join in the conversation. Maddan wasn't amused, so he continued as if he hadn't been disturbed.

"As I was saying, you can tell what direction you should go by the way the branches on certain trees bend."

Maddan rambled on with his explanation, but Kaylie had already tuned him out. His voice was simply an annoying distraction to her now as she looked out across the glade and the trees surrounding it.

Eyes half closed, she enjoyed the gentle breeze blowing through her hair. It was nice to get out of the castle, especially on a day like this. Most of the time the Rock was either musty or cold or damp. The warm sun beating down on her was making her sleepy, so she let her mind wander, wondering what it would be like to live in the forest instead of a castle. She'd like to try it some day. That's odd. The horses were nervous. Instead of eating the grass where they were hobbled, they were prancing around. Ah, well. It was probably nothing. Kaylie went back to her sun and her dreams of living in a house made of wood instead of huge blocks of stone.

CHAPTER THIRTY FIVE

DANGER

Thomas couldn't believe the lies spouting from the boy's mouth. You can make your way in the forest by interpreting the way the branches of a tree bent? The shocking thing was that most of his friends believed him, except for the dark-haired one sitting closer to the forest. She wasn't paying any attention to him at all.

Well, at least one of them had the intelligence to distinguish between fact and fiction. She really was remarkably beautiful. He wondered why she was with these people, since she really didn't fit in. He shook his head in disbelief and looked down at Beluil, who mimicked his expression. This group didn't belong in any forest, much less the Burren.

Thomas quickly rose from a crouch, turning to the west. The Ogren were moving closer, and the horses sensed them now. Thomas saw the signs of movement in the forest, no more than a quarter mile away from the glade. They were making directly for it. Thomas cursed himself. He should have been paying more attention to the Ogren he was tracking than a girl he didn't even know. It was a stupid mistake, and too late to be corrected. He'd have to move fast. Sending images to Beluil, Thomas told him what to do. In an instant, the large wolf ran into the forest.

CHAPTER THIRTY SIX

A WARNING

Rynlin rarely had the opportunity to relax. Thomas thought that Rya was only good at finding things for him to do. He was wrong. She was very good at finding things for anyone to do, including himself. Rynlin really hadn't wanted to go with Thomas, believing that it was time for the boy to be out on his own. With his weapons training, he should be able to take care of himself now. But Rya had insisted, and it was easier to just agree with her rather than argue. So he had come along, determined to give Thomas the freedom he desired, and a few peaceful hours to himself. The herbs and roots could wait.

As he lay against the bark of the tree, his mind wandered. He enjoyed not having to think or worry. Rya did enough of that for the both of them. With Beluil there, he doubted Thomas would get into any trouble anyway. Though his wife didn't believe him completely, Thomas knew how to use the weapons he carried. His instructors had confirmed it. Thomas was a quick learner and pushed himself even harder when he was in the ring.

Still, no matter how hard Rynlin tried to escape it, his mind kept coming back to one thing. Dark creatures. The Great Sharks were the minions of the

Shadow Lord. They normally didn't bother to approach boats in the channel linking the Highlands to the Isle of Mist like they had earlier in the day. Yes, they would attack a boat in open water at the first opportunity, but why try when they knew they could never reach the skiff? They weren't very smart, having nothing more in life than the kill, but they weren't stupid either. What worried him even more was that they were much more numerous than in recent years.

What had happened earlier today only substantiated what he had been hearing over the last few months from his fellow Sylvan Warriors. The creatures that formed the Dark Horde were becoming restless. Many were hunting in the Highlands and around the Breaker more often than usual, which wasn't necessarily an anomaly according to Daran Sharban, the Sylvan Warrior stationed at the point where the Highlands met the Breaker.

Nevertheless, Rynlin had a bad feeling about it. Just the other day Catal Huyuk, a Sylvan Warrior living in the mountains bordering the Clanwar Desert, had run into several Ogren. It was the first time since the Great War that the creatures of the Dark Horde had traveled so far to the west. Rynlin's mind continued to ponder the situation for several minutes, looking for a reason why, yet to no avail.

His mind continued to drift when something deep within him forced him to wake. A warning. Evil in the Burren. Ogren were moving directly toward Thomas. The necklaces that had been in his family for millennia had again proven their worth, allowing Rynlin to pinpoint the location of his grandson immediately.

Jumping up from his seat, Rynlin ran through the dense forest. If anything happened to Thomas, Rya would never forgive him, and he'd never forgive himself. With the speed of desperation, Rynlin took hold of the Talent. He hoped he wasn't too late.

CHAPTER THIRTY SEVEN

FROZEN

Kaylie's friends had moved to the edge of the lake. Having grown tired of his storytelling since Kaylie wasn't paying attention, Maddan was now amusing himself in other ways. Both he and Rohn had a hold of Nikola — one by the shoulders, the other by the legs — and were swinging her out over the water. Nikola squealed half in terror and half in delight, while Eric, Lissa and Camilla looked on laughing.

Kaylie glanced up at the branches above her, running almost completely across the lake. She had been right. The trees were almost woven together in some places, and the branches were thick enough to walk on. She thought about giving it a try for a moment, then decided against it. Maddan would probably tell her father about it, and her father wouldn't be happy. Maddan would say he was only trying to protect her, when what he was really trying to do was ingratiate himself with her father.

The soft whinnies and shuffling of hooves drew her attention. Something in the forest was bothering the horses. Kaylie rose from her seat and headed toward them, hoping a few carrots to munch on would settle them down. She stopped halfway there. Something didn't feel right. The forest had grown quiet, the silence making her uneasy. She decided it was time to go back to Ballinasloe, and as quickly as they could ride.

"Maddan," she said, turning toward the lake, "I think it's time to go—"

A roar shattered the silence, causing the horses to pull frantically at their tethers in an effort to break free. Another roar answered the first, sending a chill down her spine. Kaylie leapt back from where she stood as two monsters burst into the glade. She wanted to run away as fast as she could, but her legs wouldn't move. The beasts roared again, lifting their heads to the sky and displaying rows of sharp teeth. They had to be Ogren. They were twice the size of a man, standing at least ten feet tall.

She heard her friends scream in fear behind her, and Kaylie realized to her horror that there was nowhere to go. They were trapped against the lake. She told her legs to move, that it was time to run, but still she remained rooted to the ground. The Ogren roared again, a terrifying sound that sent shivers through her body. Not able to move her legs, Kaylie was glad to see that at least her arms obeyed her. She reached for her small belt knife and pulled it free from the sheath. She had a weapon now, though she didn't think it would do any good.

The hides of the Ogren resembled tough brown leather, and their movements belied a remarkable agility for creatures so large. Seeing that their prey had not run as they expected, the two hideous creatures moved forward slowly, enjoying the pleasure of a certain kill. Large, sharp tusks protruded from their lower jaws and curled upward, and their hands were shaped more like claws than fingers. They held large, steel maces. Gobs of saliva ran down the two Ogren's jaws as they let out more triumphant roars. Kaylie had read that these hideous beasts liked to play with their prey before killing it. Well, she refused to be easy meat.

She told herself to run again — Camilla and Nikola were now begging her to — but her legs still refused to move. If Maddan was her champion, why wasn't he here now? Irritation flashed within her. He was probably in the lake with the others. She was frightened too, but she wasn't a coward. Fine, if her legs weren't going to move, then she'd stay here. She had a knife, pitiful as it was, and she refused to go down without a fight.

CHAPTER THIRTY EIGHT

FIGHTING BACK

T homas was on his feet the moment the Ogren entered the glade, but he was too far away to run around the lake. He wouldn't get to the girl in time. The two monsters bore down on her, and her friends had moved into the lake, terrified of the Ogren. So much for those boys' fighting skills. Either the girl was very brave or too scared to move, and judging by the way she held her dagger straight out in front of her, arm stiffened, it was probably the latter. Nevertheless, she certainly had courage.

Picking up his bow, Thomas pulled four arrows from the quiver on his back and pushed their points into the soft dirt in front of him. Dropping to one knee as Ari had shown him, he nocked an arrow to the string and pulled it back to his cheek. The closer he was to his arrows, The Archer had said, the faster he could shoot.

Thomas sighted on the lead Ogren, took a deep breath and released. As the first arrow streaked across the lake, the second arrow followed right behind it, and the third and the fourth. Dropping the bow, Thomas pulled his sword from his scabbard and jumped onto a thick tree branch hanging over the lake that was about fifteen feet in front of him. Maybe he could get to her in time. Maybe.

CHAPTER THIRTY NINE

SURPRISE

The two Ogren continued their approach. Kaylie thought she was going to be sick. She had never been so afraid in her life. The first Ogren was no more than ten feet away, and she could smell him now. It was a sickening stench that resembled decaying meat. She told her arm not to shake as the dagger wavered in her hand. But it was no use. Her arms were beginning to feel like her legs.

The lead Ogren stepped closer as the other remained behind it, cutting off any hope for escape. As the creature moved closer, he swung his mace through the air. The beast let out another terrifying roar, and in that instant Kaylie knew that she was going to die. It wasn't fair, she wanted to scream. It just wasn't fair!

Strangely, the roar didn't sound the same as before. The previous ones had been to frighten her and her friends; these were roars of fury.

The lead Ogren pulled at something in its chest, then at something sticking out of its thick neck, but the best it could do was break off the parts that stuck out from its body. They were arrows, but where did they come from?

CHAPTER FORTY

APPROACH

T homas moved quickly across the branches, staying as quiet as possible. He didn't have to worry too much about detection really, as the screams of fear from the boys and girls standing in the lake and the roars of the Ogren hid his movement.

Stepping lightly across the path of branches, he saw Beluil break through the brush to his left. Right on time. Now all he had to do was get to where he was supposed to be before the two Ogren decided to attack together rather than separately.

And they would, once they realized their quarry would offer little resistance.

CHAPTER FORTY ONE

VICTORY

The Ogren roared in pain, but it still moved toward her. More slowly now, wary, scanning the surrounding forest for the source of the arrows. Kaylie had forgotten the stench. She knew that the Ogren wasn't worried about her dagger. It would take only one swing of that massive club to crush her skull. In a few steps, the beast would be able to reach out and grab her, and then that would be the end, no matter how hard she fought.

She couldn't look away from the terrible menace stepping toward her, an evil grin spreading across its hideous face as it studied its midday meal. She could almost feel the claw closing around her neck. She would never lie to her father again, she promised, if only she could escape. As if answering her plea, the Ogren stepped back a few paces.

A large black wolf appeared before her, teeth bared, an angry growl emanating from deep within its belly. It was the largest wolf she had ever seen. Normally, she would have been terrified. Yet at the moment, she felt relief. If the wolf wanted to help, that was fine with her. She focused on her legs, willing them to listen to her commands. Finally, agonizingly, as if they were stuck knee deep in mud, they listened. Kaylie shuffled back a few steps until she was at the edge of the lake, which was as far as she could go. Otherwise, she would have collapsed from fear because her legs felt so weak.

The wolf backed up with her, opening up more space in front of the Ogren. It continued to stand there, feinting an attack every so often to keep the Ogren at a distance. Though the Ogren was larger than the wolf, it had immediately become cautious. Then, a flash of light on steel streaked across Kaylie's eyes.

Thomas hurtled down from the branches above the lake. He landed between the two Ogren, wanting to take on only one at a time. One man fighting a single Ogren was risky enough; fighting two at the same time was suicidal. Thankfully, Beluil was there to help. Thomas knew that Beluil would arrive first, so the wolf's primary task was to buy enough time for Thomas to cross the lake.

Thomas moved quickly toward the unsuspecting Ogren in front of him. The creature's full attention was on the large wolf blocking the way to its prey. The Ogren guarding the path roared in an attempt to warn its companion, but failed.

Coming up from behind the first Ogren, Thomas slashed its hamstrings. The beast cried out in agony and swung its mace clumsily behind it toward this unseen foe. Thomas rolled forward on his shoulder, easily avoiding the blow. He quickly regained his feet and saw that his strategy had worked. The Ogren fell forward, first on its knees, then on its stomach, its damaged legs unable to support its heavy body. The screams of pain from the wounded Ogren washed over Thomas as the creature clutched its legs. His concentration was so intense, his mind centered on nothing else but the task at hand. He felt very much like he did when using the Talent — the total concentration, the purpose, the control. Thomas didn't think, he simply moved, letting his instincts and training lead him through the fight.

Not wanting to give the Ogren a chance to rise, Thomas bounded forward and thrust his sword deep into the beast's back, digging for its heart. Giving the blade a twist for good measure, Thomas turned to face the other Ogren. Seeing its companion's demise, the creature charged forward with surprising speed, a bloodcurdling roar splitting the air, mace raised above its head, its gruesome face twisted into a mask of hate. Beluil was already moving to the creature's side, hoping to distract it long enough to give Thomas room to maneuver. But Thomas couldn't. The girl was standing only a few feet behind him. If he dodged out of the way, the Ogren might go right for her, and she wouldn't stand a chance. He had no choice but to stand his ground.

Thomas shifted his grip on his sword, holding it like he would a staff. The Ogren charged forward, swinging its mace down toward Thomas' head with incredible force. Thomas held the sword in front of him like a shield, letting the blow slide off his blade. The Ogren's strength forced him to one knee. Though his arms were numb from the power of the attack, much to his relief the steel blade held.

Surprised that its first blow had been blocked, the Ogren raised its mace again, its shoulder muscles bunching in anticipation. But in its frenzy to attack, it had forgotten it was facing two foes. Thomas, kneeling in front of the Ogren, prepared to ward off the second blow, then saw a black blur launch itself onto the Ogren's back, its teeth and claws puncturing the beast's neck and back. The Ogren screamed in rage and spun around, trying desperately to remove this new enemy from its back.

Thomas jumped to his feet and again slashed across the back of the Ogren's legs. The monster fell forward onto its knees, his scream of agony filling the glade. Beluil jumped down from his perch, giving Thomas room. With the creature still turned away, Thomas mustered all of his strength, leveling his sword directly below the Ogren's head. His blade sliced easily through the creature's neck, its head flying several feet in the air to land by the edge of the lake. The Ogren's body crashed to the ground with a sickening thud, its blood spilling out over the grass. Beluil glided over to the first Ogren, sniffing the body, then did the same with the second. Satisfied that both were dead, it began to clean the Ogren's blood from its muzzle.

Thomas let out a deep breath. It was his first real fight, and he had come through it in one piece. If he returned home with more than a scratch, Rya would likely never let him leave the isle again. Making sure that Beluil was all right, Thomas turned away from his two kills. The boys and girls remained in the lake. Though their fear remained, they were now silent. Two of the girls cried softly. The third clung to the large boy, staring at nothing.

Feeling eyes on him, Thomas turned to the dark-haired girl standing by the edge of the lake, the only person in the glade other than himself to actually draw a blade. Up close he confirmed what he had seen from atop the waterfall. She had beautiful eyes, more beautiful than he had thought when he had seen them from the waterfall. Eyes you could drown in … just as he was doing now. Thomas cleared his thoughts. If there were two Ogren about, there could be more. Though he no longer felt any disturbance in the Burren, he didn't want to take a chance. He had learned one thing, though. From now on, he wouldn't wait for his enemy to come to him. If his blade hadn't held up against the Ogren's blow, he'd be dead. From now on, he'd attack and make his own luck.

CHAPTER FORTY TWO

SAVED

K aylie couldn't take her eyes from her rescuer. She had never seen anyone fight like that — so fast, so confident in his actions — yet he was no older than she. There was a hardness to his features that you normally wouldn't see in one so young. She had watched Kael Bellilil put Fal Carrach's soldiers through their paces several times, often because her father wanted her to do it. He repeatedly told her she had to know who she would be sending off to battle — the people, not the numbers.

Kael loved to train his men by telling stories, and the tale she remembered most vividly was the one of a single man trying to defeat an Ogren, only to fail in the end. Kael had said a single man killing an Ogren by himself would be an example of pure luck; and the fact that the man had even taken on the Ogren, an example of pure stupidity. But this one person — this boy! — had challenged two, and won, admittedly with the help of a wolf. What did that make him? The very fact that a wolf had fought with him was unbelievable. She had heard of people who could speak with animals, but that was supposed to have occurred hundreds of years in the past.

Kaylie stepped back into water of the lake. He was looking at her now, those hard green eyes taking in everything about her in a single glance. Maybe it was her imagination, but his eyes seemed to almost glow a dark green. Whatever the cause, she was entranced. It was like staring into two gems. It took a moment for her to realize that he was talking to her.

"Is anyone hurt?" He had a quiet voice, but one that you listened to.

"No. We're all right," she replied in a whisper. It sounded as if her heart was beating louder than she was talking.

"Good," he said. "I suggest that you and your friends get out of the Burren quickly. You should be safe for the moment, but where there are two Ogren, there are bound to be more."

"We'll go now," she said in a stronger voice, seeing that her friends were already coming out of the lake. Eric and Rohn were walking over to calm the terrified horses, which luckily hadn't broken free from their tethers.

The boy nodded. Their eyes locked for a moment. She could feel the intensity within him, and the strength. She found it exciting and frightening all at once, but then he turned away from her. Walking toward the wolf, he stroked its fur for a moment before they both walked off into the trees, disappearing from view.

"Thank you," she whispered, wishing she had thought to say that before, wishing that she had thought of something so she could talk to him just a little bit longer. She had never met anyone like him before.

She shook her head in frustration. At least her legs worked normally again. Kaylie hurried around the campsite, urging her friends to mount before moving toward her horse. Lissa, Nikola and Camilla were crying, and the boys were still shaken. After what seemed like an hour, but was only a few minutes, Kaylie had her friends on the way back to Ballinasloe.

Bringing up the rear of the party, she looked down at the two Ogren lying dead by the lake, and then into the trees where the boy had disappeared. There was a part of her that wanted to meet this green-eyed boy again, but now was not the time to think of that. Kaylie dug her heels into her horse and took the lead of the frightened column as they made their way home. She had wanted an adventure today and gotten more than she bargained for.

CHAPTER FORTY THREE

A NEW ROAD

T homas and Beluil walked into the forest and circled around the glade until they were back atop the waterfall. As he retrieved his bow, Thomas berated himself for not asking the girl's name. He should have, but he was nervous and he couldn't get the words out. Well, actually very nervous. It had been years since he was around anyone his own age, much less a beautiful girl.

"Thank you, my friend," said Thomas to Beluil, who stood at his side. The wolf was removing the last of the Ogren's blood from his maw. He didn't like the taste of it. Deer was much sweeter; but this, this was like rancid water.

Beluil growled softly. Thomas deciphered the wolf's thoughts, "Brothers." He understood. Brothers helped one another. Brothers protected one another. Thomas ran his fingers through the wolf's fur affectionately.

"I was wondering when you were going to appear," said Thomas, still scratching behind Beluil's ears. The wolf enjoyed the attention immensely.

"You didn't seem to need any help," replied Rynlin, stepping out from between the trees.

"Thank you."

Thomas understood how hard it must have been for Rynlin not to join the fray. His grandfather had a gruff exterior, and became irritated easily, but Thomas knew that Rynlin cared about him. Thomas was grateful that Rynlin gave him the opportunity to do this on his own. He was growing up, and Rya was having a hard time dealing with that fact. Rynlin, at least, understood what he was going through to a certain extent and was willing to extend the boundaries as needed.

Rynlin simply nodded.

"I was going to follow them to the edge of the Burren, to make sure they got out safely."

"An excellent idea," said Rynlin. "I'll go with you."

They trailed the frightened group as they made their way south to Ballinasloe. Judging from their rich clothes, they were either the children of merchants or lords.

Thomas and Rynlin were quiet for a time, entertaining their own thoughts. Beluil came and went, scouting the forest around them.

"Grandfather?"

"Yes, Thomas." Rynlin was slightly surprised, but very pleased. Thomas had only called him grandfather a handful of times in the past six years.

"I had a question for you about the Highlanders. Are they really such good fighters as the history books say? I remember watching some of the Marcher training sessions when I was younger, but I never saw them fight in a battle."

"Well, Thomas, I guess you could say that the history books are correct, at least in that respect," answered Rynlin. "You may already know some of it from your lessons. The Highlanders have always been known as warriors, and most of the stories about their legendary feats of endurance and fighting skills, like marching a hundred miles in a day then routing the opposing army the next, are true."

"All Highlanders begin their weapons training upon reaching their tenth year," he continued. "I'm sure you were about to start your training as well, if not for that cursed night. As you know, among the Highlanders is an elite group of warriors, known as the Marchers. These men are tasked with defending the borders of the Highlands. A challenge, if there ever was one, for there are not all that many Highlanders. There are, however, a lot of mountains, so they have quite a large territory to defend. Nevertheless, they have succeeded in maintaining the sanctity of their borders, at least until recently."

Rynlin's last few words burned into Thomas' heart. *"They have succeeded ... at least until recently."* The Crag had fallen as a result, and Thomas still didn't know what had happened.

"The Marchers were considered the greatest warriors in all the Kingdoms, rivaling only the Sylvana in martial skill. As a result, they often served as bodyguards for kings and queens and other notables. The Highland Lord provided the Marchers to any ruler who could afford them, as their services did not come cheaply. For centuries, they were considered the ultimate mercenaries. That all changed, though. Hundreds of years ago, before the Great War, the Marchers were serving as the bodyguards for the High King, a weak man named Midraes. The High King raped a young lady in waiting, and her family, which happened to be one of the most powerful in all the Kingdoms, demanded justice. To make a long story short, Midraes falsely accused a Marcher for the crime and had him put to death in hopes of appeasing the girl's family. The remaining Marchers knew the truth of the matter, and they would not allow such a heinous act to go unpunished. The Marchers exposed Midraes for the criminal he was and then executed him. Because of the betrayal, the Marchers refused to serve another ruler from that day forward.

"Since then, the Marchers have not ventured out of their mountainous home in their service to the Highland Lord, and with the building of the Breaker have become the first line of defense against the creatures of the Shadow Lord. Now, of course, I don't know where things stand. Since the fall of the Crag, it's been difficult to find out what's going on in the Highlands with Lord Killeran serving as regent. I'm sure none of it's to the good, which could explain why many of the Highlanders have moved to the higher peaks and passes. But they are still the best fighters in the Kingdoms, and I don't think anyone would dispute that fact."

"Are the stories true?" asked Thomas in a quiet voice.

"What stories?"

"Are the Highlanders working as slaves in the mines?"

For several months Thomas had pondered that question, as it gnawed at his soul. These were his people. Even if he was an outcast and thought to be dead, he still felt responsible for them. Yet, he wasn't sure if he was ready, or even wanted, to assume that responsibility. As a result, he wrestled with his ever-present guilt from time to time, searching vainly for a hint as to what he should do.

"Where did you hear that?" asked Rynlin casually, though the intensity of his eyes belied his interest.

"From you, a few months ago, after you came back from one of your trips."

"Oh." Rynlin realized he would have to be more careful when he discussed things with Rya. Thomas' ears were just as good as his eyes. "From what I can tell—" Rynlin stopped for a moment. He wasn't sure how to answer, knowing Thomas' impatience could often get the better of him. Now was not the time for him to go running off on some quest of honor.

But he couldn't lie, not about this. Rynlin sighed, feeling the weight of his years. He'd just have to take his chances. "Yes. Killeran has enslaved some of the Highlanders in the mines. Unfortunately, there is nothing to be done at the moment. Killeran has a large army under his control. The Marchers could probably defeat it, but they do not have any sorcerers to battle Killeran's warlocks. So it would be a lost cause to begin with."

"What about the other Kingdoms? Why don't they do something to help?"

"The other Kingdoms really don't care about the Highlands right now. They're more concerned with what's happening in their own Kingdoms. They won't turn their eyes toward Rodric until he forces his attention upon them."

"But don't they see that if Rodric expands his power—"

"—they in turn lose power. Yes, some do. They just don't know what to do about it. No single kingdom has the strength to take on Rodric directly. Your grandfather, perhaps, could have prevented it. He could have rallied the Kingdoms and stood up to Rodric. Now, there is no one who can do that. Gregory of Fal Carrach might be the logical choice, but he's got Loris of Dunmoor to worry about on his western flank. And with Loris allied to Rodric, Gregory is effectively tied down. No, there is no one who can, or would want to, help at this time."

They continued along in silence for a few minutes, but Rynlin knew what was coming next. He waited patiently.

"I'm supposed to be the Lord of the Highlands," began Thomas. "If the Marchers are the best warriors in all the Kingdoms, their leader should be the best of the Marchers."

"That would only be appropriate," said Rynlin, cringing inwardly at his own response. He didn't want his grandson to run off on some fool's errand.

"Then where do you think I would stand among them now? If I went to the Highlands right now."

It was a very important question, Rynlin knew. Probably more important than Thomas could imagine. Not just for him, but for the Highlands as well. Rynlin had arrived at the glade when Thomas leapt down from the tree and attacked the first Ogren. Initially, he had feared for his grandson's safety, ready to step in at any moment. However, Rynlin soon realized he had nothing to worry about. Thomas had learned his lessons well. He wanted to tell Thomas that he already was one of the elite among the Marchers, because he knew in his heart that it was true. Yet, he didn't want him to become overconfident. There was much he would have to do in the future, and having confidence in yourself was certainly a part of it. Yet, having too much confidence could lead to the boy's failure, or worse — his death.

Rynlin looked down at the young man walking beside him, seeing once again the little boy who first appeared in the clearing six years before, carrying a sword that was much too big for him and a scrawny wolf pup. Now the young man had grown into the blade, and the pup was the largest wolf Rynlin had ever seen.

Thomas repeated the question. "If I went to the Highlands now, where would I stand among the Marchers?"

Rynlin searched desperately for any answer other than the one he knew he had to give. But he couldn't lie. Thomas would know. He decided that again the truth was best, and that he and Rya would have to trust in the way they had raised him.

"You would be one of the best," said Rynlin.

Thomas studied his grandfather for a moment, then nodded. He just needed to know, but he saw the trace of worry in Rynlin's face.

"Don't worry, Rynlin. I'm not going anywhere. Not yet anyway."

"Good," said Rynlin, giving his grandson a wry smile, "because if you did, Rya would have me for breakfast, and then she'd come after you."

CHAPTER FORTY FOUR

ASSASSIN

Thomas, Rynlin and Beluil finally reached the edge of the Burren, where they could stop worrying about the motley group that now rode through the darkening twilight toward Ballinasloe. They would probably get home in about an hour, no worse for wear except for a few nightmares. Getting back to the boat was another matter, since they had to return through the Burren, which was now covered by the darkness of full night thanks to the overhanging trees and dense brush. Rather than trying to reach the coast, Rynlin and Thomas decided to make camp for the night about halfway through the Burren.

They had been walking for several minutes with that intent in mind when Thomas grabbed Rynlin's arm. Beluil stopped as well, ears perked for the slightest sound, his hackles standing straight. Rynlin searched the wood for danger, but only could make out the rough shapes of the trees and rocks. Instead, he trusted in Thomas' vision. What Rynlin saw as a shadow was clear as day to his grandson.

"There's something wrong," whispered Thomas, scanning the trees around them. Rynlin shouldn't have been surprised. Thomas had greater skill in this area than he did. Opening himself to the Talent, Rynlin extended his senses.

"Yes, there is," he said. He could barely feel it, this sense of pure evil.

"It's close, Rynlin. Very close."

Beluil growled into the darkness, sensing the foulness, yet even he was unsure of its location. Thomas and Rynlin continued to examine the trees. The hair on the back of Thomas' neck stood on end. He hated not seeing what was stalking them. It made him uneasy, and he fought to control the fear rising within him. His hand went to his sword hilt, ready to draw the blade. Rynlin stood there calmly, waiting. He didn't seem to be affected by the tension, but it certainly was getting to Thomas.

He nudged Rynlin and pointed to what looked like a shadow attached to the trunk of a tree no more than ten feet in front of them. The shadow had moved, and it was coming toward them ever so slowly. Thomas' sense of evil grew stronger as the shadow glided closer. Yet, even with his sharp eyes, he could barely see what approached. Cold sweat trickled down Thomas' back. He didn't know what the shadow was, but it terrified him.

Rynlin drew on the Talent, shooting a bolt of pure white light shot from his palm, striking the shadow squarely. A horrible scream tore through the night, followed by a deathly silence. The smell of charred flesh drifted to their nostrils.

Rynlin drew on the Talent again, bringing forth a ball of light that illuminated the surrounding forest.

"A Nightstalker," said Rynlin with a grimace, pointing out the pitch-black body, the sightless red eyes and the claws shaped like scythes. The bolt of energy had torn a hole straight through the creature's chest.

Beluil approached the smoldering corpse, sniffing it to make sure it was truly dead. He returned to Thomas' side quickly, revolted by the smell and shaking his head to clear it from his sensitive nose.

"What is it, Rynlin?"

"A Nightstalker is the Shadow Lord's assassin," replied Rynlin. "You normally don't see it until you're about to die, and even then catching a glimpse would be unlikely. The Shadow Lord sends them out after certain prey, and they don't stop searching until they've succeeded." Rynlin's words chilled Thomas to his very core. The Shadow Lord's assassin. "Come on. Let's get some distance from this thing before we stop for the night. I want to make sure there isn't anything else in the Burren looking for us."

The Shadow Lord sends Nightstalkers out after certain prey, and they don't stop searching until they've succeeded.

"Thomas."

Rynlin's voice drew him back from his thoughts, none of them good. The dead creature transfixed him. "Yes."

"Remember that feeling you had. That will be the only warning you'll get. With a Nightstalker, if you're not paying attention, you don't stand a chance."

Thomas nodded and followed his grandfather to the east, Beluil bringing up the rear. Rynlin said that the Nightstalker hunted for specific prey. Who was the target of this particular creature? Goosebumps rose on his flesh as a chill swept through his body. He had the nasty suspicion that it was him.

CHAPTER FORTY FIVE

MEMORIES

It was well after dark when Kaylie and her friends finally saw the lights of Ballinasloe in the distance. As soon as the sun had set, they had urged their horses to a gallop, the encroaching darkness playing off the fear that remained from their horrifying encounter in the Burren. Every shadow was an Ogren, every sound. The howl of the wind playing through the tree branches sent shudders of fear through them. Because of the fear they sensed in their riders, the horses didn't mind the extra effort, though they were lathered in sweat from the long gallop. They, too, wanted to get behind the walls of the Rock.

The group finally slowed when they entered the town, taking comfort from the lights and the people still about at the late hour. A troop of soldiers formed around them, escorting them to the Rock. News of their arrival preceded them. Kaylie's father had sent out patrols, they learned, and their families were worried.

As they made their way across the bridge and into the Rock's courtyard, soldiers took the bridles of their horses and helped the girls from their mounts. Gregory rushed out of the stronghold, dressed in full armor, sword swinging at his side. He had planned to lead the next patrol himself. The inaction of waiting worsened his temper. It was one of the few weaknesses he had as a general. Patience, or rather the lack of it. Now, after seeing his daughter safe and whole, all he felt was relief.

"Where in the blazes have you—" Gregory stopped himself. He saw their frightened faces, their exhaustion. Kaylie rushed to him and threw her arms around him, her hands clinging tightly to the cloth of his shirt that stuck out from his breastplate. He hugged her back, trying to keep the tears from his eyes.

"What happened?" he asked softly.

Kaylie clung to him for a few moments longer before pulling back and wiping her eyes with her sleeve. She was trying to regain her composure, the composure expected of a future queen. He wanted to keep hugging his little girl, to give her the protection he had provided since she was born, but was now no longer necessary. He corrected himself — not always necessary. He was pleased to see that Kaylie still needed him, no matter how much she protested to the contrary.

"Oh, father, it was the most incredible thing," began Kaylie. "We were in the Burren, when two Ogren appeared, and—"

They were in the Burren, not Oakwood Forest. So that was the lie. If only he could have figured it out beforehand. He tried to follow his daughter's story, but now all of them were babbling, telling their own versions of the adventure. Gregory held his hands up for silence, and eventually he got it, though Eric had to step on Rohn's foot to shut him up.

"You see, my lord," said Maddan, stepping in front of his friends and standing next to Kaylie. A little too close in Gregory's opinion. His daughter moved farther to the side, trying to get away from him. Gregory decided that he would have to watch Maddan carefully. Considering who his father was, he could become a very dangerous opponent. He had no doubts regarding the man's ambitions and to what lengths he would go to achieve them. "We ran into two Ogren when we stopped in the Burren. They were monstrous creatures, with huge maces." He tried to show how large the maces were by stretching out his hands. "They attacked and I kept them away from the girls for a time when suddenly this warrior, he must have been at least eight feet tall, jumped down from the trees—"

Kaylie's face grew darker and darker as she listened to Maddan's recounting of the afternoon's events. She was about to correct him, but she didn't have to.

"It's hard to fend off two Ogren when you're standing in the middle of a lake pissing in your pants from fear," said Rohn, giving his friend an angry scowl.

Maddan's face turned red with fury, and he took a step toward Rohn, but Kael stepped in front of him, blocking his path.

"Bragging, or lying, doesn't make you a warrior," said Kael, loud enough so everyone in the courtyard could hear. "Your actions do. You should spend more time improving your skills as a warrior, Maddan, because you don't have much of a future as a storyteller."

Maddan lowered his eyes. On the outside he appeared chagrined. On the inside he fumed. Two times today he had been humiliated. No more, he promised. Someday everyone in this courtyard would bow down to him. Some day—

"I will meet you at dawn in the circle," said Kael. "I think it's time to increase your training. Standing in a lake while facing two Ogren is not a strategy I would recommend."

Furious, Maddan gave a half-hearted bow before heading off to his quarters. His father was the richest man in all the kingdoms. Some day, Maddan would also be the most powerful. Then he'd be the one providing the lessons, and harsh ones they would be.

"Enough of this," said Gregory. "I want all of you to take hot baths and get some food. I'll find out what happened later."

Kaylie's friends bowed as Gregory led his daughter into the fortress. Once they were inside, she again began to explain what happened, but he shushed her, making her take a hot bath and eat a warm meal first. That done, she went to his quarters and took a chair in front of the fireplace by his desk. Gregory pulled a chair up and let the heat soak into his bones, waiting for his daughter to begin. She had been eager to explain before. Now she hesitated.

Kaylie looked into the fire, watching the flames dance across the logs. It was much like his eyes, she decided. The burning. The cold purpose with which he fought. She had never seen anything like it before.

"Kaylie?" her father asked expectantly, wanting to get to the bottom of this afternoon's events.

"I'm sorry for lying to you, father."

"We'll talk about that later." The finality of his words made her cringe. It was not the beginning she had hoped for.

Unable to delay any longer, she started with when they first left Ballinasloe. Kaylie talked of stopping by the lake and beginning to eat, and then having the Ogren suddenly appear. She told all this with calm detachment, as if she were only an observer, rather than a participant. When the large black wolf appeared in the story and the boy with green eyes, she grew more animated, using her hands and arms to better illustrate what happened. She even told him how scared she was, and that even though she had pulled her knife, she couldn't make her legs move for a time. When she finished, he just watched her, waiting for more. When she smiled, he realized she was done. It was almost too much to believe.

"So you're telling me that you were attacked by two Ogren, a huge black wolf appeared out of nowhere and came to your defense, buying enough time for its friend, a boy most likely no older than you, to leap down from the trees and in a matter of minutes kill both Ogren without getting injured."

"Yes."

She wasn't lying. He would have known. But a boy, admittedly fighting with a wolf — and that was strange enough — but a boy killing two Ogren. A veteran soldier would have difficulty just staying alive against a single Ogren. The only way to fight Ogren without decimating your own soldiers was to swarm the beasts. But a boy! And he'd killed two! It was absolutely unbelievable. Yet it had happened.

"I'm sorry, father," said Kaylie, adopting her best little girl face. "I promise I won't lie to you again." Maybe if she apologized twice, his attitude would soften.

Gregory looked at his daughter's expression, and he knew it was an obvious attempt at manipulating him. He didn't care. He'd always forgive her, no matter what. He did think about giving her a lecture, but her frightened expression when she arrived at the Rock told him that what had happened to her was probably the best lesson she could receive. Still, he wasn't about to let her off so easily.

"We'll talk about it more in the morning, Kaylie. It's getting late. Why don't you go off to bed?"

Kaylie smiled and rose from her chair, crossing the short distance to kiss her father on the cheek and then go to her room down the hallway.

After she had gone, Gregory sat in his chair for a long time, staring into the fire himself, playing her story over and over in his mind. He always came back to the green-eyed boy. It tugged at his memory for some reason. Then he had it. His body might be going because of age, but his mind wasn't. Talyn Kestrel's grandson had green eyes. That was the memory that was trying to break through. He had even seen the child once, before the attack on the Crag.

A legend had begun soon after that. At first, only in the Highlands, but then it had spread to the edges of those Kingdoms butting up against that mountainous region, and from there to all the other Kingdoms. Probably all the way to the Distant Islands, he surmised. The legend said that the grandson survived, and that the Lost Kestrel would find his way home to take the throne of the Highlands when his people needed him most. But it was only a legend, and from the reports he had received, he didn't think anyone escaped from the Crag on that cursed night, least of all a child. Still, it could be true. He wanted it to be true.

Gregory looked back into the fire. Thinking of the Lost Kestrel stirred memories of Talyn. They had been friends, good friends, fighting Ogren, Shades, Fearhounds and worse, but never with the supposed skill of this boy. A legend come to life certainly would make things interesting. After several hours of contemplation, he decided it was time for sleep, but he wanted to talk to Kael first. He left his apartments in search of the Swordmaster, only to find him coming down the hallway toward his room. The man seemed to have a sixth sense. He always knew when Gregory needed him.

"Tomorrow, I'd like you to take a squad of soldiers and check out the Burren, especially around this lake where Kaylie was attacked."

"I was planning on that, my lord. I was curious about the boy." Kael had heard the story from Eric and Rohn. He had determined that both stories were too similar to be lies.

"If you happen to run into the boy, see if you can get him to come back with you," said Gregory. "I'd like to ask him a few questions and to thank him for what he did."

Kael nodded. "I will, my lord. But if this boy did half of what those two greenears told me this evening, we won't be finding him unless he wants to be found."

"I know. But it's worth a shot, isn't it?"

"Yes, my lord. It is."

CHAPTER FORTY SIX

TARGET

T homas and Rynlin stopped a few hours after full dark, finding shelter underneath a huge willow tree, Beluil having already gone off to explore the surrounding area. Its long, full branches formed a natural hut that protected them from the cold, whipped along by a sharp, biting wind. They ate a quick meal of bread, dried meat and cheese, as Rynlin didn't want to chance a fire. Nightstalkers always worked alone, but the Shadow Lord would know immediately of this one's demise.

The howl of a wolf broke the silence of the night from the west. Then another howl echoed the first, this time to the north. Beluil had found a pack. Rynlin relaxed somewhat as the howls of wolves drifted through the night. Wolves hated the creatures of the Dark Horde. Thomas watched his grandfather closely. Rynlin was talking to himself again. He did that when he was concerned. He probably thought that Thomas couldn't hear him, but he kept catching the words Sylvana, long night and boy. He didn't know what Rynlin was mumbling about, but he had a feeling it affected him in some way.

Seeing that his grandfather was occupied, Thomas drew on the Talent, extending his senses to see what was around them. He was right. Beluil was to the west, and he wasn't alone. He had found a pack of twenty to thirty wolves. Satisfied that nothing dangerous lurked in the immediate area, he pushed his senses to the south, toward Ballinasloe.

His breath caught for a moment when he stared down at the Rock. It looked very much like the Crag in the way it was built, with the huge slabs of stone instead of blocks, the dark forbidding color, the towers located strategically at the junctures of the walls. He watched the waves crash against the rocks surrounding the fortress before circling around the great keep and examining its layout.

This must be where the girl lived. There was something about her that drew him to her. She had been terrified when the two Ogren appeared, but that was only natural. More important, she had stood her ground. She had courage, and a confidence … no, that wasn't right. It was more like an inner strength. Maybe that was what attracted him to her. That and her eyes. Thomas couldn't get the picture of this girl out of his mind. He glanced at his grandfather, who was still sitting up against the base of the tree, deep in thought and mumbling to himself. He had never tried to find someone with the Talent before. He might as well give it a try now.

Thomas formed a picture of the girl in his mind — the dark, silky hair and deep, blue eyes — then centered his Talent on the image. In an instant he was inside the Rock in a room with a large fireplace. It was a simple room, with just a few chairs and a desk. His attention was automatically drawn to the books lining one wall. A library, but not as big as the one in his home. He wondered if there were any books on those shelves he had not yet read.

Thomas focused on the other side of the room, where a large fire glowed brightly in the fireplace. Two people sat in front of it. He had found the girl. She was discussing something with a man, by the looks of him her father. But who was she? He looked at the mantle above the fireplace, and then he knew. Carved into the wall was a large shield, and on it was a bear standing on its hind legs, poised to attack. The standard of Fal Carrach. That man had to be the king; Gregory if he remembered correctly. That made the girl his daughter. A princess. He couldn't believe it. What would a princess be doing in the Burren without guards? Those boys certainly weren't there to protect her. If they'd actually thought of drawing their swords, and succeeded, they were more a danger to themselves than to the Ogren.

"Are you done eavesdropping?"

"I wasn't eavesdropping," said Thomas, letting go of the Talent. "I just wanted to make sure that the girl and her friends got back home safely."

"Uh, huh," murmured Rynlin.

Rynlin didn't believe him, but there was no reason to argue. Once his grandfather made up his mind about something, nothing could sway him.

"Anything around that we should be worried about?" asked Rynlin.

"No," replied Thomas. "Beluil found some friends."

Rynlin nodded. The howls of wolves and the sounds of other nighttime animals gave Thomas a sense of security. A silence in the forest always meant danger.

"So why did you help them?" asked Rynlin. He was certain it just wasn't because of a pretty girl, though men had been known to do stranger things for less.

"It was the right thing to do."

"So you were just doing the right thing?"

"Yes and no."

"What do you mean yes and no? Either you were doing the right thing or you weren't."

Thomas looked at his grandfather for a moment. Was Rynlin really as irritated as his voice sounded, or he was trying to get a rise out of him? The sharp-eyed sorcerer seemed at ease. His face wasn't as red as it got when he became angry. Thomas decided not to fall for the bait.

"Yes, I did it because it was the right thing to do," he replied calmly. "But there was something else as well. The fact that the Ogren were in the Burren seemed wrong. No, it was wrong. I felt the pain of the forest when I walked among the trees. That's the main reason. I wanted to eliminate the pain."

His grandfather smiled. In the darkness, even without a fire, Thomas could still see it. He had been right. His grandfather had tried to bait him.

Rynlin examined his grandson, pleased by his response. He had a feeling that might be the case, but he had to be sure. Rynlin had the distinct feeling that Thomas' dreams about unicorns were visiting him almost every night now. It wouldn't be long before it was time.

"You know, Thomas, you did a brave thing today. It was also extremely dangerous. You need to be careful in a situation like that. One mistake can kill you."

"I know, Rynlin. I was careful, or rather as careful as the circumstances allowed."

"I know you were, Thomas. I just want you to understand that you have to weigh all the risks before making a decision."

"That's why I did what I did. I didn't have time to do much else. If I had waited any longer some of those people would have died."

"You're right," said Rynlin, nodding his agreement. "But why didn't you use your Talent?"

His grandfather looked as if he had asked a trick question, so Thomas took a moment to think. If he answered quickly, and didn't give the reply Rynlin wanted to hear, he could be up all night stuck in the middle of another of his grandfather's lectures. Besides, with the excitement of the day having waned, and with it his adrenaline, he was getting tired.

"I did think about it," he began. "It just wasn't appropriate. You and Rya explained that people who used the Talent or Dark Magic could sense when another used it. I didn't want to attract any attention. Besides, with Beluil there to help me, taking on two Ogren wasn't all that difficult."

"You're bragging."

"No, I'm telling the truth," said Thomas. He was getting angry now. That was definitely one trait he had picked up from the grandfather sitting across from him — a very short temper. "Both you and Rya made certain that I knew my strengths and my limitations, and the weapons training has drilled that into me even more. When I say I can fight two Ogren, I mean exactly that, and I think I've proven it."

Again Rynlin smiled. It was good to see that all the hard work he and his wife had put into Thomas was paying off. The boy actually listened to them. Rynlin saw that overconfidence, even arrogance, were foreign to Thomas' personality. The boy knew what he could do and what he couldn't do. That knowledge would serve him well in the future.

They were quiet for a time, listening to the music of the forest provided by the crickets and the owls. A raccoon even walked into their shelter and was startled to see it occupied. Still, not viewing Thomas or Rynlin as a threat, he curled up to sleep where the low-hanging branches met the ground.

"The Nightstalker was after me, wasn't it?" Because of Thomas' cold certainty, his question came out more like a statement.

Rynlin didn't say anything. He was trying to think of the best way to reply.

"Have you had any more dreams about unicorns?" He wanted to change the subject. Talking about the Nightstalker depressed him.

"Yes, almost every night now."

Rynlin nodded. He had expected that, but it was always good to confirm what you didn't know for a fact. It definitely wouldn't be long now.

"The Nightstalker was after me."

Ah, well. Thinking that he could change the course of Thomas' thoughts was foolish. Rynlin decided that the best course was to tell Thomas everything. Where one Nightstalker appeared, another could take its place the next day, and another the day after. It was better that Thomas knew what he was up against so he could be prepared. Still, Rynlin felt sad. This young man had never had the opportunity to be a young man. It truly was a cruel world.

"Why do you ask?"

"You're dodging the question."

Rynlin studied his grandson. His green eyes flashed with remarkable intensity. Rynlin realized that it would be very difficult for someone to lie to Thomas. If his grandson didn't smell the lie from the start, the person would wilt under that hard glare. He probably picked that up from Rya, and those glowing eyes of his added an intimidation factor lacking in the glare of his wife. It was remarkable how a woman who came no higher than his chest could have such a commanding presence.

Rynlin chuckled inwardly as his thoughts turned to his wife. "It could have been after me, you know."

"Do you really believe that, Rynlin? I've been off the Isle of Mist for less than a day, and the Nightstalker immediately appears. You've gone off the island many times, and you never once mentioned running into something like that. You and Rya never let me off the island. Ever. I know you've got wards all around the island, hiding us from those who can use Dark Magic, and that must hinder a Nightstalker's abilities as well. The Nightstalker hunts until its prey is found, you said. It found me."

The boy was smart. He had pieced together the puzzle very well, and he didn't even have all the pieces. What surprised Rynlin, though, was the way Thomas explained it. There was no fear in his voice, as there should have been. At least Rynlin thought so. If you told a battle-scarred veteran of a dozen wars that a Nightstalker was after him, he'd wet his pants in fear. But Thomas wasn't afraid, he just wanted to know the truth.

"Yes, the Nightstalker was most likely after you."

"Why?"

"For the same reason that you can't return to the Highlands yet. If you ran into the wrong people, you would be killed on sight."

"Killeran?"

"Yes, probably Killeran, since he's in league with the High King. Rodric most likely arranged the attack on the Crag and your murder, but I'm sure you've already thought of that possibility. If you had died like they wanted, Rodric would now rule the Highlands and probably a few other Kingdoms as well. Because your death has not been confirmed, he must wait, at least a few more years, before he can put into motion whatever plans he might have."

"Why don't the other rulers do something to stop him?"

"That would be the logical solution, wouldn't it?" said Rynlin, shaking his head sadly. "But some Kingdoms don't care because their rulers lack any political acuity, some might be in league with Rodric and too blind to see that he will stab them in the back as soon as he can, and some probably have already guessed at what Rodric wants to do, but until there's actual proof, there's nothing they can do."

"If Rodric is behind all this, how could he have the power to control a Nightstalker? He's just a man."

"*He* doesn't," said Rynlin.

"So he has another ally, a hidden ally," said Thomas. "One who has the power to control a Nightstalker."

"Very good, Thomas. You've done better than most of the people who consider themselves experts in political maneuvering."

"That leaves only one possible ally."

Rynlin nodded.

"But why would he want me dead?"

Rynlin shrugged. He thought he knew the answer, he just didn't want to tell Thomas. Not yet, anyway. Not until he was sure. His grandson had enough to worry about for now. But soon he'd have to know. And then the hard decisions would have to be made, decisions that would affect not only Thomas, but everyone around him as well. It was really a frightening thought, which was why Rynlin didn't burden him with it.

"I won't run from him," said Thomas, his voice filled with cold determination. "I won't."

If you really enjoyed this story, I need you to do me a HUGE favour – please write a review. It helps the book and me. I really appreciated the feedback.

Consider a review on Amazon or BookBub at https://www.bookbub.com/profile/peter-wacht.

Follow me on my website at www.kestrelmg.com to keep an eye out for the nest book in the series… or perhaps even a new story.

Made in the USA
Monee, IL
08 September 2021

77618160R00184